BLOOD SUCKING SERIES NO. 5

THE DEATH CHAMBER

NORMA LINENBERGER

America Star Books
Frederick, Maryland

© 2015 by America Star Books.

All rights reserved. No part of this book may be reproduced, stored in a retrieval system or transmitted in any form or by any means without the prior written permission of the publishers, except by a reviewer who may quote brief passages in a review to be printed in a newspaper, magazine or journal.

First printing

All characters in this book are fictitious, and any resemblance to real persons, living or dead, is coincidental.

America Star Books has allowed this work to remain exactly as the author intended, verbatim, without editorial input.

Hardcover 9781681228549
Softcover 9781681223094
PUBLISHED BY AMERICA STAR BOOKS, LLLP
www.americastarbooks.pub
Frederick, Maryland

Dedication

This book is dedicated to my husband, Leo, and family, Cheryl, Elva, Deborah, James, Valerie, Jacqueline and Jeff. Grandchildren Milah, Morgan, Dayton and Cayden.

Introduction

"The Death Chamber"

Recently, a species of weird, eccentric, mechanically behaved people have infiltrated their society in Calgary, Canada with horrible, terrifying, ghastly encounters upon guiltless victims. They are involved in death defying rendezvous' throughout Calgary and beyond adding to the macabre plot of frequenting a variety of cemeteries for their morbid pleasure. They are also engaged in feeding on corpses' besides grisly, ghastly encounters at nightly haunts, events, banquets etc………….. A variety of assaults, are eventually revealed as the vampires, zombies, mummies and witches plot is disclosed in a macabre resolution. The unusual killings are shrouded in a mysterious sequence and the forthcoming pages will keep you in suspense. Continue reading!!! Autobiography Norma Linenberger

Norma Linenberger is an aspiring, upcoming author and poet on the writing scene with her fifth book, "The Death Chamber." Her most recent book is preceded by The Final Floor I, Dripping Blood II, Blood Banquet III and Six Feet Above IV. This is the fifth part of a "murder mystery" series titled "Blood Sucking Series" etc…………… She is also a published poet with a book titled "Norma Jean's Poetry" by Norma Linenberger. She is originally from Victoria, Kansas home of the "Basilica of the Plains." She married Leo Linenberger April 28, 1962 and are the parents of four children Deborah, Cheryl and twins James and Jacqueline. They have four grandchildren, Milah, Morgan, Dayton and Cayden.

Contents

Chapter 1 What Has Befallen Jean? 9
Chapter 2 Jean's Court Case 12
Chapter 3 A New President 14
Chapter 4 A Blood Sucking Rendezvous 17
Chapter 5 Witches in the New Haven Cemetery 20
Chapter 6 Witches!!! 23
Chapter 7 Beware of the Witches 25
Chapter 8 Witches Again!!! 28
Chapter 9 Horace the Vampire 31
Chapter 10 Who wants to go to the Theater? 34
Chapter 11 Earthquake! 36
Chapter 12 Rebuilding Calgary, Canada 38
Chapter 13 Bang! Bang! Bang! 40
Chapter 14 Poheta Cemetery 43
Chapter 15 July 4th, 2015 45
Chapter 16 The Next Day 48
Chapter 17 Confiscating Caskets Only 50
Chapter 18 Another Trip to the Poheta Cemetery 52
Chapter 19 Company??? 55
Chapter 20 Labor Day, September 4th, 2015 58
Chapter 21 An Encounter with the Witches 61
Chapter 22 A Basement Blood Sucking Encounter 64
Chapter 23 Buried Alive!!! 67
Chapter 24 A Swimming Escapade? 70
Chapter 25 Are You Ready to Go? 73
Chapter 26 A Vampire Club Meeting 75
Chapter 27 Mummies Galore!!! 77
Chapter 28 Mohegan Cemetery Again? 79
Chapter 29 The Media 82
Chapter 30 Living Underground 85
Chapter 31 Halloween Preparations 89
Chapter 32 A Mummy Attack 92
Chapter 33 Thanksgiving Day 95
Chapter 34 The Blood Sucking Mummy Rampage 98
Chapter 35 A Mausoleum Rendezvous 101

Chapter 36 Christmas Eve 2015 104
Chapter 37 A Blizzard Monday Morning.. 107
Chapter 38 New Year's Day--2016 109
Chapter 39 A Valentine's Haunt 112
Chapter 40 Let's Attack the Witches!.. 115
Chapter 41 What Happened to Steve?... 118
Chapter 42 Depressed? 122
Chapter 43 Poheta Cemetery Again? 125
Chapter 44 The Poheta Cemetery Once More? 128
Chapter 45 Confiscating Another Corpse!... 131
Chapter 46 A Labor Day Celebration 134
Chapter 47 Where are the Victims? 137
Chapter 48 "Last Day at Work"... 140
Chapter 49 A Delayed Vacation... 142
Chapter 50 Vacation Time 145
Chapter 51 A Variety of Activities 148
Chapter 52 Back in Calgary, Canada 151
Chapter 53 Partially Intoxicated... 154
Chapter 54 Dead Witches... 157
Chapter 55 Another Vampire Meeting... 160
Chapter 56 "Rest in Peace" Cemetery 163
Chapter 57 Rest in Peace Cemetery 166
Chapter 58 Some More Christmas Shopping? 169
Chapter 59 The Onslaught of the Storm.. 172
Chapter 60 Whatever Happened at the Mohegan Cemetery? 175
Chapter 61 A Valentine Party.. 178
Chapter 62 Another Rendezvous 181
Chapter 63 Calgary Ski Resort 184
Chapter 64 Barnum and Bailey Circus.. 187
Chapter 65 Memorial Day 190
Chapter 66 Gilbert Drowned.. 193
Chapter 67 In Honor of Gilbert! 196
Chapter 68 How About the Mausoleum? 199
Chapter 69 A Vampire Meeting... 202
Chapter 70 Mummies on Patrol 205
Chapter 71 One More Swimming Escapade? 208
Chapter 72 A Broken Down Hearse.. 211

Chapter 73 Calgary State Fair..214
Chapter 74 Roller Coaster Rides..217
Chapter 75 Two New Stragglers...220
Chapter 76 The Witches Return? 223
Chapter 77 The Encounter Release 226
Chapter 78 A Speedy Recovery...228
Chapter 79 The Retrieval of Joe and Ryan!..231
Chapter 80 An Informal Meeting..234
Chapter 81 Thanksgiving Banquet 237
Chapter 82 New Year's Day...240
Chapter 83 Blood Sucking Escapade—Ronton Mortuary? 244
Chapter 84 Is There Any Interest? 247
Chapter 85 Roller Skating Anyone?..251
Chapter 86 An Easter Banquet and Hunt 253
Chapter 87 The Alleyway Haunts 256
Chapter 88 Memorial Day...259
Chapter 89 Dancing, Anyone? 262
Chapter 90 A July 4th, 2018 Banquet..265
Chapter 91 The Calgary Bowling Alley 268
Chapter 92 New Bowling Balls!...269
Chapter 93 A Nightly Haunt...271
Chapter 94 "Joseph and Mike"...273
Chapter 95 "Time to Swim Again?"...275
Chapter 96 Mausoleum Rendezvous 277
Chapter 97 Blood Sucking Rendezvous-2018 278
Chapter 98 Silent Meditation Only..279
Chapter 99 Lurking Behind the Tombstones!..280
Chapter 100 Next to the Last Chapter 282
Chapter 101 The Last Chapter..283

Chapter 1
What Has Befallen Jean?

An eerie mist is draping the environment as the vampires are huddled together in front of the television set in the basement, hopefully, awaiting a possible midnight news report about the disappearance of Jean Benson, Albert's sister. Jean departed at 8:30 PM for the New Haven Cemetery by herself, arriving at 9:00 PM, transporting her equipment, tools, lantern, etc... She trudged past several mausoleums en route to the only mausoleum left on the cemetery grounds. At this point, Jean is planning on either confiscating or mutilating the corpses' bodies beyond recognition. Possibly, after the inevitable has taken place she might even consider salvaging their innards to be used at future meal sites, holiday banquets and events the vampires and she are sponsoring. Maybe she can kill three birds with one stone! Right? We'll see! Jean asked Earl, Chris and Ryan to accommodate her on her short expedition to the New Haven Cemetery but they declined the invitation making the remark, "I'm sorry, but we have extracurricular and recreational activities this week that require our immediate attention." Earl, Chris and Ryan thanked Jean for the honor of asking and warned her to be "extra cautious" because you never know who is slinking behind the tombstones at the cemetery after hours. Jean reciprocated the warning saying, "I can assure you I'll be "extra cautious" of anyone or whatever I encounter."

In the meantime, after Jean didn't return by midnight the vampires decided to make a trip to the New Haven Cemetery in search of her. After all Jean reiterated, "If I'm not back by midnight please come to the New Haven Cemetery in one of our extra vehicles in search of me although I'm sure I'll be fine." The vampires walked through the cemetery gates at 12:45AM Friday morning, frantically scouring the cemetery grounds in search of Jean but to no avail. They could not search the mausoleums and other small, outside buildings because they were all securely locked. They continued roaming the hallowed grounds but Jean was nowhere in sight. Only her blue hearse was parked two blocks north of the New Haven Cemetery, nothing else. Bryan made the remark, "We might as well leave now and report Jean's disappearance to the Calgary Police Department later on this morning. I'm sure they'll do a thorough search and evaluation sometime today.

As soon as daylight appeared the vampires made a phone call to the Calgary Police Department speaking to the Chief of Police. Earl reported the complete story of Jean Benson's disappearance at the New Haven Cemetery last night. The Chief of Police said, "I will send several of my policemen to the New Haven Cemetery this evening before dark to see what transpired." When the policemen arrived Officer Robb dispersed them to different areas of the cemetery grounds in search of the body of Jean Benson. In the meantime, dusk is beginning to settle on the city of Calgary as the policemen continue scouring the cemetery for any clues that would lead them to the body of Jean Benson. Finally, Officer Robb decided to investigate the last mausoleum on the farther end of the cemetery. He banged and clanged on the older mausoleum door with his tools in tow managing to release the latch, thereby, opening the door. It creaked slightly emitting a foul, filthy stench permeating the room. Standing at the open casket was an unrecognizable man dressed in typical black, vampire attire, cape included, sporting perfectly coiffed hair, pale skin, red, glazed eyes to match his bloody, red lips and elongated fingernails. Officer Robb and his policemen pointed their guns at the vampire while questioning him repeatedly if the ashes in the casket were that of Jean Benson to which he replied, "Arg! Arg! Arg!" meaning "Yes! Yes! Yes!" Upon hearing this Officer Robb immediately ushered him to a waiting patrol car to be transported to the Calgary Police Department. He was escorted into a private cell where he will be incarcerated until his trial and sentencing.

Inurement

January 25, 2015

Earl, Chris and Ryan are vampire morticians currently employed at the Ronton Mortuary because of increased business sooner than the February 8, 2015 date previously set. They made arrangements to have Jean's ashes transferred to the Ronton Mortuary for a memorial service tomorrow morning at 9:30 AM at the New Haven Cemetery. Pastor Crane gave a eulogy in Jean's honor and several songs were song.

Jean's ashes was slowly lowered into the grave and is now considered a closed case. Prior to departing from the New Haven Cemetery Earl and the vampires invited everyone to a meal at the Green Garden Restaurant on the outskirts of Calgary. He also announced, "If you are interested in the upcoming trial and sentencing the week of Monday, February 7, 2015 at 9:00 AM in the Calgary County Courthouse please be aware of this information. Thank you! Good afternoon."

Chapter 2
Jean's Court Case

Jean's murder case is reaching full capacity in the Calgary County Courthouse. February 7, 2015, Monday has arrived with the courtroom filled to the brim with Jean's friends and acquaintances she mingled with over the years.

Albert and Jean's vampires are sitting and waiting excitedly for the court case to begin. Every once in a while their eyes fill up with tears as Jean enters their minds. Slowly the door opens and the bailiff escorts a vampire prisoner wearing an orange jumpsuit with his hands and feet shackled walking to the table. He has a lean build encompassing his six foot frame and his short, blonde, thick hair was neatly styled which is similar to that of a vampire. His appearance incorporated the utmost style in regards to that of a vampire. He flashed a pleasant smile to his attorney, Mr. Lamar, as he sat next to him. Everybody arose as Judge Jones entered the scene seating himself in the center of the courtroom in an elevated position. Immediately several of Jean's friends were called to the witness stand to testify on Jean's behalf. Eventually, the vampire prisoner appeared on the witness stand with Judge Jones asking him his name. He said, "My name is Carl Hanley and I'm originally from Calgary, Canada. Judge Jones questioned Carl intermittently in regards to Jean's death. Carl admitted, "I stabbed Jean in the heart once with a knife which automatically kills a vampire. I immediately flung her corpse into the casket not knowing what to do in such a short amount of time. Later, I returned to the cemetery and burned Jean's corpse depositing the ashes in the casket. When I was apprehended by the Calgary Police Department I had completed my mission in regards to the knifing and burning of Jean's ashes. I was momentarily glaring into the casket proud of my most recent achievement but it didn't last.

Judge Jones said, "Very well. Your last statement answered all my questions. Court will adjourn until February 15, 2015 at 9:30AM for the last sentencing of Carl Hanley in the death of Jean Benson. Case No. 274 dismissed.

As before, Carl Hanley is shackled once again and removed from the courtroom to a waiting patrol car. He is being transferred to the Calgary County Jail to await his final sentencing February 15, 2015 at 9:30AM.

Final Sentencing

February 15, 2015

Again, Carl was accompanied into the courtroom by a bailiff sitting next to his attorney, Mr. Lamer, for court to convene.

Judge Jones appeared in court asking everyone to be seated so the sentencing can begin. With Judge Jones permission Carl Hanley presented himself in court for the final sentencing of life in prison to be served, consecutively, for the first degree murder in the death of Jean Benson. The sudden impact of the verdict caused Carl Hanley to collapse in a heap on the floor with two prison guards removing him from the courtroom after he recovered.

The last court order that was applied was Carl Hanley will be transferred to the Calgary State Prison for Men in Calgary, Canada February 22, 2015 to serve a life sentence, consecutively, for the first degree murder of Jean Benson.

Chapter 3
A New President

Besides conducting their busy lives as morticians at the Ronton Mortuary on a daily basis Chris, Ryan and several other vampires have decided to submit Earl's name as President of the Vampire Club. Blair Jones and Isaac Hamlon are also on the presidential submission list besides Earl. Their names will be on the presidential ballot to be voted on next week February 23, 2015, during their belated Valentine party. The vampires had a variety of other issues on the agenda of utmost importance at this time, therefore, the Valentine party was cancelled until February 23, 2015.

February 23, 2015, the day of the belated Valentine party arrived with a vengeance. A crippling snowstorm which is typical every year about this time in Calgary, Canada. This evening the streets are darkened and packed with snow with a blinding snowstorm raging throughout the city and immobile transportation at this time. A power outage is also prevalent for the last several hours incorporating the city of Calgary, Canada. The vampires are hurriedly scurrying around in the closets with their flashlights searching for candles to lighten the basement in preparation for their oncoming company. The vampire's friends arrived sporadically due to the inclement weather this evening hindering their transportation. They came clomping and stomping onto the threshold screaming for joy, "Happy Belated Valentine's Day" with their arms loaded with gift's, cards, etc………. Likewise, the vampires reciprocated the favor. Their company was immediately seated by their name card anticipating an assortment of Valentine desserts, including a Valentine cake commemorating the occasion, a wide variety of candy, chocolate pie, anything edible in the line of chocolate. Goblets of red, crimson, succulent blood will be available at each placemat for the vampires to quench their thirst. "Sounds delicious, doesn't it?"

After the "dessert feast" was consumed the vampires exchanged gifts, cards, etc………. to everyone's delight drawing names and numbers in the process.

Naturally, the last event on the program this evening is the passing of the ballots with the president making an appearance before the vampires introducing themselves as Earl, Blair Jones and Isaac Hamlon. Within several minutes the ballots were collected and presented to the secretary, Joe Conley, for an evaluation of the winner. Joe announced, "The winner in tonight's election is Earl our new President of the Vampire Club. Everybody cheered, clapped and congratulated the new president, with Earl giving his final speech thanking the vampires for the honor bestowed on him, which he wasn't anticipating on winning. Earl bowed to his vampire friends and immediately seated himself at the presidential table continuing the meeting. He made several announcements to the club members saying, "The next meeting will be April 1, 2015 which I'm sure everyone will be in attendance. Thank you and good evening!"

At the conclusion of the meeting everyone arose, bundled up, thanked Earl and the vampires for the wonderfully spent evening and proceeded on their way. Earl and the vampires related their "thanks" likewise.

After such a long, eventful evening they were very fatigued and decided to retire to their caskets soon resuming their cleaning tomorrow. "Sounds good to me! How about you?"

Shoveling Anyone?

The vampires arose earlier than usual because of the cleaning procedure they had to follow while several of the vampires decided to start shoveling since it had stopped snowing for the time being. Evidently, this morning the power outage has been restored and their neighbors could be seen shoveling their porches, sidewalks and walkways after the onslaught of a blackout blizzard that ravaged the entire city. The vampires shoveled in 15 degree weather with a brisk wind following them and a light snow beginning to lazily drape the environment. Eventually, Carl said, "I'm beginning to freeze with this cold wind enveloping us. Is anyone interested in going inside like myself? I'm ready for some warm air! How about you?" The other vampires gladly accommodated him back into the house at a moment's notice. After they warmed up they came back outside to finish what they had begun while there was still some daylight left. By the time they headed back into the house again a heavy snow was falling which eventually covered the complete landscape. Tomorrow they will be out shoveling again for most of the day to complete as much as they can before another blizzard moves in. "Bad, Bad Weather!"

Chapter 4
A Blood Sucking Rendezvous

April 15, 2015

By now, the inclement weather has subsided and Earl and the vampires are eagerly anticipating a blood sucking rendezvous at the New Haven Cemetery in the near future. Earl reiterated to the vampires, "Since the weather is more accommodating at the present would anyone be interested in accompanying me for an outing at the New Haven Cemetery this coming week at an available time? Please raise your hands." All the vampire's hands shot up and their faces sported a gleeful grin as if to say, "We're ready to go! You name the night!" Earl said, "I'm considering vandalizing Mortimer's grave this coming Friday night since we have never been able to locate him. His casket was empty the last two times we unearthed it and we are still not sure who broke into Jean's house and terrorized one of the vampires. Was it Mortimer? Who knows?" The vampires had a questionable, puzzled look clouding their countenance. Could they possibly have forgotten that it could've been Mortimer that invaded Jean's house instilling fear in the remaining vampires that night? Are they experiencing short term memory loss? Surely not! Earl remarked, "Nevertheless, anyone that is interested in a blood sucking rendezvous this coming Friday night please meet me at 5:OO PM at my blue hearse accompanied by the usual tools at our disposal. It will be dark and after hours when we return from the New Haven Cemetery. Thank you!"

Friday Night

Four vampires, Blair, Joe, Alvin and Isaac, are patiently awaiting for 5:00 PM to roll around for their trip to the New Haven Cemetery with Earl, the President of the Vampire Club, for their blood sucking rendezvous at Mortimer's gravesite. Here comes Earl, lock, stock and barrel, transporting a variety of tools, at his convenience, to be used in the event they encounter any problems with the casket lock, other incidentals, etc............. "To come prepared is better than unprepared! Right?" The vampires are taking their respective seats in Earl's blue hearse, originally belonging to Albert and Jean, which has automatically been transferred to Earl because of his present position as President of the Vampire Club. 5:30 PM finds the vampires entering the gates of the New Haven Cemetery parking adjacent to Mortimer's grave in the newer part of the hallowed grounds. They exit the hearse and approach Mortimer's grave which gives the appearance of never having been desecrated. Never! By this time of the evening the cemetery lights have been illuminated casting a bright glow over the complete cemetery to the delight of the vampires. One by one they frantically start digging on Mortimer's grave with Earl keeping a watchful eye on any intruders that might possibly be infiltrating the cemetery at this time of the night.

By now the vampires have shoveled a depth of six feet into Mortimer's grave with Isaac screaming, "My shovel is banging on the lid of Mortimer's casket. Please help me with the remainder of the shoveling!" Earl immediately adjusts the lantern into the grave for better vision as the vampires attempt to break the lock with their tools. All of a sudden, they heard a slow, creaking sound as the casket lid automatically lifted to expose the corpse of Mortimer exactly as he appeared the day they buried him. Only this time both his eyes and mouth were wide open with cockroaches and beetles climbing in and out. A rancid, vile, stale odor incorporates the casket and permeates the air as the lid is slowly lifted higher. A small rattlesnake is nestled under Mortimer's arm making a rattling sound in the stillness of the night. Isaac is making an attempt to lift Mortimer's head into an upward position where he can adjust his mouth onto Mortimer's left jugular vein for the sucking sensation he is generally accustomed to by this time. Everything is falling into place as Isaac gorges himself on Mortimer's crimson, thick, succulent blood as it gushes from Isaac's mouth in a constant overflow onto Isaac and Mortimer's clothing, the casket, etc……….. Blair is next in line for the bloody feast that he was looking forward to stating, "It was well worth the effort!" Joe and Alvin took their turn respectively enjoying the bloody encounter and power they had over Mortimer's corpse. After all four vampires had effectively drained volumes of red, succulent blood from Mortimer's left jugular vein as they slammed the casket lid in haste and hurriedly shoveled the remainder of the soil into the grave. They scampered up the dirt walls of the grave glancing nervously around the New Haven Cemetery for fear of hidden intruders invading their privacy. Earl was still at his position, slinking behind a decomposed tombstone, keeping abreast of anybody entering or exiting the cemetery grounds at this time of the night. As they were getting ready to leave a light, eerie, filmy mist is beginning to infiltrate the tombstones, cemetery landscape, mausoleum, etc............ Earl and the vampires can be seen traipsing around the cemetery tombstones carrying their tools, equipment, etc............ headed for Earl's blue hearse parked two blocks north on Cemetery Road. As Earl and the vampires were driving back to Calgary he engaged them in a conversation regarding tonight's excursion to the New Haven Cemetery for their palatable pleasure. Isaac was the first to make the remark, "In the near future I would sincerely consider returning to the New Haven Cemetery for another rendezvous similar to this evening. Is anyone else interested at this time?" Blair, Joe, Alvin and Isaac expressed their desire to unearth more grave sites once they are absolutely positive the corpses' have been embalmed at a local mortuary which is standard procedure.

Chapter 5
Witches in the New Haven Cemetery

Three weeks have passed since Earl, Isaac, Blair, Alvin and Joe have made a nightly excursion to the New Haven Cemetery for a blood sucking rendezvous on Mortimer's bedraggled, decomposed frame. Earl approached Isaac, Joe, Blair and Alvin asking them, "Are any of you interested in frequenting the New Haven Cemetery again for a bloody, refreshing drink at any of the available, not embalmed corpses' that we have access to?" Since Earl, Chris and Ryan are currently employed as morticians at the Ronton Mortuary in Calgary they specifically are aware of the corpses' bodies that are embalmed and those that have been drained automatically of all bodily fluid. Earl again remarked, "I can recall a young man's body, Oliver Stone5 that was buried three days ago by the Ronton Mortuary of which I was in attendance. This individual is not embalmed, therefore, creating no problem whatsoever. Earl reiterated the question about frequenting the New Haven Cemetery again some night in the upcoming days? Joe, Blair, Alvin and Isaac, along with Earl, were eagerly anticipating their next outing to the New Haven Cemetery in a couple of days according to their plans. Isaac said, "I am basically speaking for our small group. I will say we are all looking forward to another bloody escapade, similar to three weeks ago, to increase our palatable desire. A date and time would be greatly appreciated before we depart. Earl said, "How about 8:00 PM this coming Friday night? Please meet me at my blue hearse parked in the garage with our equipment, tools, etc.........Thank you!" The vampires were in agreement and will proceed with the forthcoming plans.

Oliver Stone

Earl, Joe, Alvin, Blair and Isaac are in the process of traveling to the New Haven Cemetery to unearth the grave of Oliver Stone that was buried three days ago in an undisclosed, remote area of the cemetery. The unearthing procedure was a simple process which left little to the imagination. By this time, the vampires were scampering to the foot of the grave, ready to exhume the corpse of Oliver Stone, for their palatable preference. After Earl and the vampires quenched their soluble thirst which consisted of thick, crimson, succulent, bloody fluid overflowing from the left jugular vein in volumes they hurriedly cast his frail, young, frame back into the casket. Already ants, spiders and cockroaches were infiltrating Oliver's eyes and mouth as his eyelids kept closing and opening intermittently. No wonder! A small reptile had nestled on Oliver's suit for the night because no amount of coaxing could eliminate the situation. By now, Earl and the vampires are slithering up the walls of cold earth into the dark, eerie environment encompassing them. The lights are embracing the cemetery with their sheer brilliance flooding the tombstones with a bright beam of light. Earl and the vampires shoveled the top of the grave to perfection exiting with their tools and equipment onto Cemetery Road and Earl's blue hearse. Oh no! As they were leaving the New Haven Cemetery a group of vile, bedraggled, filthy women of all ages passed Earl and the vampires snickering and snarling to themselves. Upon passing they eyed the vampires with creepy, bewitching, shifty glances. Their hair were long and unkempt hanging limp and shapeless onto their neck. Adding to their creepy disposition was their formal attire which consisted of long, ankle length dresses which left a lot to be desired. Besides, leaving an unpleasant appearance they snickered, screeched and snarled with shrill, boisterous laughter as they traipsed on by. Are they witches? Are they fortune tellers? Where do they come from? Are they canvassing the New Haven Cemetery with their supernatural magic powers? I'm sure no one has ever encountered them before! Who are they capable of captivating and who will they approach? I'm assuming they are associated with witchcraft, magic spells, demonic powers, etc............ What is your opinion? Earl and the vampires stealthily walked to his blue hearse, seated themselves, with Earl quickly exiting Cemetery Road headed to Calgary. What an eerie, unpredictable evening! The bloody rendezvous incorporating Oliver Stone was a wonderful, exhilarating experience but the witches prowling makes the vampires apprehensive about frequenting the New Haven Cemetery again! "I wouldn't want to approach them in a dark alley, would you? The vampires had no idea that witches existed in Calgary, Canada! Did you?"

An Emergency Meeting May 6, 2015

Earl and the vampires posted meeting signs on the basement walls about tonight's gathering at 7:00 PM in the meeting room in the basement. All the vampires filed in at approximately 7:O0 PM with the exception of a few latecomers. Earl immediately approached the subject of the "witches" and their escalating fear as they passed them by on such short notice. Earl mentioned, "Please be cautious the next time you visit the New Haven Cemetery because this might be a new phase the "witches" are going to explore if, they indeed, reside in the city of Calgary! They might just be passing through! We can't be sure of that! Any questions so far?" Joe raised his hand saying, "Are we going back again sometime soon? I enjoyed the time we spent up there but not our return trip." Earl made the remark, "We will bide our time for a while, in the event, the same encounter occurs again. I will inform you when I will instigate our next trip. Thank you! This meeting is adjourned for this evening. Goodnight!"

Chapter 6
Witches!!!

Several weeks have passed since Earl and the vampires frequented the New Haven Cemetery after hours in search of a good old fashioned, gory, bloody encounter with a corpse that has gone through the process of internment some time ago. Upon entering the cemetery gates this evening, Earl led the vampires to the gravesite of Horace Kenison which Earl remembers was not embalmed prior to his burial because he was in attendance as a mortician at that time already. Earl and the vampires are positive Oliver Stone's body is devoid of any superfluous blood encased in Oliver's corpse. As I mentioned earlier, Earl and the vampires have moved on to the next non embalmed corpse on hand which is Horace Kenison. As they neared Horace's tombstone a group of slimy, filthy, vile appearing witches are desecrating the gravesite with their chopping and banging antics. Horace's tombstone has been once removed and lying on top of the barren earth. The coven of witches have replaced the tombstone with a cauldron on top of Horace Kenison's grave and are frantically boiling a concoction of watery, aromatic oils, leaves, etc………..to enhance a pleasant, becoming odor. Steadily, a distinctive fragrance permeates the night air as several witches keep stirring the bubbly cauldron to insure an even mixture throughout. In the meantime, Earl and the vampires are hidden behind several rows of tombstones, unnoticed by the witches working in a weird, emotional, frenzied state, oblivious of anything that is taking place at this point in time. Hearken! The witch's coven is babbling incoherently to each other indistinguishable in layman's terms. Several witches have moved the cauldron off the gravesite and are religiously beginning to shovel the barren earth to one side. What does this indicate? It appears to me they are shoveling towards the vault intent upon opening the casket lid exposing the corpse of vampire Horace Kenison! By this time, the aromatic aroma has been diminished but is still capable of emitting a sensation when the sense of smell is quickened.

Unearthing Horace's Grave

The casket lid is slowly creaking open while releasing a vile, loathsome, foul stench which quickly permeated the casket and its surroundings. The witches are continuing to snicker and giggle among themselves as they hurriedly apply the aromatic oils to Horace's bare vampire hands, arms and face in the hope of reincarnating him on their return trip. After Horace was thoroughly lathered with the aromatic oils the witches swiftly slammed the casket lid, proceeding to exit the earthen grave, while shoveling mounds of dirt to cover their tracks. After smoothing the gravesite they collected their tools and equipment leaving on foot with their ankle length robes and long unkempt hair blowing in the evening breeze. Similar to a band of fortune telling gypsies invading a community at night. After Earl and the vampires witnessed this atrocious behavior while positioning themselves behind a tombstone besides the witch's manner of speech they quickly exited the New Haven Cemetery for the city of Calgary. "I don't blame them! Do you? Who wants to be associated with a coven of witches with their magical spirits and powers? Not me!!! Will they be back next week? Will they continue to wreak havoc besides desecrating tombstones? Who knows? I'm not interested in finding out! Are you?"

Chapter 7
Beware of the Witches

As Earl was stating he is biding his time before the other vampires and himself go on an excursion at the New Haven Cemetery again. He was remarking to the vampires, "We can always resort to our downtown haunts to perform our dastardly deeds, thereby, avoiding the witch's coven at the New Haven Cemetery. We don't want to get involved with them. Is everybody agreed?" The vampires smiled and nodded their heads saying, "You set the time and date! We're ready!" Earl suggested, "How about tomorrow night? The weather is accommodating with a superfluous amount of people milling about through the main thoroughfares and downtown alleys for their strolling pleasure. I'm sure we can rustle up a straggler or two for our blood sucking passion, possibly, dragging them along back in the process. Meet me at the blue hearse at 7:00 PM for a night out on the town." The vampires are looking forward to the inevitable, as usual. They woke up at 4:00 PM the next day, their regular time, as they prepared to bathe and shave besides getting dressed in their formal attire which consists of black suits, no capes, because of recognition and white shirts. Their hair are perfectly coiffed, flawless makeup with their nails professionally manicured. An appealing aroma clouds the vampires as they prepare to exit their home for a downtown rendezvous. As they enter the downtown alleyways of Calgary throngs of people can be seen swarming the streets enjoying the midsummer night's air. Music is blaring in the background, drifting out of the business area, to accommodate their clientele. At present, Earl and the vampires are strolling the walkways between the business buildings in search of homeless people, transients, shiftless bums loitering the area besides sleeping in the doorways of businesses and restaurants. Numerous transients can be seen sifting through the refuse containers in the back alleys. A rotten, decaying odor is escaping the containers because newer methods of sanitation are lacking. A group of shiftless bums can be seen sitting in a circle, warming their hands, while conversing with each other intermittently. Every once in a while a smile is etched across a homeless person's face but basically they portray a sad, forlorn, destitute appearance. As the evening takes on a darkening gloom the vampires are scouring the filthy alleyways between business buildings laden with papers, cigarette butts, discarded cheap wine containers, leftover food, etc………….. A light, misty film is beginning to encompass the area as vagrants are huddled together in a desperate attempt to shield themselves from the elements. Earl and the vampires are meandering through the back alleys, hopefully, to encounter anyone that is destitute and desperate enough to comply with their demands. Earl, unexpectedly decided to approach an intoxicated young man wandering through the walkways between two buildings. He crept up stealthily behind the man saying, "Hah! I think I recognize you from somewhere!" When the intoxicated man turned around Earl grabbed him by his slimy, wart infested throat sinking his sparkling, white fangs into his withered neck. Earl sucked his succulent, crimson, bloody fluid that gushed out of his left jugular vein violently. The excess spilled on Earl and his victim besides splashing on the outside business walls, concrete, etc………….At this point, it was totally dark as Earl decided to transport the vagrant back to their home on 2125 Melbourne Street. The remainder of the vampires dragged him to the blue hearse for the ride back. When they arrived Earl instantly gave the vagrant a shove which landed him at the bottom of the basement floor to lie there until the next day. Earl made the remark, "We'll check on him tomorrow." Everybody nodded their heads in agreement and went to their respective coffins for the night.

A Quiet, Peaceful Night Until?

A soothing, restful slumber was had by everyone until a bumbling, mumbling sound could be heard at daybreak echoing from the basement walls. Is the vagrant incoherent, stumbling around in the basement, oblivious of what has transpired? Evidently he resuscitated after Earl flung him down the basement stairs. Now the vagrant is stealthily creeping up the stairs in search of Earl since he was nowhere to be found in the basement coffins. The vagrant immediately encountered Earl as he charged into his room grabbing him by the neck while sinking his fangs into Earl's withered, brown neck. Earl's violent outburst of fear screaming, "Get away from me!" besides his ranting and raving immediately awoke the vampires in the basement prompting them to dash upstairs in response to Earl's screams for help. Earl was beside himself with fear as Isaac forcefully yanked the vagrant's frame from Earl's bedraggled, mangled body. The vampires slowly escorted the vagrant to the basement placing him in a coffin for the night while attending to Earl's emotional needs upstairs. Earl was still beside himself with fear and unease as the vampires tried to console him but to no avail. Each vampire took their turn observing Earl for one hour during the night to make sure there were no problems.

The Next Day

Once again, after Earl and the vampires awoke the next afternoon Earl had regained his composure while eating his meals and visiting with the vampires on a regular basis. He made the remark, "It's my own fault the vagrant attacked me during the night with his sucking rampage. I should have known better than to bring him back here. I can't believe I made a stupid mistake like that. This is the first time I can ever recall something like this taking place since we have been transporting derelicts back here etc………….. What do you think?" The vampires kept their private opinions to themselves for fear of upsetting Earl emotionally again. "You can never really be sure how a situation can escalate! Follow me?"

Chapter 8
Witches Again!!!

Earl and the vampires, Isaac, Joe, Alvin and Blair have decided to frequent the New Haven Cemetery in search of Horace Kenison's grave which was desecrated by a coven of witches several weeks ago. The witches lathered Horace's body with aromatic oils in the hope of reincarnating his body back to life. Earl and the vampires were mysteriously huddled outside a mausoleum on the outskirts of New Haven Cemetery awaiting the arrival of the coven of witches. Suddenly, there appeared a small group of slightly bent, dirt infested hags sporting billowing robes and pointed hats. They were speaking gibberish to one another unaware of their surroundings at the present moment. In spite of laughing and snarling at each other they seemed to be in a pleasing frame of mind. They hurriedly uncovered Horace Kenison's grave with their spades while continuously shoveling to the bottom of the vault. Hastily lifting the lid of the casket they encountered an empty tomb void of any remains. The witches were amazed at the outcome of their problem at the New Haven Cemetery. Evidently the lathering of Horace Kenison's corpse reincarnated his decrepit body back to normal. The witches are repeatedly interrogating their friends, "What happened to Horace Kenison? Was he reincarnated? How did he scrabble his way to the top of the grave?" The witches stared at each other in disbelieving shock as they began the process of shoveling the earth back in place and scampering up the ladder to the entrance of the grave tools and all. Unbeknown, that they were being observed by Earl and the vampires in close proximity of the mausoleum they quickly exited to the New Haven Cemetery in sheer silence for fear Horace Kenison might be in the vicinity. "Is this possible?" After the witches passed through the New Haven Cemetery gates Earl and the vampires proceeded to follow the darkened path en route to Earl's blue hearse parked north of the hallowed grounds. On the way back to Calgary Earl made the remark, "I'm surprised at the outcome of tonight's rendezvous since Horace Kenison's body was absent. Did someone remove the body? But who, may I ask?" The vampires were reminiscing what transpired the last several hours. By this time, Earl was pulling into the driveway at 2125 Melbourne Street minus their bloody encounter at the New Haven Cemetery. Besides, practically being confronted by the coven of witches, alias gypsies, on their way out. At this time of the evening the vampires are not interested in the aforesaid only in a good night's slumber in their respective coffins. "Goodnight, everybody!"

Another Meeting? June 17, 2015

Earl posted several meeting signs for this evening at 7:00 PM in the All Purpose Room in the basement encouraging everyone to attend. The vampires were slowly filing in at 7:00 PM with Earl positioned at the president's table calling the meeting to order. After the Pledge of Allegiance was recited the vampires resumed their respective seats for the ongoing meeting that was on the agenda for the evening. Earl immediately asked, "Is there any old business on the docket that needs to be reviewed or taken into consideration at this point? Please raise your hand if you have information that has not been brought to our attention." None of the vampires raised their hands in regard to Earl's suggestion indicating "all is well." Earl continued, "Is there any new business on the agenda that needs to be evaluated this evening? Please raise your hand." Isaac raised his hand indicating he had something of interest to present to the Vampire Club. Isaac made the remark, "Several weeks ago Earl, Joe, Blair, Alvin and myself decided to frequent the New Haven Cemetery on an outing in regards to Horace Kenison's grave that was being desecrated by a coven of witches the last time we were there. We were nestled outside of a mausoleum observing the coven of witches entering the hallowed grounds walking directly to Horace Kenison's grave site. They shoveled the earth until they were able to lower themselves into the tomb to exhume Horace's corpse. The witches lathered Horace's body with aromatic oils in the hope of reincarnating his body back to life. Earl, Joe, Alvin, Blair and myself observed the inevitable while we were positioned at the mouth of the grave without their awareness of this. After the coven of witches scampered up the earthen walls they finished their shoveling escapade and hurriedly exited the hallowed grounds of the New Haven Cemetery by the pearly gates. Several nights ago, Earl, Alvin, Joe,

Blair and I went back to the New Haven Cemetery again encountering the coven of witches at Horace's grave once more. According to their gibberish conversation they indicated Horace Kenison's corpse is missing from his grave." Isaac asked, "Was he reincarnated with the lathering of the aromatic oils on his body by the witches? What happened to him? Did someone kidnap him? Surely not!!! Do you suppose he is wandering around the New Haven Cemetery tonight? Who knows?" The remainder of the vampires have no answers for the aforesaid questions and are constantly whispering among themselves despite the fact they weren't even present at the actual gravesite. "That's rather strange, isn't it?' Earl asked, "Does anybody else have any input on Isaac's story of our encounter with a coven of witches? Please raise your hand or come forward at this time." None of the vampires made a motion to move, therefore, Earl said, "At this point in time, we do not have any further information on the whereabouts of Horace Kenison. If anyone decides to frequent the New Haven Cemetery for a bloody rendezvous please be on your guard since you are aware of the fact that Horace Kenison is missing from his grave as we speak. Thank you! This meeting is adjourned for this evening. Our next meeting will be July 6, 2015. Refreshments are available on the back table for those of you that so desire. Goodnight!"

Chapter 9
Horace the Vampire

Indeed! Horace the Vampire is scouring the New Haven Cemetery in the eerie, misty night time hours searching for the possibility of an opened grave, a deceased body at random unattended, anything of blood sucking value! "Will he get lucky? Read on!!! Horace has decided to walk north on Cemetery Road toward a few homesteads that are scattered in this farming region of Calgary, Canada. He is walking aimlessly toward the first home he encounters in the dead of night as he begins to rattle and bang on the door and windows for warmth and a place to lay his head. The longer he waits the more agitated he becomes since no one will answer their door during the nighttime hours. "Can you blame them?" He continues to rattle and bang unceasingly until soft footsteps can be heard slithering across the floor. All of a sudden, the room is ablaze with light and movement can be heard within. Gibberish voices can be heard, laughing and snarling at each other but fearful of opening the door. "Oh no! It's a coven of witches!!!" By this time Horace is beside himself with anger since it is beginning to rain lightly which could materialize into something heavier. Once again Horace yanked on the door forcing it to open voluntarily while several witches snarled and glared at him besides spitting in his face. Horace screamed at them while grabbing one of the witches by her yellow, withered, slimy neck and sucking her left, jugular vein till it was void of all blood. Horace slurped the red, succulent, bloody concoction until he couldn't retain it any longer. Eventually, volumes of blood spilled out of his mouth onto his and the witch's clothing, landing on the floor. In the meantime, Horace collapsed on the floor in a dead heap at the witch's feet. They dragged him to an extra bed for the remainder of the night. "Goodnight Horace! Don't let the witch's bite!"

A Bloody Encounter

All of a sudden, Horace the Vampire lay wide awake devising a morbid scheme to brutally attack several of the witches while they were fast asleep in their private bedrooms. As he stealthily crept down the long, dark hallway he could hear loud snoring escalating from either side. Horace decided to step into the first bedroom he passed observing a witch sound asleep oblivious of anything going on as he grabbed her slimy, spindly neck with both hands jerking her in an upright position. Her eyelids flew wide open as she screamed and flailed her arms in discontent and fright at the outcome of Horace's demeanor. He opened his tantalizing lips and voluptuous mouth to incite pleasure into her person in spite of her continuous clamoring for help. After Horace sucked her left jugular vein until it completely collapsed he flung her filthy, moldy specimen of a human being onto a bloody heap on the floor. Since daylight is fast approaching Horace has decided to exit the witch's hideaway and trudge back to the New Haven Cemetery and the safety and shelter of his coffin six feet underground. Horace has easy access to the shovels and equipment in the storage shed which will be no problem. On second thought maybe Horace doesn't need to sleep in his casket! Maybe he can sleep in the mausoleum that was just constructed several weeks ago at the far end of the cemetery. It is filled with new caskets, never been used, or so he thought! Horace worked on the lock and managed to pry the door open to gain entrance. He checked all ten caskets and they were empty, except one, which was occupied by an older man. The mausoleum, itself, had a pleasant aroma, climate controlled and powered by electricity. Horace thought, "What more do I want? I can always eat out of the refuse containers along the road. It's better than digging myself in and out of a grave every night. Hah! If the witches come back to the New Haven Cemetery they'll never find me! It sounds like Horace has it made, doesn't it? Sleeping in a new casket in a new mausoleum every night! Eating your free meals out of a refuse container along the road! Since Horace has the characteristics of a vampire he will have easy access to the non- embalmed corpses in their caskets besides all the derelicts, transients and stragglers in the downtown alleyways, behind the business buildings and otherwise. Maybe, he will even encounter the witches again on one of his nightly haunts? What do you think? You never know! Stranger things than that have transpired in this world! Right? Just keep on reading!!!

How About Roller Skating?

It's been several years since Earl and the vampires have been seen at the Calgary Skating Rink back to the days when Albert and Jean were in authority. "Remember?" Earl decided to call this afternoon and make reservations for the vampires and himself for an evening at the skating rink. As Friday night drew closer the vampires were meticulously groomed to the nines, their hair were perfectly coiffed, not a hair out of place, flawless makeup and sporting a flashy smile, emblazoned with stark, white teeth to complete their appearance. As they entered the Calgary Skating Rink there were shrieks of laughter penetrating the air as they were being fitted with roller skates. Everybody, including Earl, was trying to balance themselves with their skates on. Isaac said, "I can't hardly stand up with these skates on. How about you?" Joe made the remark, "I'm sitting on the floor oftener than I'm standing up!" Blair insisted, "We need to hold on to the hand rail longer until our balance has improved." Everybody agreed with the aforesaid and proceeded to uphold their balance. After they skated for two hours they decided to take a snack break before entering the skating rink again. By the time 10:00 PM rolled around, most of the vampires had improved their skating techniques immensely. It was just a matter of lack of practice in between their trips to the Calgary Skating Rink. Earl insisted, "We need to come to the skating rink oftener. Practice makes perfect!" The vampires smiled and nodded in return. Before the vampires left the skating rink Earl scheduled another skating excursion for the following week.

Chapter 10
Who wants to go to the Theater?

In the meantime Earl is scanning their agenda for different activities to keep the vampires occupied this summer while Chris, Ryan and he are employed as full time morticians at the Ronton Mortuary in Calgary, Canada. This morning Earl was conversing with several of the vampires, at random, concerning a variety of recreational activities they would like to pursue while they are at work this summer. Joe mentioned, "We haven't been to the Redwood Theater for over a year and I'm sure we would all like to see a good, classical movie that is currently being advertised as a box office hit." When the vampires heard Joe's suggestion they were elated breaking out in smiles and whispering among themselves. Joe asked them, "Is every one in favor of a "night at the Redwood Theater?" Please raise your hand!" By this time most of the zombies and vampires had accumulated raising their hands in favor of a "night at the Redwood Theater." Earl was pleased at the outcome of the survey and would immediately schedule a 'night at the Redwood Theater" within the next week. "Incidentally," Joe suggested, "If our preference is to sit farther back in the upstairs balcony of the Red Theater our chances are better at encountering several younger women for a blood sucking rendezvous. There might even be a possibility that we can transport them back with us if we bide our time. Does this appeal to everyone? Please raise your hand if you are in favor of my suggestion!" Everybody present raised their hand in favor with Joe saying, "Very well. I will make the necessary arrangements when a popular, well, advertised movie is featured. The vampires were thrilled at the prospect of going to the Redwood Theater once again and a possible blood sucking encounter. "Good luck, vampires!" Today is June 17, 2015 with a clear, balmy night and not a cloud on the horizon. The vampires, including Earl, are primping and pruning themselves, as usual, to present their best, possible appearance while in the public eye. After they bathed and shaved they are attired in their black suits, no capes for fear of recognition, and white, dress shirts with neckties to match. Their hair are perfectly coiffed, flawless makeup, gleaming white teeth with their vampire fangs unnoticeable.

Their elongated fingernails are excellently manicured while their red, flashing, blood shot eyes hold one spellbound as it completes their appearance. At present they are positioned in their movie seats in the upstairs balcony of the Redwood Theater awaiting the movie, currently featured titled, "Armageddon 111."In the proximity of their own seats two younger women are seated adjacent to Earl and the vampires. Towards the end of the movie Joe and Isaac decided to approach the two younger women. They mildly stroked their necks while slowly opening their blood thirsty mouths and sinking their snow white, canine fangs into their lily, white necks incorporating their left, jugular vein. They sucked their blood vehemently, gorging themselves to the point of an overflow of blood on their clothes, floor, etc..........While very few people were leaving the Redwood Theater Earl and the vampires ushered the two, younger, unnoticed women to the vampire's vehicles for the trip back to 2125 Melbourne Street. When they reached the aforesaid address they exited their vehicle immediately flinging the two, young women downstairs to lie on the barren, cement floor until the next afternoon.

The Next Day

After the vampires arose at their customary time, which is 4:O0 PM they checked on the two women they had flung downstairs previously the night before. They seemed to be fine other than a few scratches they acquired when their frame hit the barren, concrete, basement floor. "Ouch!" So far they have not spoken when spoken to nor have they eaten anything when asked. They have been transferred to private coffins where they will continue to lie until they express interest in being up and about. "Fair enough?"

Chapter 11
Earthquake!

Earl and the vampires decided to frequent the New Haven Cemetery this evening on one pretext or another. Possibly scouring the cemetery for new gravesites with corpses' that have not been embalmed. They can be seen at dusk traipsing through the New Haven Cemetery studying the newly tilled gravesites forcefully yanking the mausoleum doors in hope of gaining entrance besides anything else they set their mind to. As they continue traipsing through the cemetery they are met with an ominous rumbling, constant rattling and horrific cracks in the hallowed, cemetery grounds. The rumbling is increasing at an alarming rate as Earl and the vampires seek shelter next to the mausoleum. At this point in time, the roof of the mausoleum is blown away and numerous tombstones have been yanked off the gravesites and deposited in other areas of the cemetery. The cracks in the cemetery are getting increasingly deeper with gravesites being blown completely open to reveal the caskets six feet underground with their lids ajar. Several of the corpses' were missing from their caskets apparently scattered throughout the New Haven Cemetery. Earl and the vampires are screaming, "It's an earthquake! It's an earthquake! How will we make it back to Calgary? Is it safe to drive?" Earl made a remark, "We better wait here in the cemetery for a while until the earthquake subsides, before we go on our way. When we get back I will immediately notify Ronton Mortuary about the displaced corpses' on the cemetery grounds because I'm sure they are unaware of this." The vampires waited for a while before departing the New Haven Cemetery for Calgary. When they arrived back KIBX television station was announcing severe damage throughout the city of Calgary. There was destruction at several cemeteries, numerous businesses and homes were completely destroyed and hundreds of injuries, plus twelve deaths. Their home at 2125 Melbourne Street was unscathed but two homes in the neighborhood were demolished beyond repair. Earl and the vampires were shocked at the devastation the earthquake left in its path. "No one expected anything like this tonight!" They could still feel the aftershock and tremors after the earthquake had subsided. Everyone stayed awake watching television late into the night as reports kept filtering in regarding the earthquake that left the city of Calgary, Canada in ruin and despair.

Chapter 12
Rebuilding Calgary, Canada

"Are the vampires and zombies getting lucky or what?" While they were watching their local, television station KIBX the broadcaster diligently announced, "Construction workers are in high demand in the city of Calgary due to the onslaught of the earthquake that severely devastated an enormous part of the businesses, homes, parks, etc............ If anyone is interested in the above mentioned please apply at the office, No. 412, in the City Hall on Harper Street for further consideration. The sooner an application is filed the sooner you will be accepted. All phases of construction will be deliberated on such as roofing, siding repair, painting, electrical, sheet rocking, heating and cooling, etc.............. Experience is very helpful but not necessary. Doors open at 9:00 AM. When Joe, Blair and Isaac became obvious of this sudden influx of labor Joe made the remark, "I think I'll apply for a construction job with the city tomorrow. All we have to do is complete our household chores earlier and be on our way to the construction site which sounds like it's within walking distance. Are either of you interested in getting another job?" Blair said, "I think I'll submit my application for a construction job also because the extra money will come in handy especially at Christmas time." Isaac was in total agreement saying, "I could always use the extra money so I'm in game for an extra job, even construction. We will have to get around pretty early tomorrow morning getting our household chores completed then catching the bus to City Hall on Harper Street."

Rise and Shine

Joe, Blair and Isaac got an early morning start on their chores, therefore, they are ready to leave to catch the bus for City Hall. When they approached City Hall they encountered several long lines waiting for the doors to open at 9:00 AM. They got in line with the rest of the applicants and patiently awaited their turn. After they completed the application they were told, "We will notify you next week in regards to the status application of your form." The vampires smiled and nodded saying, "Thank you" and proceeded to exit the City Hall building. Joe, Blair and Isaac experienced a "fast week" considering notification of their pending construction jobs. They each received a call this morning telling them, "Your application form has been reviewed and accepted for a job with Berg Construction Company starting on Gilmore Avenue. When are you able to start?" They said, "Tomorrow morning" while receiving further instructions in regards to specific training, time frames, building codes, etc...............

Construction Work

Upon arrival at the Berg Construction site, Joe, Blair and Isaac were immediately referred to the training department for the evaluation of the different areas they would be positioned in. At this point in time the vampires were in the same area in their respective positions gleaning information as to what is expected of them in the forthcoming days. This afternoon they were trained in the replacement of new siding on the devastated homes and tomorrow they will grasp certain techniques to facilitate the roofing process. The above mentioned is a "far cry" from your "regular household chores." Correct?

Chapter 13
Bang! Bang! Bang!

As the temperature soared to one hundred and five degrees this afternoon Joe, Blair and Isaac could be seen in the "hard hat" area replacing demolished siding or standing on a slanted roof applying new shingles. The heat is intensifying as the days wear on and the vampires are "sweating bullets" so they say. At the present they are taking a break enjoying a refreshing, cold drink to quench their humongous thirst then back to work until five o'clock. Joe, Blair and Isaac will meet the bus this evening to transport them back to Earl and the vampires because they are too tired to walk that long trek. "I don't blame them! Do you?" Tomorrow will be more of the same and the day after that! This is what they chose! You are responsible for what you choose! No one twisted their arm! This was their own decision! Right?" I would say, "It's a wise enough choice plus more money. It just takes some getting used to!" New Haven Cemetery Again?

Earl and the vampires are gathered around their television set in the basement this evening watching an old nineteen fifties movie, a rerun, that's been featured several times for the pleasure of the older crowd. All of a sudden Earl spoke up saying, "Who would like to go to the New Haven Cemetery tomorrow night for something to pass the time? We haven't been there since the earthquake happened." Blair said, "I guess I can also speak for the remainder of the zombies and vampires when I say we would all be interested in frequenting the New Haven Cemetery once again for our sheer pleasure. It seems like there is always something going on there! Right?" Earl said, "That's for sure! Meet me at my blue hearse at seven o'clock tomorrow night with your spades and extra tools in the event that we need them." As they were coasting towards New Haven Cemetery tonight in Earl's blue hearse Isaac blurted out, "I wonder if all the corpses' have been placed back in their caskets since some were scattered around the cemetery due to the earthquake." Earl remarked, "I'm sure the caretakers have taken care of everything by now. I also expect the tombstones to be back on their respective graves." By this time, Earl and the vampires have parked the blue hearse two blocks north of the cemetery and have passed through the gates en route to view the different areas that were desecrated by the earthquake. So far everything seems to be intact in regards to the bodies being back in their caskets and the tombstones back on their graves. The roof of the mausoleum has been repaired and everything else seems to be back in place. Joe and several of the other vampires are prowling around the cemetery on their own this evening disconnected from Earl and the others, "Just for nosiness sake!" Suddenly Joe encounters a corpse lying at the eastern end of the New Haven Cemetery in an open field. Evidently the caretakers missed him when they buried those that were scattered all over the cemetery. His open grave is situated a distance from the location of his course. Joe screamed as Earl and the vampires came forth to view the mangled corpse with his eyes wide open and blood trickling from his mouth.

Has the Corpse Been Embalmed?

The utmost question on the vampire's minds, at this point, is, 'Has this corpse ever been embalmed?" The only way to be sure is to initiate a sucking procedure that will indicate whether the presiding mortician proceeded with the inevitable. Who wants to be the first person to make this determination? Please step forward." Logan, a new member of the Vampire Club, came forth indicating he was willing to make an attempt at withdrawing human blood from the mutilated corpse in their midst. Logan violently jerked the corpse by the neck with his bare hands while positioning his thick, bloody lips on his left, jugular vein in hopes of gorging himself with crimson, succulent blood to his liking. The transition went smoothly from the corpses' left jugular vein to Logan's palatable, juicy, blood thirsty lips. Logan was beginning to feel the full, bloated effect on his stomach indicating that he had gorged himself with more blood than his body could contain. He immediately dropped the disfigured corpse to the cemetery grounds making him available for the other vampires to feast their hungry fangs thereto. At present neither Earl nor any of the other vampires are interested in a blood sucking rendezvous to satisfy their craving for human blood. "Have you got any interest in the above mentioned? If so, please come forward!" Since the New Haven Cemetery is desolate at this hour of the evening Earl and the vampires have decided to "call it a night" and proceed to the blue hearse for the ride back to Calgary. Besides an eerie, heavy mist is beginning to drape the tombstones and everything in sight.

Chapter 14
Poheta Cemetery

Several days have passed since Earl and the vampires have frequented the New Haven Cemetery. Just as recently as today Earl approached the vampires asking them, "Would any of you be interested in visiting the Poheta Cemetery sometime in the near future? It is an Indian Cemetery that has been there for years located several miles out of Calgary. Actually I remember going out there one night while Albert was still living with a few of our other vampires for a "night on the town," like they used to say. Do any of you remember this?" The vampires smiled and nodded saying, "Yes. That was a fun night. We're raring to go again! Just tell us when!" Earl remarked, "How about this coming Friday night? We will be leaving at 7:00 PM in the blue hearse parked in the driveway. Please bring extra shovels and equipment in the event we have to gain entrance unexpectedly. You never know! Please come prepared with light jackets since the evenings are cooler in the outskirts of Calgary. Not only that, a heavy mist is not uncommon later in the evening. Is everybody in agreement with my terms of an outing at the Poheta Cemetery this coming Friday night? Please raise your hands, if so." All the vampires raised their hands indicating they were very interested in the outing on Earl's terms.

Friday Night

Friday night is upon the vampires as they are frantically making preparations for the "upcoming bloody rendezvous" at the Poheta Cemetery this evening. They ate a light supper in the event they will be feasting on corpses, possibly, scattered around the cemetery after the earthquake. Who knows? Earl and the vampires left at 7:00 PM for Poheta Cemetery arriving at 7:30 PM. Upon parking the blue hearse two blocks north of the cemetery they noticed a strange car parked adjacent to their hearse unrecognizable by anyone. They proceeded to pass through the cemetery gates with everyone dispersing in different directions to familiarize themselves with the cemetery. They are aware of the earthquake wreaking havoc at the Poheta Cemetery with a variety of corpses' dispersed in different directions. The onslaught of the earthquake resulted in displaced tombstones, partial and completely opened graves, total collapse of several outbuildings, etc………… Once again Earl's vampires located numerous corpses' blown out of their graves to lie in open fields and the edge of the Red River a short distance from the cemetery. Earl said to the vampires in regards to the corpses, "Help yourselves! They are at your disposal! First come! First served!" Several of the vampires stepped forward with their blood sucking anticipation only to be met by a dry, parched mouth void of a drop of blood. How disgusting! These corpses were embalmed prior to their internment and burial. Earl made the remark, "I vaguely remember them being embalmed because I assisted in the procedure at the Ronton Mortuary. After the vampires became aware of the "embalming process" they nonchalantly flung them back on the hallowed ground in search of another prospect. The vampires wandered out to the open field where numerous corpses' were strewn sporadically for their delight. None of these corpses had been embalmed and the vampires will surely help themselves.

   Logan is going to press his luck again tonight as he will make an attempt to engage in another bloody rampage on the corpses! He grabbed the first female corpse he laid his eyes on, his bare hands jerking her frail, spindly, withered neck towards him. His eyes were feasting hungrily on her lily, white jugular vein as he thrust his white, canine fangs into her neck. Logan is sucking horrendously with crimson, succulent blood flowing violently as he gorges himself with volumes of the juicy, sticky substance to satisfy his palatable desire. As his overwhelming desire for blood has ebbed away he immediately flung the corpse on a mound of earth and wandered aimlessly away. Earl and the vampires strolled from one corpse to another sprawled in the open field seeking to satisfy their sucking desires before the evening ends. Poheta Cemetery is one of the few cemeteries that has not yet been evaluated in regards to the devastation and destruction caused by an earthquake several weeks ago. What a calamity!"

Chapter 15
July 4th, 2015

The Fourth of July is fast approaching for the vampires in regards to sponsoring a free for all community meal for anybody that is interested in attending this event at Mitchell Lake. After the evening food extravaganza there will be numerous fireworks on display for the entertainment of the general public in the larger area encompassing Mitchell Lake. Music will be provided by Les Brown commonly known as the Band of Renown. A variety of fifties and sixties music will be presented for their musical pleasure throughout the evening. At present the Death Chamber at 2125 Melbourne Street is housing several decomposing corpses' suspended from the ceiling with their eyes wide open and several deceased bodies are stored in closed coffins. The vile, loathsome stench is unbearable since they have been in this position for several years. When a community event is imminent Earl, more than likely, will select a corpse that is suspended from the ceiling in the last stages of decomposition. Earl has accomplished the above mentioned task this morning and is soliciting the assistance of the remainder of the vampires this evening for the dissection process to follow. This evening after supper the vampires hurriedly scampered to the Death Chamber in the basement to assist Earl in the dissecting process of a decomposed male corpse. His complete body was sliced into one and a half inch fleshy cubes to be barbecued tomorrow evening as the main entrée of the meal. The remainder of the meal consisted of beef gravy, mashed potatoes laced with dead beetles, blood bread, moldy carrots, a salad which consisted of rotten lettuce, fresh onions, boiled, slimy tomatoes, croutons, sliced, decayed cucumbers, and filthy dish water for salad dressing. Dessert is Blood Pound Cake and Vomit Ice Cream. This scrumptious meal is accompanied by goblets of fresh, crimson, succulent blood to everyone's liking! "A free meal! Can you beat that? Where else can you get a free meal like that tonight? Nowhere!"

A Free Meal

The vampires were out of their coffins bright and early this morning to make the necessary preparations for the community meal which will ensue at 6:00 PM. After that a fireworks display will follow accompanied by Les Brown's Band taking center stage for the remainder of the evening for the public's enjoyment. "Sound's interesting, doesn't it?"It is 5:30 PM and the public is slowly filtering into the area of Mitchell Park, encompassed by Mitchell Lake, where the free, community meal is being sponsored by the Vampire Club. Picnic tables have been set up and the barbecue cooker is slowly roasting the human, flesh eyeballs, etc............ The barbecue flavor is wafting through Mitchell Park while a starving community is anxiously awaiting the food extravaganza so popularly advertised. By now the vampire waiters have started seating the public at the picnic tables while beginning to serve goblets of the bloody concoction everyone was anticipating. Plates of the main entrée were passed up and down the tables accompanied by mashed potatoes, beef gravy, carrots, a vegetable salad, blood bread, etc........... Dessert consisted of Blood Pound Cake and Cherry Vomit Ice Cream. Everyone was eating to their heart's delight while praising the food set before them with remarks such as, "What a wonderful meal and elaborate setting." Another man said, "This is better than any restaurant I've ever eaten in. I wonder if they cater meals, also. I'll have to inquire!" After the meal was completed the general public dispersed to different areas of Mitchell Park to be serenaded by Les Brown's band of Renown with their 1950 and 1960's "oldies music" for their sheer pleasure! Songs frequently played were from the "Elvis Presley, Fats Domino, Johnny Cash era of time," etc............ The cement platform encompassing the stage was reserved for their dancing expertise. A variety of young and old couples were swinging and swaying to the beat of the music while other couples were clapping their hands in a festive mood.

Fireworks Galore

Dusk is fast approaching as the vampires are working diligently to position their fireworks with the intention of lighting them in a blaze of glory. "Bang! Bang! Bang!" Everybody was craning their necks upward as the sky exploded in a brilliant, sparkling, radiant light only to dissipate in a few minutes. After a couple of hours of fireworks display the vampires had depleted their explosives and were willing "to call it a night." About this time they resorted to cleaning the grounds in the park they were affiliated with while the public thanked the vampires for the free meal, music, dancing and fireworks display. They were very appreciative. Earl and the vampires were glad when they pulled in the driveway at 2125 Melbourne Street because they were very tired after long, tedious hours of waiting on tables, creating the fireworks display, clean up, etc…………..They welcomed a good night's rest after they retired in their coffins. "Goodnight, guys!"A light rain is pelting down as Isaac distinguishes the last light in the basement. Occasionally a clap of thunder can be heard resonating in the background throughout the evening.

Chapter 16
The Next Day

Since the Fourth of July has passed the vampires are back in their construction work while Earl, Chris and Ryan are employed as morticians at the Ronton Mortuary in Calgary. Currently the remainder of the vampires are assisting Earl in the household chores that have been assigned to them. Typically Earl and the vampires are still exceedingly tired today after the July 4th holiday yesterday in regards to the free, community meal, fireworks display and clean up. This evening they congregated around the television set in the basement to enjoy a good, old fashioned movie from several years ago. To accompany the movie Earl served them cold, bottled blood to quench their thirst. The movie started at 8:O0 PM and ended at 10:O0 PM with the vampires immediately retiring to their coffins for the night. "Good idea!"Actually the hours have changed since Earl, Chris and Ryan are employed as morticians at the Ronton Mortuary. Instead of arising at 4:O0 PM in the afternoon they arise at 7:O0 AM in the morning to report for work at 9:O0 AM. The vampires that work for Berg Construction Company arise at 6:O0 AM in order to report for work at 8:O0 AM. The vampires that perform household chores are still able to sleep till 4:O0 PM in the afternoon because of their position at home. The hours are a little more accommodating for the vampires at home but a little more taxing for the morticians and construction workers. "What is your opinion?"

Back to Poheta Cemetery Again

Since Earl and the vampires have taken a break for several days Earl suggested, "Who is interested in frequenting Poheta Cemetery again?" The vampires smiled and nodded their heads saying, 'We're raring to go! You set the time and day!" Earl said, "How about tomorrow night at 7:O0 PM? Meet me at my blue hearse in the garage." The vampires said, "We'll be there!" Earl continued, "I have a plan that I have devised in my mind. I would like to accumulate some extra corpses' in the Death Chamber for our own personal barbecuing pleasure.

Would any of you be willing to assist in the removal of a body or two from the Poheta Mausoleum tomorrow night? It is imperative that we are equipped with the correct tools in the event the mausoleum door is locked. Is everybody in compliance with the following request?" The vampires smiled, nodded and agreed wholeheartedly to Earl's suggestion. Earl said, "Very well. Then it's settled!" As Earl and the vampires were en route to Poheta Cemetery this evening he discussed the trip with them at length. "I am explicitly encouraging everyone to collaborate with each other, as a group, while we are in the process of finalizing the transferal of the corpse from the casket to the hearse. At any time please do not stray from the mausoleum or cemetery grounds to other unknown areas. As you exit the hearse bring the tools with you that you have in your possession. Thank you!" the vampires smiled, nodded their heads and said, "We understand." By this time Earl and the vampires have reached the Poheta Cemetery departing the hearse en route to the two Poheta Mausoleums. As dusk is fast approaching Earl is making the first attempt at breaking the mausoleum lock with no luck. Joe tries his luck also using a different wrench and immediately hears a crack and movement within the lock. He turns the handle and opens the door with the greatest of ease displaying stacks of caskets on top of each other. The vampires opened a casket to their liking with Earl and Isaac removing the corpse of an older man to transport to his hearse and back to their home at 2125 Melbourne Street. Actually it was a simple procedure with no one on the hallowed, cemetery grounds to take advantage of the ongoing process. The vampires moved the hearse closer to the Poheta Cemetery to shorten the walking distance for conveyance of the corpse. After the corpse had been positioned in the hearse Earl and the vampires left the Poheta Cemetery en route to 2125 Melbourne Street and the privacy of their own home. The vampires transferred the corpse to the extra coffin in the basement for future use. Earl and the vampires retired soon because they were worn out and tired from their usual day's work besides their jaunt to Poheta Cemetery.

Chapter 17
Confiscating Caskets Only

Upon arising from their nighttime slumber this afternoon Earl informed the vampires, "I'm planning on making another excursion to Poheta Cemetery this week but it will be of a different nature. Instead of confiscating bodies and conveying all of them back to our home I am planning on confiscating caskets only, in this attempt, and more corpses' later on. I am aware that we are getting low on caskets. How does this appeal to you?" The vampires smiled and said, "We are willing to assist you in this venture. Just tell us what night and what time. Also, how will we make enough room for the caskets?" Earl remarked, "I am planning on removing the seats from the hearse to accommodate the caskets for the return trip. I decided I will leave Wednesday night at 7:00 PM. Anyone that is interested in going please be at the hearse at 7:00 PM. The vampires agreed saying, "That sounds like a splendid idea. Those of us that are planning on going will be at the hearse at 7:00 PM. Thank you!"

Wednesday Night

Dark, menacing clouds are encompassing the horizon as Earl and the vampires are edging their way towards the Poheta Cemetery with the intention of confiscating several, empty caskets for future use. "No corpses' involved." As they entered the cemetery gates they are met by a coven of witches strolling through the hallowed grounds in search of the inevitable. They are shrieking and giggling to each other besides eyeing Earl and the vampires in hopes of attracting their attention. Basically there is nothing about the witches that would attract another human being's attention. Their wardrobe leaves a lot to be desired! They are attired in flowing, ankle length robes with scarves adorning their heads. A coven of witches are typically women with supernatural powers, supposedly dark haired and dark skinned, the wandering type of a Caucasian nature. Witches are known for trying to impress people with their demonic powers and evil actions that will follow. Earl and the vampires have no desire, whatsoever, to associate with the witches.

They are agitated and in a poor frame of mind because of the trip they made to Poheta Cemetery with the intention of confiscating a few caskets for their personal use. They are unable to enter the mausoleum with the witches present in the cemetery. Earl said, "We will leave the cemetery now and come back at a later date." The vampires gathered their equipment and tools heading for Earl's blue hearse. In the meantime the witches were watching them slyly while giggling and pointing their fingers at them. On the way back to Calgary Earl said, "When we come back next week we'll just have to take a chance and hope the witches aren't at the cemetery again." The vampires agreed wholeheartedly.

Chapter 18
Another Trip to the Poheta Cemetery

Another week has passed since Earl approached the vampires about taking another excursion to Poheta Cemetery in hopes of confiscating several, empty caskets from the mausoleum for their personal gratification. Their attempt was thwarted last week, due to the fact, that a coven of witches have been frequenting Poheta Cemetery, in their quest to wreak havoc on the gravesites, tombstones, cemetery grounds, etc……………Because of their position at the cemetery Earl and the vampires were unable to gain entrance to the mausoleum to continue their blood sucking rendezvous and confiscation of several caskets.This coming Friday night Earl and the vampires will make another arduous trek through the Poheta Cemetery in an attempt to gain entrance to the Poheta Mausoleum to ransack the caskets at their disposal. At the present moment they are trekking through the cemetery en route to Poheta Mausoleum with the coven of witches nowhere in sight. A dark, cloudy, stormy night is fast approaching with Earl and the vampires hurriedly transferring the empty caskets to the hearse for the trip back to Calgary. Before they departed Earl and the vampires indulged in a blood sucking rendezvous on the corpses' that weren't embalmed. "You might as well kill two birds with one stone! Right?" After their task was completed they left immediately for Calgary and the safety of their home at 2125 Melbourne Street. After they arrived back Earl and the vampires transferred the caskets to the basement, in case, they will need them in the near future for the disposal of corpses' they plan on annihilating to supplement their meals. When the tedious procedure was completed everyone retired to their respective coffins for a good night's sleep which they deserved.

A Tornado!!!

As Earl and the vampires were resting peacefully ominous, menacing, threatening clouds are beginning a formation in the eerie darkness of the night sky. Suddenly they are awakened with several claps of thunder resonating in different areas of the basement and upstairs. A pelting rain is descending on the city of Calgary with fingers of light scrapping the atmosphere, a form of lightening. The vampires are scurrying and scampering out of their coffins with Earl descending the basement stairs saying, "Hurry, turn the television set on to station KIBX for the local weather!' The vampires followed Earl's command with everybody gathering around the television set to absorb the weather report at this hour of the night. The announcer was very nervous, fearful and jittery as he started announcing the reports as they came filtering in regards to the onslaught of weather plaguing the city of Calgary, Canada this evening. Earl and the vampires were listening intently and craning their necks towards the outside for a materialistic view of the inevitable. According to the announcer "a tornado is imminent and heading straight for Calgary, Canada arriving at approximately 4:00 AM. Please take shelter immediately in the lower level of your house, preferably, a basement. If a basement is not available an upstairs closet or bathtub will suffice. Don't delay! Leave immediately! Stay away from all doors and windows!" Earl and the vampires were where they needed to be so they continued watching television for any other new, forthcoming news in regards to the tornado. All of a sudden, as it was getting closer to 4:O0 AM, the vampires heard a loud roar, like an oncoming train, accompanied by a high, shrieking wind following. The sound of the train was the tornado, itself, as it approached Melbourne Street. Prior to reaching the vampire's home it switched directions and headed east. The vampires could distinguish the characteristics of a tornado having been exposed to them before. Everyone was thankful the tornado switched directions giving thanks to God for the inevitable that no one was hurt.

The Next Morning

In the early dawn, the next morning, the vampires were outside evaluating the damage to the structure of their home. The siding was plummeted with baseball size hail which left gaping holes in the siding accompanied by holes in the roof which needed to be replaced. At this point the vampire's home needs new siding, a new roof and a completely new paint job. Earl made the remark, "Our home insurance will cover three fourths of the damage and we will have to pay the balance out of our bank account. I'm glad we have enough money in there to pay the remainder of the bill." The vampires smiled and nodded their heads in agreement.

Chapter 19

Company???

August 15, 2015

At present, Earl has had the old roof and siding replaced on the complete house. The vampires are painting the house after hours when they are finished working on their construction job plus their employment at the Ronton Mortuary. Earl and the vampires decided to take a break from the house repairs and scour the thoroughfares and alleyways of downtown Calgary for an old fashioned blood sucking escapade to their heart's content. It's been awhile since they have been "out on the town!" After a light supper the vampires watched a two hour movie and decided to retire early because of their night, "out on the town" tomorrow night. During the wee hours of the morning Earl and the vampires were awakened by muffled voices and soft, shuffling feet slithering in the dark on the basement floor. All of a sudden, several of the vampires are screeching and screaming, as they are being bitten in their left, jugular vein draining them of their life's blood. Once again several of the other vampires in the other part of the basement can be heard with a shrill, piercing cry resonating in the entire house as the coven of witches are plunging their white, canine fangs into their left, jugular vein. Volumes of crimson, delectable blood are being continuously released, as the witches suck the vampire's blood vehemently' gorging themselves to the extreme. Upon finishing their blood thirsty escapade on the vampires the witches plunged them to the cement floor to lie there of their own accord. Eventually the vampires were meekly able to raise their mangled bodies in protest as they fiercely snatched the witches dragging them up the basement steps and flinging them out the door! En route to the door, Joe asked, "How did you gain entrance into our house this evening?" They showed him a silver key and said, "With this skeleton key. It unlocks all doors." The vampires also asked, "How did you know where we lived?" They said, "We followed you home one night from the Poheta Cemetery. Remember?" The vampires shrugged and gave them an even harder shove out the door saying, "Get out of this house and don't ever come back again because we don't tolerate people like you!" The witches hurriedly departed on foot walking towards The New Haven Cemetery and their own home. By now the vampires have had their sleep broken, since it's almost 5:O0 AM, by a coven of witches. At least they got rid of them and they won't ever be back! They hope not!!! Well they might as well stay up now because it will be time to go to work before long. Earl and the vampires have completely forgotten about their escapade tonight in the thoroughfares and alleyways of downtown Calgary because of the invasion of the coven of witches. "Where did they come from? Calgary, Canada? Did they come walking into the city? How old are they? I still think they are walking in from the outskirts of Calgary, Canada! What do you think?"

A Downtown Haunt

Now that the witch's episode is past Earl and the vampires are anxious to go on a blood thirsty encounter in the alleyways and thoroughfares of downtown Calgary. It's been quite a while since they have been on a blood sucking rendezvous and are looking forward to it. This evening they bathed, shaved, dressed to the nines in their black suits, no capes, hair meticulously groomed, flawless makeup, snow white fangs and blood red lips. They are sporting elongated fingernails, neatly manicured, besides being lathered all over with heavy cologne. They positioned themselves in Earl's hearse for the ride downtown, hopefully, transporting several people along back. As they departed from Earl's hearse they dispersed in different areas of the alleyways to see whom they could encounter at this time of the evening. Isaac approached an older woman walking in between two buildings as he snatched her decrepit, wrinkled neck while sucking her left jugular vein in an attempt to satisfy his craving for some tasty, delicious, succulent, juicy blood to his liking. The older woman screeched and howled, pleading for mercy on Isaac's behalf, which he didn't relent to. "How cruel can you get? Really!" Isaac continued "slurping and gurgling, slurping and gurgling," until his stomach was gorged with blood from devouring the excessive fluid. His insatiable, sucking rampage prompted an overindulgence causing the release of volumes of blood to flow sporadically upon Isaac and the older woman. In the meantime Isaac regained his composure while his victim collapsed at his feet in a mangled mess. Since there was no one in the immediate area Joe and Isaac were able to transport the body, unnoticed, to fling in Earl's hearse for the ride back home. Joe made a remark saying, "I also encountered a mentally challenged young man that succumbed to my vampire advances at a moment's notice. I sucked his left jugular vein voraciously until his blood was totally depleted." After Joe and Isaac deposited the bodies in Earl's hearse they continued meandering through the back alleys of the main thoroughfare in search of any stragglers that might be frequenting the area. At this time of the evening the derelicts, homeless and disconnected people are beginning to thin out especially in the walkways between the business buildings. They decided to retreat to Earl's hearse awaiting the rest of the vampires. By 10:O0 PM everybody was accounted for as Earl sped off into the night with the vampires making small talk among themselves to pass the time. As they approached the basement entrance, Joe and Isaac flung their victim downstairs to lie all night until the next afternoon. Thereafter, they will be evaluated and dealt with accordingly.

Chapter 20
Labor Day, September 4th, 2015

As the end of summer is fast approaching Earl and the vampires are sponsoring a free Labor Day, community meal that is open to the public, mingling with their friends, besides partaking the scrumptious meal that is set before them. The meal site will be Monday September 4th, 2015 at 6:00 PM in Berkley Park, adjacent to Berkley Lake. Incidentally the elderly woman that Isaac confronted several weeks ago during a nightly haunt downtown passed away unexpectedly of an unknown, mysterious condition during the night. Earl decided to use her body for the main course of the meal. They will be dissecting her body soon to be used for Earl's famous, human, flesh stew meal. It will be accompanied by potatoes, moldy carrots, celery, peas, onions, stew seasoning, etc………….. The balance of the meal will be rotten, moldy potato salad, blood bread, Cherry Jello that has been frozen several years, goblets of crimson, tempting, thick, juicy blood and vomit Butter Brickle ice cream for dessert. "Sounds delicious! Yummy! Are you ready to eat? I am!" Entertainment will be provided by the Berg Heinz Orchestra permanently in Calgary, Canada. It is a well, known 1950's rock and roll orchestra providing music from different eras of time. A dancing platform is also available in front of the bandstand for those of you that like to participate in a variety of styles of dancing from the past. "Sounds interesting, doesn't it?"

Monday, September 4, 2015

The vampires are up bright and early this morning due to the fact they will be in the process of assisting Earl in the basement kitchen. They will be dissecting the corpse of the elderly woman that Isaac transported back to the house when they were on their nightly haunt in the back alleys of downtown Calgary last week. Earl has started the dissecting procedure but is failing to rinse the blood off the chunks of human flesh before he stores them in containers. "Won't that be a bloody mess? Oh no! Let's be a little more cautious there, boys!" At present the dissecting procedure is completed and Earl and the vampires are loading the hearse with the necessary food, supplies and barbecue equipment required for the preparation of the festive meal they will be serving this evening. Earl's Famous Stew

Earl and the vampires are unloading their food preparations in the Berkley Park shelter reserved for general seating plus kitchen facilities. Today there is an outnumbering of modern society frequenting Berkley Park to participate in the free, elaborate, community meal sponsored by Earl and the vampires. A variety of residents from the immediate city of Calgary, Canada are lined up at the outskirts of Berkley Park to share in a stew meal plus additional trimmings to complete the fancy feast.

By now the diners are beginning to filter in to take their respective seats at the reserved tables. Earl and the vampires concocted an enormous amount of stew earlier today which they are transporting to the meal site sooner than expected. In spite of this they still have extra stew in reserve at their home in Calgary, just in case! The diner lineup at the outskirts of Berkley Park seems to be increasing instead of decreasing. "Oh no! I hope they don't run out of food! I haven't eaten yet! Have you?" While all the diners are partaking of the fabulous meal Earl and the vampires have prepared in honor of their expectation, the Berg Heinz Orchestra is serenading them in the background from the Berkley Grandstand. They are playing renditions of Elvis Presley's "Love me Tender, Blue Suede Shoes, Don't be Cruel, Jerry Lewis' Great Balls of Fire" etc............ Several couples are trying their luck at their dancing expertise, only to be met by two left feet in the process. "Ha! Ha!"Once again Earl and Isaac can be seen exiting Berkley Park for Calgary to transport their last supply of Earl's famous stew for the remainder of the diners that happened to file in at the last minute. Earl remarked, "This is the last supply of stew. I hope this will feed the extra diners that sauntered up to the table." Isaac said, I'm sure it will because there weren't that many plates to fill anymore." Earl said, "Yes, I vaguely recall that."

A Closing Poem

At the closing of tonight's entertainment agenda, a local author and poet Myrna Lowell, read a Labor Day poem for the pleasure and enjoyment of the people that were still in attendance in Berkley Park. After the poetry reading concluded numerous people thanked Earl and the vampires for the scrumptious meal exiting the park for their departure. After all the diners and Berg Heinz Orchestra had dispersed Earl and the vampires cleaned the shelter houses and picnic tables, loaded their hearse and departed Berkley Park for Calgary. Everybody was exceedingly fatigued and anxious to return to the privacy of their own home.

Chapter 21
An Encounter with the Witches

Earl and the vampires are laying low for a while because of the tiresome, busy day they encountered on Labor Day. They weren't expecting such an influx of people but a free, community meal always draws a large crowd. Everybody has been going about their daily chores, eating their meals and relaxing in front of the television set, watching a movie, a musical, whatever is on schedule for the evening. Eventually they retire for the night in their respective coffins sleeping soundly until the next day.

The Mausoleum

Earl came up with a bright idea relating it to the vampires while eating supper this evening. "Would any of you be interested in making an excursion to the New Haven Cemetery some night in hopes of confiscating some corpses', for possible use at a meal site? It would be similar to the elderly woman we dissected last week for the Labor Day meal! Please raise your hand if you are interested." The vampires looked at each other grinning and nodding their heads in anticipation and back at Earl. They yelled, "You name the time and the night! We're raring to go!" Earl replied, "How about tomorrow night, Thursday, at 7:00 PM?" They yelled again, "We'll be at the hearse waiting!"

Thursday Night

Thursday night arrived in a flash with the vampires anxious for a blood sucking rendezvous at the New Haven Cemetery in the mausoleum of their choice since there are several available. It is a misty, eerie, creepy night this evening with a light rain draping everything in the cemetery. Upon entering the iron gates several people can be seen meditating and weeping at certain gravesites. Normally Earl and the vampires cannot enter a mausoleum unless they are in the presence of a cemetery caretaker. Evidently, the light rain is distracting the weeping meditators since they have left the

New Haven Cemetery. Earl and the vampires continue to meander around the cemetery biding their time until dark. In the meantime, they are looking at gravesites behind the mausoleum for their strolling pleasure unable to see anyone entering the iron cemetery gates. All of a sudden, they came in full view of a coven of witches strolling through the cemetery grounds oblivious of their presence. When they viewed the vampires "they immediately snapped at attention" snickering and giggling while pointing their fingernails and shrieking at the top of their lungs. They could be heard yelling, "Vampires! Vampires!" Earl and the vampires have an "instant dislike" for the witches because of the attack that occurred on themselves some time ago. Remember? They edged closer to the witches while they backed away. As the vampires came closer to the witches they yelled and screamed at them besides chasing them out of the cemetery. The witches had a horrified, fearful look on their faces as they hurriedly slithered out of the cemetery gates bemoaning their plight and rushed to their car. They quickly sped away without taking a glance back. By now the vampires are assuming the "coast is clear" since there is no one meditating, casually strolling through the tombstones or canvassing the cemetery generally speaking. Earl and the vampires came prepared with their usual tools and equipment plus extra cloths to cover the corpses' when they convey them from the mausoleum to the hearse since they are parked much closer to the New Haven Cemetery grounds tonight. Finally, the darkened cemetery is all ablaze with lights since a new lighting system has just been installed this past week. Prior to that many areas of the cemetery are dim and spooky due to insufficient lighting. Earl and the vampires take one more, swift look around the cemetery before their attempt to break the lock on the mausoleum door. They banged, clanged and twisted on the door knob but it offered too much resistance to open up. Gradually Morris, a new vampire, forcefully broke the lock causing immediate entrance to the mausoleum. They positioned vampires outside the mausoleum for observation in the event mourners might enter the iron gates at the New Haven Cemetery, unnoticed. The other vampires are diligently conveying two cloth covered corpses' to Earl's hearse for the trip back to Calgary. When they arrived back they swiftly transferred them to their coffins where they will lie in repose indefinitely. The vampires also retired to their respective coffins as soon as they accomplished their task. "If you are interested in future volunteer work please submit your name to Earl."

Chapter 22
A Basement Blood Sucking Encounter

Earl made the remark one day, "Since the corpses' are decomposed, if I remember correctly, their bodies were not embalmed, therefore, they remain intact. If any of you in the near future are interested in a blood sucking rendezvous please notify me as to your desire and I will make the necessary arrangements.

Several days later a few of the vampires expressed interest in a bloody escapade in the basement "for old time's sake." They reported this to Earl with him making the reply, "If you so desire please report to the Death Chamber at 7:00 PM this evening to perform your blood sucking encounter. The vampires entered the Death Chamber this evening at 7:00 PM, as Earl suggested, to partake in the blood sucking encounter on the corpses' they confiscated from the New Haven Cemetery. Joe gently picked up an older man by his neck while sinking his white, canine fangs into his pale, withered, dirt infested left, jugular vein. Joe sucked violently and greedily gorging himself until he could not tolerate anymore. He positioned the older man back in the coffin amidst gallons of lost blood in the process. Isaac decided to hoist a middle aged woman out of the coffin while gorging himself on her left, jugular vein, devouring her red, succulent, moist blood ravaging. Isaac placed the middle aged woman back in the coffin, in spite, of her blood stained face and clothes. "Can you imagine that?'Ryan had a blood thirsty urge this evening to try the inevitable as he grabbed a young man's neck, yanking him forward, as he thrust his white choppers into his slimy, swollen left, jugular vein with volumes of blood gushing forth. Ryan sucked voraciously until he could not control his desire any longer, therefore, flinging his body into the casket. Joe, Isaac and Ryan opted for an early retirement to their coffins this evening because of the blood sucking rendezvous they encountered this evening in the Death Chamber.

What Happened to Joe?

Joe, the vampire, decided on the spur of the moment to pay his respects to his best friend, Milford Morton, that passed away a couple of months ago from an unexpected heart attack at the age of 49. Isaac and Morris asked Joe, "Do you want us to accompany you to Poheta Cemetery while you pay your respects to your best friend that passed away?" Joe replied, "No, that won't be necessary, but "thank you" for the offering." Isaac and Morris asked, "Are you sure, Joe?" Joe said, "Yes, I'm positive. I'll only be gone a little while. You'll see me when I return. Isaac and Morris said, "Okay!" `

Joe left for the Poheta Cemetery after supper, around 6:30 PM, telling the vampires, "I'll be back by 8:00 PM. In the meantime, Earl and the rest of the vampires starting watching a new movie at 7:00 PM that was just released some time ago. Everybody was so engrossed in the movie that time was swiftly getting away from them. All of a sudden Isaac said, "Where's Joe? It's 8:00 PM and he still hasn't arrived back from Poheta Cemetery. Do you suppose he also lost track of the time?" Earl remarked, "That could've possibly happened that he got sidetracked and is running late tonight!" Isaac said, "If Joe isn't here by 11:00 PM tonight I suggest we go to Poheta Cemetery in search of him." The vampires had a worried look on their faces and were in agreement with the 11:00 PM deadline. They continued watching another 9:00 PM movie which lasted until 11:00 PM. If Joe isn't back by then Earl and the vampires will make a trip to Poheta Cemetery in hope of finding Joe.

Where is Joe?

In the meantime after Joe arrived at Milford's gravesite and meditated on the plot of ground covering the grave he knelt on his knees and haunches in a relaxed form reading Milford's epitaph on the tombstone. As he was reading he became aware of a brisk wind whispering through the trees with shadows clinging to the foreground. Suddenly Joe is mesmerized by an unknown, strong force within the grave pulling vigorously at his frame. Eventually his body slides slowly underground until he is completely out of sight. As his body

65

slowly slid to the bottom of the grave he is catapulted into a casket with the lid snapped and locked as his body lies motionless oblivious of time. By this time, the vampires have arrived at Poheta Cemetery and are dispersing in different directions in search of Joe. Eventually everyone met at the Poheta Mausoleum but still "No Joe!" Earl asked the vampires, "Did any of you encounter Joe's friend, Milford Morton's gravesite, while you were meandering around?" Morris said, "Yes, but there was no one at the gravesite so we walked on." Earl said, "Joe is nowhere in sight so we might as well go back to Calgary and report this to the Calgary Police Department tomorrow."

Chapter 23
Buried Alive!!!

At the present time Joe is encased in a tomb, six feet underground with mounds of soil overhead, with no means of breaking free, escape or survival. Joe is banging, "Bang! Bang! Bang!" and clanging on the interior of the casket lid in hopes of loosening the lock and lifting the lid but no luck so far. He is unable to tell the time of day or night on his watch due to the darkness of the casket. Occasionally, he drifts off to sleep only to be awakened by pangs of hunger gnawing at his stomach. It is not only uncomfortable in his position, but stifling hot, with sweat beads protruding from his forehead. What is he to do? He has no means of escape from this grave because no one can hear his cries for help, due to the fact, there are very few people that frequent Poheta Cemetery on any given day. His chances are slim! "Oh no! What will happen to Joe?" Once again, Joe is thumping, clanging and banging on the casket lid ferociously to disengage himself from the confinement he is subject to. He is fiercely shoving the lid with all his might and strength from inside but to no avail. The casket lid refuses to budge, thereby, entombing Joe inside the casket six feet underground. Joe ponders to himself, "Oh, no! I'm buried alive! How will I ever escape? I cannot even move myself much less, open the lid. Please, dear God, help me!"

It's raining!!!

Joe is thinking to himself, "What is this I hear? It sounds like the rumble of thunder! It's beginning to rain!" Luckily, it rained all afternoon with Joe dozing periodically in the casket. Upon awakening he decided to give the casket lid another shove again because of the moisture content that had begun to accumulate within the casket and grave. Suddenly, the lid gave a shrill, piercing sound as it slowly lifted in an opening position. Naturally, Joe took advantage of the inevitable. As the soil came folding in all sides of the grave Joe continued shoveling with an abandoned shovel and scrabbled his way to the top of the grave relieved that God answered his prayers. Eventually, he was standing at the top of the grave, smoothing the soil and preparing to walk several miles back to Calgary. It was still light outside and it had stopped raining so the timing was just right!

A Tiresome Walk

It is 6:30 PM in the evening and Joe has started his wearisome trek back to Calgary. He continues his walk with nary a car passing him or offering to give him a ride into Calgary. "What a shame." All of a sudden, a Calgary Police Department car slows down asking him, "Are you coming from the Poheta Cemetery?" Joe said, "Yes." The policeman said, "We're en route to the Poheta Cemetery to recover the body of a man by the first name of Joe that supposedly slipped underground while meditating at his friend's grave." Joe identified himself to the policemen and was immediately transported to the Calgary Police Department and then directly on to 2125 Melbourne Street.

Welcome Home

Earl and the vampires welcomed Joe wholeheartedly asking him, "What happened to you at the cemetery?" Joe answered them saying, "I bid farewell to all of you that night and drove to the Poheta Cemetery to meditate at my best friend's gravesite, Milford Morton. Remember?" The vampires acknowledged the statement with a nod of their heads. Joe continued, "That was the first time I had been to the cemetery since Milford was interred several months ago so I decided it was time to make another visit. As I was meditating, kneeling on the gravesite soil, I felt an unknown force pulling vigorously at my frame until I slowly started slipping underground catapulting into an open casket. The casket lid snapped shut, immediately locked and was beyond my control." Earl asked, "How long were you confined in the casket?" Joe remarked, "About two days." Isaac asked, "How did you finally manage to escape?" Joe replied, "After the heavy rain decreased moisture content accumulated under the ground, eventually, releasing the tightness of the lock accompanied by my incessant thumping, banging and clanging." Carl asked, "How did you manage to shovel your way to the top of the grave?" Joe replied, "The caretaker accidentally forgot to place the shovel back in the tool shed which was a good thing for me. I shoveled and scrabbled my way to the top of the grave. I immediately started walking towards Calgary with the Calgary Police Department picking me up en route. Earl and the vampires expressed their heartfelt gratitude and happiness that Joe was back among them, safe and sound, in spite of the circumstances involved.

Chapter 24

A Swimming Escapade?

Recently, Earl mentioned to the vampires, "Who's interested in a "swimming outing" at the Calgary Swimming Pool one more time before the pool closes for the season? Please raise your hands." All the vampires were smiling and nodding their heads as they raised their hands in sheer glee at the thought of swimming and splashing in the cool, refreshing water at the Calgary Swimming Pool. Not to mention, jumping off the diving board, playing games and races in the pool, making new acquaintances and a snack and cold drink beside the pool. "Does anybody have any other suggestions?" Leonard said, "The vampires and myself are ready to go on a moment's notice," with all the vampires laughing. "You set the day and time and we'll be ready to roll." Earl said, "Fine! I will make the necessary arrangements and notify all of you. It will be probably be some evening next week. Thank you!"

Friday Evening Earl approached the vampires this morning telling them, "The swimming outing is scheduled for this evening from 7:00 PM to 10:00 PM at the Calgary Swimming Pool. Is everybody in agreement with the day and time?" Everyone said, "Yes" and they will be meeting Earl at his hearse at 6:15 PM, beach towels and all!Everyone was raring and anxious to dive off the diving board into the cool, refreshing, crisp, clear water since the heat had soared up to 98 degrees today. Many people were hurrying to the swimming pool to immerse their overheated, scaly bodies into the cool, clear water. The vampires were stomping and tromping up the diving board as they jumped head on into the water. The vampires are frolicking about with their friends and new acquaintances splashing each other mercilessly as the evening wears on. "Remember, the vampires are not there only for their swimming expertise but in the hope of confronting one or two loosely, disconnected vagrants that don't conform to human standards. Do you get the message?"As dusk is fast approaching a majority of the swimmers are leaving the Calgary Swimming Pool en route to their homes. Ominous, menacing clouds are beginning to form on the horizon with claps of thunder resonating in the area. Everyone is gone with the exception of Earl and the vampires plus two vagrants lurking around at the edge of the pool. They were in a darkened area of the pool as the vampires floated towards them, grabbing them fiercely by their neck while vehemently sucking their left, jugular vein to their heart's content. They gorged themselves violently with their blood besides spilling volumes on themselves and their victim. After the vampires were finished with their blood sucking escapade they hastily transported them to the confines of Earl's hearse to be transferred to 2125 Melbourne Street. When they arrived they flung both vagrants to the base of the stairs to lie there until the next afternoon. The next day at 4:00 PM when the remainder of the vampires arose they transferred the vagrants to their coffins to be evaluated for several days as to their condition. They were fine the next day, up and about, releasing personal information as they were asked. Their names are Samson Helton and Andrew Ford, both from Calgary, Canada. Samson is 34 years old while Andrew is 32 years old. They are unemployed at the present time and living on the streets. In spite of being labeled vampires now they are looking forward to being a part of their vampire family. "After all, what have they got to lose? In this respect they have a place to live and three meals a day to look forward to. You can't beat that! Can you?" Earl can always use extra help doling out chores when he is running low on vampires. After all, several of the vampires are employed as construction workers since the earthquake and Earl, Ryan and Chris are employed as morticians at the Ronton Mortuary. This leaves only several vampires to complete the chores, inside and outside. This is where the two, new vampires come in handy! Right? "By the way, is there anybody out there that wants an extra job? Just call Earl!"

A Respite

Earl and the vampires have, most recently, taken a respite from the flurry of activities that have been plaguing the city of Calgary. Everybody needs to revitalize themselves in regards to their position in the work force and at home. Even though, Earl himself is currently employed as a mortician at the Ronton Mortuary he is still official presider of the vampire household with his governing authority to prevail. At this point their evenings are mainly spent watching a movie on television in the basement, a game of billiards, chess, a game of cards etc……………. "There is always a form of entertainment to impress everyone." By 11:00 PM in the evening the vampires have retired to their coffins for a long night of restful sleep! Goodnight, vampires!"

Chapter 25
Are You Ready to Go?

During the course of watching a rerun of an old movie in the basement this evening Earl confronted the vampires asking them, "Who is interested in frequenting an Indian Cemetery, called Mohegan Cemetery, that I totally forgot about? Please speak up!" Simon, the one eyed vampire, said, "I think all of us would be exceedingly happy to be visiting our nightly haunts that we have not frequented for any length of time. Is everybody agreed?" The vampires were laughing and nodding their heads while whispering among themselves in regards to Simon's suggestion which they were all in favor of. Simon noticed the vampires expressed sheer interest in the aforesaid as he made the remark, "Then it's settled! Since everyone is interested in our nightly haunts, once again, we are in agreement with resuming our activities starting in the Mohegan Cemetery." Earl said, "Thank you for the response. The date is set for tomorrow night, Friday September 17th, 2015 at 7:00 PM. Please be at my hearse at 6:15 PM. Are there any more questions? Thank you!"

Mohegan Cemetery

As the vampires exited Earl's hearse at the Mohegan Cemetery the weather has changed directions turning sharply colder with a fine mist spitting on the tombstones etc…………..Streaks of lightening are beginning to illuminate the sky as claps of thunder can be heard resonating in the area. Several mausoleums can be seen at the farther end of the Mohegan Cemetery. A few families are meditating at gravesites, weeping, etc…………….. By now, they are departing the Mohegan Cemetery due to the influx of oncoming bad weather in the proximity of the cemetery. In the meantime Earl and the vampires are making an attempt to pry the lock open on the mausoleum door with the tools and equipment they brought along. As the mist is slowly enveloping the graveyard it has settled on the lock itself making it more flexible. Suddenly, a grinding sound emanated from the lock as it slowly turned open revealing stacks of sealed caskets, except one!" 'What happened? Why is the casket lid wide open? Where is the corpse? Oh, no! He's gone!" Earl said, "Let's scour the cemetery and see if we can observe a lone, reincarnated, mummified corpse casually walking through the hallowed grounds. If so, be prepared to confront him bringing him back with us." The vampires were in agreement with Earl's statement as they strolled through the complete cemetery with no one in sight. What happened to the corpse? He disappeared into thin air. There he is! Walking towards Calgary, Canada! Let's catch up with him!" The vampires crept stealthily behind him, grabbing his neck, while twisting him around, confronting him face to face. The corpse mumbled incoherently with a fearful look clouding his countenance. "Is this a vampire or a zombie? Is this possibly a mummy? Oh boy!!! Was he buried alive?" The vampires corralled the corpse positioning him in the hearse for the ride back to Calgary. After they reached 2125 Melbourne Street they flung him down the basement steps to lie there until the next afternoon. They will evaluate him according to his needs, etc……………….

The Day After

The next day after the remaining vampires woke up they escorted their new found mummy friend from Mohegan Cemetery to the table for a meal and preferably "light conversation." The mummy corpse ate very little food and no conversation ensued because all he could do was mumble and growl with nothing materializing. After supper he watched television with the vampires while constantly glaring at them, the basement and pointing at the coffin indicating that he wanted to rest for the night. During the night around 3:00 AM, the vampires preferably Earl, were awakened by their "so called mummy friend," from Mohegan Cemetery. Earl was fiercely grabbed by "the mummy friend," while he protruded his canine fangs into Earl's left jugular vein for a fast and furious sucking rampage which, once again, didn't materialize. Earl jumped up and slapped "his mummy friend to the floor" screaming, "Get out of here! Don't ever come back! Get!" His friend lifted his body off the basement floor, crept stealthily up the basement steps and out the door. Earl and the vampires assumed he stumbled back to Mohegan Cemetery and into the casket. "What do you think?"

Chapter 26
A Vampire Club Meeting

Earl, Chris and Ryan have been posting signs on the basement walls, etc.................. about a meeting that will be conducted tomorrow night at 7:00 PM encouraging everyone to attend. A few minutes before 7:00 PM the vampires started filtering into the basement for the meeting to be conducted by Earl, Chris and Ryan. The first issue on the agenda was the "attack" on Earl by their so called "friend." The "inevitable," as it occurred was discussed with Earl making the following statement, "I'm sure he will never be back!" Several other issues were discussed at the meeting besides the above mentioned. At this time Earl, Chris and Ryan arose facing the vampires while Earl announced, "Chris, Ryan and myself are in the process of renting a building in Calgary to open a new mortuary which will be owned and operated by all three of us under the title "The Canadian Mortuary." We look forward to being open for business December 25, 2015. We will brief you as time extends. Are there any questions?" Nobody raised their hands indicating there were no questions at the present time. Earl concluded the meeting for the evening bidding everyone "Thank you and Goodnight!"

In spite of Earl ordering the lone, reincarnated mummy out of his basement quarters he still has a sublime interest in their past history. What Earl and the vampires encountered was an actual corpse, in a mummified form, unfamiliar to the mortuaries under any circumstances. Mummies are specifically embalmed with an ancient, Egyptian heritage in their background. Mummies are dry and shriveled up besides being sealed with bands of tape to cover their affliction from the general public. "Where did the mummies come from? Are there more mummies in the remaining caskets at the Mohegan Cemetery? There's only one way to find out and that's to go back and check the other caskets. Right?" Earl related his train of thought to the vampires this evening at the supper table asking them, "Are any of you interested in frequenting the Mohegan Cemetery again in regards to a thorough search of the caskets for more lone, reincarnated actual corpses in a mummified state? This captivates my interest immensely!"

The vampires said, "Yes, this sparks our interest also. We would be willing to accommodate you to the Mohegan Cemetery again for a further search in regards to more mummies in the remaining caskets. Stipulate a day and hour and we will be ready to leave." Earl said, "How about this coming Saturday night at 5:00 PM, since dusk is arriving earlier?" The vampires said, "We will be ready! Once again Saturday night approached fast and furious for the vampires since they are going on a mummy excursion to Mohegan Cemetery this evening. They arrived at the cemetery at 5:30 PM with their tools and equipment in tow. At this time of the evening there was no one in the cemetery meditating, strolling from tombstone to tombstone, etc............. They immediately went to the Mohegan mausoleum entering through the front door which was still unlocked from their former episode four days ago. Upon entering the mausoleum they noticed all the lids on the caskets were wide open with the caskets void. Earl made the remark, ""Evidently mummies filled every casket and now they are empty. They are probably on their way to Calgary to see whom they can victimize in the process. Normally this will cover an influx of people, due to the fact, that the inhabitants of Calgary, Canada are 636,104. We will have to read the newspaper and view the news on the KIBX station for further details on this upcoming issue. I'm sure the Calgary Police Department has become aware of this and will do everything in their power to curtail this atrocious behavior in the city of Calgary, Canada. What is your opinion on this subject?" The vampires raised their hands saying, "We're sure the Calgary Police Department is aware of the imminent danger forthcoming and are placing extra policemen on duty to compensate for those in the outlying areas of Calgary." Earl reminded the vampires, "Refresh my memory this evening in regards to viewing the 6:00 PM news. Thank you!"After Earl and the vampires arrived back from Mohegan Cemetery the next hourly news was 10:00 PM which they will be observing for further, detailed news about the mummies killing escapades throughout the city of Calgary, Canada.

Chapter 27
Mummies Galore!!!

At 10:00 PM Earl and the vampires were hunkered down in front of the television set in the basement, awaiting the 10:00 PM Newscast for the day. It was very interesting and informative, in regards to the World News, besides the city wide news pertaining to Calgary, Canada and the surrounding area. The announcer elaborated, "Mummies that were encased in caskets at the Mohegan Cemetery have reincarnated, escaped and are currently infiltrating the city of Calgary, Canada at an alarming rate. So far, they are responsible for 152 deaths and counting. Please be aware of this situation if problems arise in the near future. Extra, staffed policemen will be on duty to answer all incoming calls and dispense patrolmen where needed. Calls will be directed to 1—649—260—2902. Thank you!"The regular news was as follows which didn't interest the vampires. Discussion about the announcement followed after which Earl and the vampires slowly edged their way to their coffins for a peaceful night's sleep!

3:00 AM

Earl and the vampires were achieving their "beauty rest" which they so desperately needed when Ryan awakened to a clamoring on the basement stairs. He yelled, "Whose there? Please answer or I will be forced to take action immediately". No answer! Ryan crawled out of his coffin and was confronted by a group of mummies that began to encircle him for the inevitable. "I think you know what that is!" Several mummies held Ryan down while the other mummies took their turn sucking the life's breath out of Ryan's left jugular vein with him ranting and raving, pleading for mercy, etc.............. The mummies continued sucking his crimson, juicy, delectable blood to their heart's content while the overflow spilled on Ryan, the mummies and the basement floor. The mummies finally relented when their stomachs were gorged with blood. By this time, other vampires could be heard climbing out of their coffins to see what the commotion was about. Earl was coming down the basement stairs also. In the meantime, the mummies hurriedly mumbled to each other while scampering up the stairs and outside. Earl and the vampires tended to Ryan's needs on his neck while making him comfortable for the remainder of the night. In spite of the attention Ryan was still moaning and groaning at the pain involved and the plight he was subject to this morning. The Next Day

Earl and Chris reported for work at the Ronton Mortuary this morning but not Ryan. They excused Ryan, involving an illness of sorts, which automatically clarifies him with the Ronton Mortuary. Earl and Chris were very busy at the mortuary today, due to the fact, that the reincarnated mummies from Mohegan Cemetery have killed four more victims since the last count was announced on television several days ago. As usual, any leads are referred to the Calgary Police Department at 1—649—260—2902. Earl and the vampires have no interest, whatsoever, in reporting the mummies escapade in their basement because the police would come out to make a report. Upon seeing the conditions they are living under, sleeping in coffins all night, canine fangs towards the back of their mouth's etc............... The police would recognize them immediately as typical vampires and consequently they would be arrested at a moment's notice. The vampires cannot take any chances!!!Rest and Relaxation October 15, 2015

Cool weather is fast approaching with the vampires taking a break from all their activities, haunts, excursions to the local cemeteries, etc............. but no breaks from construction work, a mortician's job and daily household chores. Lately, after supper they have been sitting outside and relaxing, discussing different aspects of their work, unusual ideas related to downtown haunts and excursions at their favorite cemeteries. When sponsoring holiday meals how about a blood thirsty rendezvous behind a grandstand unseen, an outbuilding, in a darkened parking lot after hours, or in a dimly lit carnival area? Earl continued, ""When we assume our nightly haunts please keep the aforesaid in mind. After all, some of our coffins in the basement are lacking bodies at the present moment." This prompted a crackle of laughter from the vampires while expressing their different views and ideas that can be applied in their upcoming activities.

Chapter 28
Mohegan Cemetery Again?

Earl and the vampires are resuming their usual haunts at Mohegan Cemetery again this evening in spite of the cold, eerie, dark, atmosphere they are being exposed to. They haven't been to the Mohegan Cemetery for several weeks and are itching and raring to go. Earl briefed the vampires, "We will be departing at 5:00 PM for Mohegan Cemetery this evening," to which they were all ecstatic. The vampires were ready to leave well in advance this evening while Earl was still in the process of accumulating his tools and equipment. When they arrived at the Mohegan Cemetery the weather and atmosphere surrounding the hallowed grounds was one of a morbid, misty, scary scene depicting frightening, eerie shadows and evil creatures of the night. In spite of this Earl and the vampires sauntered in an easterly direction while observing a variety of gravesites they were not aware of. Evidently it was an older area of the cemetery they had never encountered because Mohegan is an Indian Cemetery which is quite large with numerous tombstones incorporating the cemetery itself. As they were standing at a gravesite, meditating, the soil started moving back and forth for no apparent reason. The vampires stared at each other in horrid disbelief, as the soil began to form an opening through which a mummy corpse projected out of the soil, halfway screaming, with his mouth wide open. His dry, withered features were gross to behold while his arms were flailing in the air. His wretched, deteriorating mummy corpse was covered with filthy, disgusting, ragged bands of tape. Evidently, his frame was unable to progress any farther while being positioned unable to move in advance. By this time Earl and the vampires were beside themselves with fear, contemplating their next move, which was the swiftest way out of the Mohegan Cemetery. Hoofing It?

Earl and the vampires were running top speed down Mohegan Road, two blocks north towards Earl's blue hearse, which was easily identifiable in the dark of night. Looking back while Joe was running, he caught sight of the mummy corpse in hot pursuit after Earl himself and the vampires. Evidently, the mummy corpse was hurriedly writhing to and fro in an attempt to release his body from the position he was confined to and it worked!!! That's why he was chasing Earl and the vampires, helter skelter, down Mohegan Road. He is "hot on their trail" with the vampires quickly jumping into the hearse and taking off at breakneck speed with Earl at the wheel. Isaac looked back saying, "The mummy corpse is standing in the middle of the road and staring at us!" By now, Earl and the vampires have arrived back home and are eagerly anticipating a long night's rest till morning. Some will arise for their construction job, three vampires are employed as morticians at the Ronton Mortuary and the remainder performing daily, household chores. Everybody is assigned to a specific task they are willing to participate in with their best interests at heart. Before they retired for the evening Earl had a suggestion to make, "I know you are all tired and so am I, because of what transpired this evening, so I will make this brief. Chris, Ryan and I would like to inspect the gravesite where the mummy corpse crawled out of. Is anyone interested in going along at this time? Please raise your hand so I know." Several of the vampires raised their hands exclaiming their interest. Earl said, "Very well, we will be leaving this coming Monday night at 4:30 PM because nightfall will descend on us sooner. Please meet us at my hearse in the driveway. Thank you!" The vampires replied "Thank you!" in return.

Monday Night

Since Earl, Chris and Ryan are unemployed at the Ronton Mortuary on Mondays they couldn't have chosen a better night to frequent the Mohegan Cemetery for an outing. They left in the hearse a few minutes ago supplied with tools and extra equipment because you never know what type of problems you might encounter. After they reached the gravesite where they had the confrontation last week with the mummy corpse chasing them the vampires meditated for a few minutes. In the meantime, Earl, Chris and Ryan investigated the immediate gravesite area for any unusual circumstances that might lead to the inevitable. While the vampires walked north two blocks to retrieve the remainder of the tools and equipment Earl, Chris and Ryan stepped on the actual gravesite where the mummy corpse protruded out of the soil from last week. All of a sudden, the soil completely opened up and swallowed Earl, Chris and Ryan in one huge gulp. The opening filled in continuously with more soil, until eventually the gravesite was filled up and smoothed over. "Where did Earl, Chris and Ryan go? They have never reappeared out of the gravesite! Are they ever coming back?" One of the vampires, Gilbert, happened to stay behind and witness this atrocity. He was weeping and lamenting the plight of Earl, Chris and Ryan and the finality of the procedure. The remaining vampires were aghast and appalled at the gruesome, inexplicable, horrific phenomena that had just occurred. As they were discussing the situation among themselves Isaac said, "We have never called their names! Let's try that!" They yelled, "Hah! Earl! Chris! Ryan! Answer us, please, if you can.! Where are you? Are you underground?" There was no sound! Dead silence! At this point there was nothing the vampires could do except go back to their home in Calgary and hope for the best and prepare for the worst. "Right?" When they came back Joe decided "It is in the best interest of Earl, Chris and Ryan to report the incident to the proper authorities, namely, the Calgary Police Department, which I will do in the morning personally or by phone." Everybody decided it was "a splendid idea" before they retired to their coffins.

Chapter 29
The Media

Instantly, after the vampires arose this afternoon, Joe decided to report the incident about Earl, Chris and Ryan's disappearance at the Mohegan Cemetery last night. When Joe, Isaac and Gilbert arrived at the Calgary Police Departmentthey were politely escorted to the Chief of Police's office. Mr. Clyde Senton introduced himself as the Chief of Police of Calgary, Canada. Joe, Isaac and Gilbert also introduced themselves, being careful not to expose their canine fangs for fear of being recognized as typical vampires. As the conversation ensued between both parties, the Chief of Police, Mr. Senton, requested information in regards to the complete incident. The vampires, Joe, Isaac and Gilbert, described carefully and scrupulously the episode to the best of their knowledge. Joe also related the following encounter to Chief of Police Senton, "The following event also took place last week at Mohegan Cemetery about 8:00 PM. Suddenly, while we were meditating, the soil started shifting to and fro, with an opening gradually forming. Abruptly, without any forewarning, a filthy, dirt infested, slimy, mummy protrudes out of the soil, exposing monstrous facial features, while flailing his arms, screaming and wailing. He was encased in soil to his waist, bound by grimy, ragged bands of cloth. The vampires hastily ran to their hearse, two blocks north of the cemetery, for their ride back to Calgary with the mummy standing in the middle of Mohegan Road glaring after them." Joe continued, "Yesterday, Earl, Chris and Ryan decided to go back to Mohegan Cemetery for a thorough investigation of the gravesite in question, asking us if we would care to go along? We said, "Yes" and that's when the formidable incident took place! We were meditating at the same gravesite where the lone mummy protruded out of the opening in the soil, when suddenly, an opening formed again in the soil swallowing Earl, Chris and Ryan in one humongous gulp! We called their names repeatedly, but no answer! When this transpired they had been in the process of doing a thorough investigation of the main gravesite involved and the immediate area. When we were unable to recover their bodies and proceed any further we hurriedly came back to Calgary and have not been back since. We are skeptical of a repeat performance of this nature happening again." Police Chief Senton was wary of the descriptive information the vampires had disclosed in regards to the disappearance of Earl, Chris and Ryan. Newspaper, Television and Radio

Police Chief Senton had no desire to make a house call to the vampire's home since he has accumulated a variety of information from the vampires. It will be transferred to the Calgary News Department, KIBX television station and Calgary's local radio station for the interest of the general public. Upon their dismissal from the Calgary Police Department, Police Chief Senton remarked, "If I have any further questions in regards to this matter I will be calling you at this number you released to me. Please be tuned in to the newspaper, television and radio for further details about this incident as it becomes available. Thank you!" Joe, Gilbert and Isaac reciprocated the formality by repeating, "Thank you!" also.

The Local News

Several nights later the vampires are gathered in the basement watching the local 6:00 PM KIBX television station news in regards to the disappearance of Earl, Chris and Ryan at the Mohegan Cemetery. An announcer is at the scene of the actual disappearance, describing the facts, as the vampires related them to Police Chief Senton. The Calgary News carried a full report of the incident plus a photograph of the gravesite itself.

The Mummies Reincarnated!

The local Calgary Radio Station has been broadcasting the disappearance of morticians, Earl Morton, Chris Baker and Ryan Coles at the Mohegan Cemetery periodically throughout the day. Different conflicting reports have been filtering in to the radio station in regards to various sightings around the city of Calgary. All conflicting reports have been misleading and referred to an "insufficient file."

A Gravesite Digger

Since the misguided reports are all "dead leads" the Calgary Police Department has decided to contact the Mohegan Cemetery Caretakers in regards to the problem at hand. They have decided to make arrangements, relating to an excavation of the gravesite in question, for tomorrow afternoon while the weather is still accommodating for the month of October. Joe, Gilbert and Isaac are on their way, en route to the Mohegan Cemetery, for the excavation process that will proceed. The bodies of Earl, Chris and Ryan were engulfed within the gravesite yesterday afternoon and have not been heard from since. As Joe, Gilbert and Isaac entered the cemetery gates, the grave digger was steadily excavating the gravesite, hollowing out a cavity deeper and deeper into the bowels of the earth. At one point, the caretaker manning the grave digger made the remark, ""We have excavated the depth of twelve feet with no results. We will continue until it gets dark and then resume this procedure tomorrow. Thank you! Good evening!" Joe, Isaac and Gilbert heard the inevitable and are on their way back to Calgary to relate the news to the rest of the vampires.

Chapter 30
Living Underground

Again, Joe, Isaac and Gilbert are anxiously awaiting the outcome of the hollowing procedure by the grave digger this afternoon in Mohegan Cemetery. So far, the results are the same, nothing! Eventually, dusk will be fast approaching accompanied by a few, light sprinkles on the tombstones, etc………………..giving the cemetery grounds a creepy, eerie, scary atmosphere. Hearken! Joe, Isaac and Gilbert are looking at each other in horror and disbelief as they hear murderous screams and screeching emanating from the huge opening the grave digging machine hollowed out! "What happened? What does this indicate?" The caretaker, manning the grave digging machine, discontinued the operation and stood staring into the huge, black pit he had created. He urged his coworkers and Joe, Gilbert and Isaac to step forward since it was relatively safe to stare into the humongous, black, pit confronting them. As they kept gazing down which seemed about twenty five feet or more they encountered what appeared to be a ground laden, lower surface that is capable of withstanding traffic. Now at this point, the grave digging caretaker said, "We will be back tomorrow afternoon to finish our investigation into the realm of the earth and make our conclusion. Thank you and Goodnight!" The vampires also said, "Thank you, and we will also be back tomorrow." Once again, Joe, Isaac and Gilbert are entering the cemetery gates en route to the gravesite that poses the impending problem. Signs have been posted throughout the cemetery, intermittently, due to underground exposure at this time. The caretaker that operated the grave digging machine said, "We are going to lower a ladder into the lowest part of the pit which will be manned and controlled by extra cemetery caretakers while we enter the area. Joe, Isaac and Gilbert decided they would also like to view the lowest part of the pit for their personal gratification and possibly a glimpse of Earl, Chris and Ryan?

Descending the Ladder

In the meantime, the grave digging caretaker was the first to climb the ladder to the bottom. Several other caretakers followed suit with Joe, Gilbert and Isaac following. When everyone had reached the ground laden, lower surface they meandered around as a group from area to area, with living conditions crude and simple, reminiscent of the Stone Age. "There was no Earl, Chris nor Ryan!!! No mummies in sight!!! What happened to everybody? Where are they? This is a strange, weird situation!!! Yes, this is definitely the correct gravesite!"Since there was nothing to keep the caretakers nor Joe, Isaac or Gilbert in the darkened pit they all escalated the ladders until they reached the top. At this point, there was nothing more to do regarding this situation. Evidently, the mummies have been reincarnated and are living as human beings the same as Earl, Chris and Ryan. From what Joe, Gilbert and Isaac observed this is the only explanation they can give the remainder of the vampires. "What is your opinion?"

Back in Calgary

After Joe, Gilbert and Isaac arrived back home in Calgary they proceeded to relate to the rest of the vampires what transpired at the gravesite at the Mohegan Cemetery this afternoon. The vampires were aghast and appalled at the idea of entering the darkened pit along with the caretakers for moral support in spite of not finding anyone, especially, not Earl, Chris and Ryan. Joe said, "We are going back again tomorrow to put closure to the case in spite of the fact that everyone might still be alive. There's nothing that can be done because of the circumstances, environment, locality, etc…………….. We're sorry!" The vampires expressed their condolences in regards to Earl, Chris and Ryan's disappearance. They will contact the Ronton Mortuary about a memorial service in their honor. Several of the vampires contacted the Ronton Mortuary later this morning with them being unaware of this forthcoming dilemma. The mortuary was shocked and mortified at the outcome of being completely engulfed in the soil and being transported to the bowels of the earth. They also offered their sympathy with a service scheduled for Friday night at 7:00 PM.

Memorial Service Friday Night 7:00 PM

Since the radio, television and newspaper have been commenting on the disappearance this past week of Earl, Chris and Ryan nothing has changed in regards to the inevitable. The media and press have released current reports of reincarnated mummies living in an underground tomb which swallowed Earl, Chris and Ryan at the Mohegan Cemetery. Joe, Isaac and Gilbert will relate the latest occurrence regarding Earl, Chris and Ryan to everyone in attendance this Friday night at 7:00 PM.

Joe, Isaac and Gilbert were seated in mourner's row accompanied by the remainder of the vampires for the memorial service to be conducted at 7:00 PM by the reverend John Style, minister at the Calgary United Methodist Church. Numerous family members, relatives and friends filtered into the memorial room adorned with beautiful bouquets of flowers and photographs of Earl Morton, Chris Baker and Ryan Coles at various stages of their lives. Prayers were led and recited by Reverend John Style, intermittently, throughout the evening. Some latecomers are continuing to file in, in spite of the overflow of mourners in the memorial room. The presiding mortician has referred them to an adjoining room with speakers etc…………..Joe is stepping quietly to a small podium centered in the front of the memorial room. He proceeds to explain the circumstances involving the disappearance of Earl, Chris and Ryan. He reiterates the facts as they unfold into view, including their ladder descent, twenty five feet underground, to the bowels of the earth. According to Joe their bodies were engulfed in the soil on top of the gravesite as they were meditating Monday night. At this point, Isaac stepped forward to continue the discussion and answer period. A variety of questions were presented to Isaac which he answered to the best of his ability. For instance, one man asked, "Can you explain, in detail, the environment as you encountered it at the base of the tomb when you descended by ladder?"

Isaac answered, "When we descended the tomb by a ladder it was totally bare, no furniture, nothing. It was empty, void." The man continued to ask, "How many rooms did it consist of?" Isaac said, "I believe there were three or four." The man asked again, "Did you see any living being, in human form, creature, a strange, abnormal being etc…………….. Isaac said, "No." By this time, Gilbert approached the microphone to conclude the question and answer session for the evening. A woman stood up, identified herself and asked, "Will there be any other descents by ladder into the tomb because I think there would be several people among us this evening that would be interested in going down, namely myself?" Gilbert made the remark, "No, the descent into the tomb is, basically, for our immediate group and the Mohegan Cemetery caretakers. Sorry! A look of disappointment clouded her countenance. She immediately said, 'Thank you" and proceeded to sit down. Gilbert asked, "Are there any more questions left unanswered?" No one spoke up so he concluded the memorial service and thanked everyone for their attendance. He also said, "If further information becomes available it will be publicized by the media in Calgary."

Chapter 31
Halloween Preparations

Neither hide nor hair has been seen of Earl, Chris or Ryan nor the mummies as of to date. The vampires are going about their daily business of construction work eliminating Earl, Chris and Ryan from the scene. They have been swallowed into a black, mummy pit at a gravesite in Mohegan Cemetery. The remainder of the vampires are tending to the household chores at hand. In regards to the status of the Vampire Club a meeting was held Tuesday night in the basement installing Joe as the presiding President of the Club. The vampires discussed different aspects, decorations, etc.............. for Halloween night. They arrived upon a decision that several vampires would remain at home doling out candy. The rest of the vampires were interested in canvassing door to door or approaching individuals on the street in the darkened areas of the city. Everybody was in agreement with the above mentioned and proceeded to decorate the home Albert had purchased years ago for the vampires and himself. They hung a lit up skeleton on the front door, an orange candle was lit in every window of the house including the upstairs, several imitation witches riding on broomsticks in the front yard and spooky, lit up Halloween faces perched in the trees. A Halloween basket of goodies was setting on the front porch for the ghosts and goblins to help themselves. There was also a basket of goodies setting on the back porch for the ghosts and goblins that stroll through the alleyways looking for victims to confront if there expectations weren't met.

Halloween Night

Joe, Isaac and Gilbert decided, on the spur of the moment to meander through the back alleys downtown behind the main thoroughfares. They were frequented by the numerous homeless, derelicts and street people, besides a variety of night people sitting in a circle with their hands outstretched over a fire taking the chill off their numb fingers. Also, some of the night stalkers are patiently waiting for the local eateries, before closing time, to deposit leftover, uneaten food they are unable to sell into the large, outside receptacles. The night stalkers will go "dumpster diving" to retrieve anything that is edible on their part. As the evening wears on it is getting increasingly colder, after all it is Halloween night, October 31, 2015. A slight mist is beginning to drape everything in the back alleys with a slight rumble of thunder in the background and fingers of lightening streaking the horizon. Joe, Isaac and Gilbert are hurriedly scurrying around in between business buildings looking for someone to victimize at this late hour. Suddenly, Gilbert and Isaac conveniently approached two older men, grabbing their slimy, dirt infested, yellow necks, with their protruding, left, jugular vein intact for a quick and furious blood sucking escapade. They gulped their crimson, blood voraciously and vehemently till their blood started spilling onto their clothes, the outside walls of the business buildings, the cement pavement in the alley, etc……………….. At this point in time, Joe, Isaac and Gilbert decided to deposit them into the back seat and transport them back to the house. When they arrived at 2125 Melbourne Street they flung the two older men to the foot of the basement stairs for a good night's rest. Tomorrow afternoon at 4:00 PM they will check on their condition to see if everything is satisfactory. If that is the case, they will be transported to a coffin until they are in a mobile, mental and sociable state of mind. Actually, Joe is anxiously looking forward to extra victims to occupy the coffins in the spare bedroom in the basement. After all, victims are always used for holiday meals, especially, Thanksgiving Day coming up. The vampire's meals are the cannibalistic style meaning they prepare and consume the flesh of deceased, human beings. "Are you interested in enjoying a Thanksgiving meal prepared by the vampires? If so, let them know. The more, the merrier! Right?"

Is Everybody Awake?

Its 4:00 PM and the remaining vampires are just beginning to crawl out of their coffins to check on the two older men that are laying at the foot of the basement stairs. Too bad! One of them must've died during the night and the other older man is barely alive. "Can the vampires revive him? I don't know." They are frantically working on him to sustain his life but it is slowly ebbing away. As he slowly drew his last breath the vampires transported them to the Death Chamber and suspended them on poles by their necks since they are now available for future holiday meals. This completes a total of five bodies suspended in the Death Chamber! "Not too many, are there?"

Chapter 32
A Mummy Attack

Several weeks have passed since the mummy episode at the Mohegan Cemetery. Everything is subdued and quiet in the vampire household with several of the vampires applying themselves to their construction jobs while the remainder to their household chores on a daily basis. Actually, for the past week they have been living in a more relaxed, sheltered atmosphere with nothing hindering their lifestyle. They have been taking a break from their current attacks, episodes, Halloween preparations, etc............. to focus on more important issues on hand. The Thanksgiving holiday is just around the corner and they are planning a free, community meal for the public in a building, not designated, as of yet. Their evenings are currently spent viewing nationally, accredited movies on television that spark their interest. Once in a while, a vampire can be observed sleeping while watching a largely, advertised movie due to the overwhelming labor entailed at their construction job.

"Is it Earl, Chris and Ryan?"

At this point, the vampires are sleeping peacefully with no distractions to disturb them other than a heavy rain pelting the outside of the house. Once in a while, a sudden streak of lightening can be seen across the western horizon. Suddenly, Isaac is awakened by a soft, shuffling noise at the top of the stairs, yet seeming to come closer, as he lies there in his coffin rigid and fearful at the impending disaster that could prevail. The room is exceedingly dark because Isaac is unable to distinguish clearly the other coffins, objects, etc............... in the room. Unexpectedly, the headlights from several cars flashed through the basement windows emanating light throughout the basement. By this time, 3:30 AM, most of the vampires have awakened to someone walking with a constant repetitive, clumsy gait. Also, eerie, mummified forms are standing and glaring into the coffins at the vampires lying before them. The vampires are extremely frightened and alarmed at these horrid creatures in their midst, "Who are they? Where did they come from bound with cloth strips covering their body? What are they saying? They are mumbling and grumbling to themselves! Are we able to chase them out of the basement? Oh, no! Let's give it a try!" By now, the vampires are screeching and screaming at the mummies, besides wrestling with them, since they have a firm grip on their necks. The mummies must've been vampires at one time since several of them are gorging themselves in their left, jugular vein with volumes of blood they are contending with. The mummies are sucking vigorously and vehemently down to the last drop. Eventually, they discontinued their sucking rampage when the blood flowed out of their mouths and onto their cloth strips covering their body. In the meantime, Joe confronted one of the mummies asking him, "Are you Earl, the vampire? I'm Joe. Remember me?" The mummy had a quizzical look in his right eye, acting very strange while gurgling and mumbling to himself. Joe asked, "Where are Chris and Ryan?" The mummy pointed at two other mummies several feet away indicating they were Chris and Ryan! Eventually, the vampires were able to round up the mummies, herd them up the stairs and out the basement door. They were unwilling to leave, fighting the vampires off, but they lost the battle in the end. At least, the vampires are sure that Earl, Chris and Ryan died in the process of being engulfed in the gravesite soil only to be reincarnated several days later. At this point in time, the vampires are apprehensive about meditating at the Mohegan Cemetery or the New Haven Cemetery for fear the same incident might occur to them the same as Earl, Chris and Ryan. "That would be terrible!"

The "At Home Mummies"

The mummies, including Earl, Chris and Ryan, have retraced their steps back to Mohegan Cemetery to the gravesite they emerged from. At present, they are underground living in an area that is "off limits" to everybody except the mummies. It was also "off limits" to the caretakers and vampires with a steel door, cement floors, etc................ The mummies reside in the area they are accustomed to with their wooden, Egyptian, body formed cases for sleeping, a minimum supply of food, plus other incidentals. They actually exist on the bare essentials. By way of the grapevine, the mummies acquired the address of the witches! "Remember them?" It sounds like the mummies will be paying the witches a blood sucking visit in the near future. "Sounds interesting, doesn't it? I can't wait to see what happens! Can you?"

Chapter 33
Thanksgiving Day

November 23, 2015

Tonight is the evening before Thanksgiving Day, which is tomorrow, November 23, 2015. The vampires are in an anxious and excited frame of mind anticipating Joe's dissection of a male cadaver that has been suspended for several years in the Death Chamber. Joe made the remark, "I have decided to dissect this particular cadaver for our private Thanksgiving Day meal because I observed a foul, rancid odor emanating from the body itself. I'm sure after we dissect the body into bite sized chunks for barbecuing that should eliminate any odor involved in the process." The vampires smiled while looking at each other and nodding their heads in agreement to Joe's suggestion. Joe's help tonight will consist of Isaac, Gilbert, Oliver, Steve, Peter and Colton. They will need six vampires to assist Joe in the complete procedure they are about to undertake this evening. The meal will be prepared in the confines of the basement area, due to the fact, that it has been snowing since early this morning and presumably will continue for the remainder of the day.

Dissection process

By now, Joe and the vampires have completed the dissection procedure and packaged the bite sized chunks, preserving them until tomorrow, when they will barbecue the chunks of flesh in the basement, barbecue cooker. The main entrée will be the barbecued, human flesh accompanied by baked, rotted, moldy potatoes, hot, kernel corn laced with a variety of beetles, a salad with slimy, dish water for dressing, blood bread and goblets of juicy, crimson, delectable blood. Dessert will be Albert's prized vomit, vanilla ice cream. "Sounds delicious, doesn't it? Do you think we'll get invited to the meal? I hope so!" Joe and the vampires are up bright and early tending to the barbecued, human flesh chunks, plus the remainder of the meal, while others are outside sweeping and shoveling the snow that had accumulated during the night for their pleasure. "Hah!"The vampire waiters are hurriedly dressing the dining room tables elaborately with candles, place cards, silverware and goblets of savory blood. After the vampires were seated Joe conducted a nondenominational Thanksgiving Day prayer in everybody's honor with the vampires answering "Amen."After the vampires had partaken of the delicious, holiday meal, with mountains of praise circling the dining room tables they tackled the task of cleaning the kitchen, dining room tables, etc……………… before they relaxed for the evening. Some of the vampires watched television, others played cards and some opted to play a game of billiards. "I think Joe retired to his coffin for a short, cat nap after the activities of the day!" After a quick, late supper in the evening which consisted of the 'left overs" from dinner most of the vampires watched another movie and then retired to their respective coffins for the night. "Sounds like quite a day, doesn't it? Considering, they might have to shovel again tomorrow afternoon when they arise from their coffins for the day. Oh, no!"

Back to Normal

Now that Joe and the vampires have put Thanksgiving Day behind them they are observing their neighbors diligently beginning to decorate the outside of their homes for the Christmas season. "Why shouldn't they? Christmas is only a month away!" The weather in Calgary, Canada is very accommodating for the season considering they received two inches of snow already. "It sounds like it might be a snowy season! I'm looking forward to winter, aren't you?" Joe and the vampires decided to decorate the inside of the house first because of the cold and snow outside. Steve and Colton went about the task of setting up the Christmas trees in the different areas of the house while the other vampires decorated them with lights, figurines, colored Christmas decorations, etc……………… They also hung decorative, holiday signs throughout the house for their pleasure. After they completed the inside of the house they proceeded to decorate the outside trees with Christmas decorations galore. When the trees were decorated they brought an end of the year, clearance, sale item outside that had been purchased but too late to display. It was a large sled with Santa Claus at the helm and a bag of Christmas presents in the back of the sled harnessed by six reindeer. Steve and Colton positioned the sled in the front yard, as nightfall is fast approaching, while lighting up the front yard in all its array and beauty for the pleasure of the remaining vampires. "Busy day! Right?"

Chapter 34
The Blood Sucking Mummy Rampage

In regards to the mummies habitation, including Earl, Chris and Ryan in an underground dungeon, located under a gravesite twenty five feet under the bowels of the earth in Mohegan Cemetery. They are still continuing their barely, nonexistent lives. As you can probably fathom the inevitable, the mummies were vampires at one time because they are prone to encounter varieties of people for a blood sucking rendezvous whenever they become available. A perfect example is: The mummies confronted Joe, Isaac, Gilbert and the rest of the vampires at 2125 Melbourne Street some time ago for a blood sucking rampage during the night. Luckily, the vampires herded then up the stairs and chased them out the door with them trekking all the way back to Mohegan Cemetery close to the crack of dawn in a slight drizzle. Hah! Incidentally, within the last several days the mummies received an anonymous tip from an undisclosed source regarding the address of the witches on 2429 Tyler Road on the outskirts of Calgary. If my recollection serves me correctly the witches also have a past history of thriving on human blood until nourishing food becomes easily accessible. The mummies are in the right frame of mind this evening to trek to 2429 Tyler Road for a blood sucking rampage on the coven of witches that reside there. In spite of the cool, misty, drizzly night the mummies once again, including Earl, Chris and Ryan, are shuffling along east of Mohegan Cemetery towards the witches residence at 2429 Tyler Road. They are getting extremely fatigued as they lumber along towards the witches living quarters in the inclement weather at the untimely hour of 2:00 AM in the morning. It is one mile from the Mohegan Cemetery to the witch's dwelling having finally reached their destination. Their home was constructed on the crest of a hill overlooking their neighbors surrounded by a wooded area flowing with an abundance of trees, shrubbery, flowers, etc……………… similar to a park in the middle of nowhere. As the mummies approached the coven of witch's home it was totally dark with an eerie, sinister, foreboding atmosphere surrounding the entire landscape. Suddenly, a front porch light flickered on as if someone became aware of an unusual sound, a strange animal, an intruder, etc................. The mummies immediately took refuge by the side of the house as not to be seen. Eventually, the light was diminished and everything became dark, quiet and creepy again. The mummies waited a while before entering their abode until everything was settled down and the witches had gone to sleep again. Suddenly, they grabbed the ugly witches by their weathered, yellowed, slimy, dirt infested necks, twirling them around so they would come face to face with them. They jerked their necks upward towards their mouth as they sunk their gleaming, white canine fangs into their filthy necks. The witches cried and lamented, "Please let us go! Leave us alone! What are you and where did you come from? Get away from us! Get out of here!" The mummies continued on their sucking rampage, gulping every drop of succulent, delectable morsel of blood they could muster. Like they say, "Good to the last drop." As soon as the mummies satisfied their insatiable desire, which is their lust for blood, they quickly exited the witch's residence for their mile long trek back to Mohegan Cemetery and the safety of their Death Chamber underground. After they were in their private residence underground they proceeded with their nightly ritual of resorting to their formed, wooden coffins with an accompanying lid for closure. They reclined for the remainder of the night only to be awakened some time the following day. The mummies, Earl, Chris and Ryan, naturally, adopted the same lifestyle as their counterparts at this point in time.

Mummy Communication

Unbeknown to us, the mummies have a means of communicating among themselves which we were never aware of until now. Incidentally, before they retired for the evening last night they designated, Silvan, as the mummy with the authority and responsibility to conduct future, blood sucking rendezvous, rampages, escapades, etc...................... "Good idea! Right?" The mummies are planning on resting and relaxing for a day or two after their encounter with the witches on Tyler Road. Since several, new bodies not embalmed due to a car accident have been placed in Mohegan Mausoleum the mummies are interested in a late night rendezvous with the aforesaid.

Silvan quotes in his mummy communication, "That he is taking full responsibility for all stages of the rendezvous and assures them there will be no problems."

Chapter 35
A Mausoleum Rendezvous

Silvan and the mummies decided among themselves that this evening, Friday night, would be the ideal night for a blood sucking rendezvous at the New Haven Cemetery after dark. The weather was cool, crisp and eerie with a slight, rustling wind throughout the cemetery accompanied by dim lighting and the hollow sound of a hoot owl in the background. "What a combination!" Actually, it wasn't quite as ideal as the mummies surmised. Evidently, it was colder than they thought because of the velocity of the wind and the three mile trek to the New Haven Cemetery and Mausoleum. Three miles is quite a jaunt in twenty degree weather with blasts of cold air on your back. The mummies are also transporting tools to open the mausoleum door, just in case, it is locked. Luckily, the mummies are wrapped in strips of clear, linen cloth which keeps them quite warm on nights such as this. "I think I would rather be wearing my winter coat, wouldn't you?" When they reached the mausoleum door it was securely locked as the mummies banged and clanged to gain entrance. Finally, the door slowly creaked open with a disgusting, foul, decrepit, stench emanating from the mausoleum. While they were inspecting the coffins two mummies were posted outside in the event there are onlookers or intruders, etc................. at the New Haven Cemetery.

A Blood Sucking Rampage

At present, the mummies are busily canvassing the caskets since some of them are stacked on top of each other not knowing which corpses' are embalmed and which ones are not embalmed? In spite of the fact, that ex morticians, Earl, Chris and Ryan, formerly employed at the Ronton Mortuary have been transformed into mummies. They are unable to predict the embalming procedure because they have been characterized as mummies for some time now. The way the situation unfolds it's just a matter of trial and error. As the mummies scaled their way through a mountain of caskets for non- embalmed corpses to feed their hungry stomachs on they finally encountered a total of twelve non embalmed corpses' they could relate to. The mummies grabbed the corpses' necks while jerking them out of the casket and thrusting their slimy, rotten, claw like fangs into the corpses' neck. The mummies sucked the corpses' thick, crimson, succulent, tasty blood to their heart's content. They drank volumes of their blood horrendously and vehemently, besides, spilling some on their clothing and floor. Eventually, their sucking escapade ceased with them flinging the corpses' back into the caskets, slamming the lid and exiting the mausoleum. By now the weather has turned to heavy snow as the mummies start their three mile trek back to Mohegan Cemetery in the dead of winter. "I wonder if it was all worth the time and effort? With the oncoming weather, uncomfortable, bloated stomachs, etc………………. It doesn't appear that way to me! How about you? I could think of better ways to pass the time!"

Back to the Vampires

Christmas day is fast approaching with the vampires decorating their house, inside and out, right after Thanksgiving was over. Joe held an unexpected Vampire Club meeting last night in regards to extracurricular activities on the agenda pertaining to the Christmas holidays, etc……………. He brought the meeting to order with the recitation of the Pledge of Allegiance. He immediately mentioned, "With Christmas just around the corner we will be taking several shopping expeditions to downtown Calgary in the evenings after supper like we have done in the past years. Raise your hand if you are interested in going along again this year." Everybody had a profound interest in going since all hands were raised. Joe said, "Good! We will be going this Thursday night at 5:30 PM. Please meet me at the hearse at the appointed time."

Joe brought their private Christmas meal to their attention, also, saying, "We are having a gift exchange on Christmas Eve in the gathering space here in the basement for the benefit of all of us. I suggest a limit of $15.00 to be spent on the gift of your choice. Does anybody have a different suggestion?" Nobody spoke up indicating $15.00 was within everybody's limit.

Joe mentioned, "I will be dissecting one of the suspended corpses in the Death Chamber several days before Christmas. It will be for barbecued chunks the same as Thanksgiving Day. The meal will be accompanied by potatoes, a vegetable salad, goblets of blood, frozen, moldy bread and dessert. Possibly some soft Christmas music in the background?" Joe said, "How does that appeal to everybody?" The vampires were ecstatic with glee because they are always looking forward to Christmas.

Chapter 36
Christmas Eve 2015

Tonight is Christmas Eve, with Joe and the vampires ecstatically making holiday preparations in regards to the gift exchange and last minute decorations in the All Purpose Room in the basement. They are also preparing extra Christmas snacks plus a Christmas Ice Cream Cake that was delivered earlier this morning. Several of the vampires are wrapping gifts for the exchange at 7:00 PM this evening while others are diligently checking to see if there is an ample supply of blood for tonight's celebration. Steve made a remark to the vampires, "There is abundant amount of blood under refrigeration for the occasion this evening plus our Christmas Day dinner tomorrow. That isn't a problem. But, a problem can arise if, after tomorrow, we are unable to confiscate any extra, human blood to sustain ourselves indefinitely since that is what we thrive on. Are there any questions?" None of the vampires raised their hands in spite of displaying a bleak look on their faces. Steve said, "If anyone has any idea in regards to this situation please contact me at once at your earliest convenience. Thank you!" The vampires continued their preparations for the private holiday get together this evening. They are placing a wide variety of holiday snacks on the table accompanied by goblets of crimson, luscious, delectable blood to satisfy the vampires craving and lust for the above mentioned. At the other end of the table an assortment of Christmas gifts will soon be opened to the ecstatic fervor of the vampires that have been patiently waiting.

A Gift Exchange

It is 7:OO PM and Joe and the vampires are gathered in the All Purpose Room in the basement for their own, private, Christmas celebration among themselves this evening. Joe hired a small, personal, five piece string orchestra to provide the Christmas, background music for himself and the vampires. As the vampires filed into the All Purpose Room the orchestra, The Fabulous five, was serenading them with soothing, Christmas melodies from days gone by. The vampires were crooning gently in their low voices to the sound of the orchestra. This evening place cards were placed at the table and everyone sat accordingly. After everybody was seated, two vampires distributed the gifts, by name, to complete the gift exchange. They were all exceedingly happy as they hastily removed the Christmas paper usually revealing a gift to their liking. By now, everyone is getting famished for something edible. They are lining up at the table to partake of the Christmas snacks and goblets of juicy, thirst quenching, bloody fluid that awaits them. They are visiting among themselves and sharing the camaraderie while enjoying the different variety of Christmas snacks and goblets of blood they were exposed to. They also had a movie screen on the wall depicting a short film of Albert and his sister, Jean, when they were President of the Vampire Club before their deaths. The film brought tears of sorrow to their eyes and a sad, dejected look on their faces as their minds traveled into the past. After the film ended they had a happier outlook and, once again, resumed their joyous nature. As the evening's Christmas celebration reached its climax the vampires thanked each other for their gifts, food, music and the wonderful camaraderie they experienced. Everybody assisted with the final cleaning of the All Purpose Room before retiring to their coffins for a good night's slumber.

Christmas Day

Merry Christmas!!! Everybody was up bright and early to prepare the barbecued chunks of human flesh that Joe dissected several days ago in the basement kitchen. The corpse that Joe used in preparation for the Christmas meal had been suspended in the Death Chamber for several months. The vampires transported two men back to the house from the downtown alleyways where they had been on a "nightly haunt." The corpse that Joe dissected is one of the men. A spade was used to pound into the corpse' heart never to be reincarnated again. Joe is hurriedly barbecuing the chunks of flesh while the vampires are preparing the rotted, mashed potatoes, slimy, green gravy, frozen corn which they forgot to thaw out, a cucumber salad laced with cockroaches, blood rolls and vomit, vanilla cupcakes for dessert. The meal will be complimented by a serving of thirst quenching, savory, tasty goblets of juicy blood. The orchestra, "The Fabulous Five" is serenading the vampires again as they eat their scrumptious, nourishing Christmas meal at 11:30 AM. After the vampires finished their meal they assisted Joe in the cleaning process that was involved. After that was completed they viewed a Christmas movie with "The Fabulous Five" orchestra serenading them all afternoon. After the movie they ate a light supper and watched another movie on television. By now the vampires are dead tired with full, bloated stomachs as they retired for the evening in their coffins with a smile pasted on their lips. "Goodnight, vampires! Sweet dreams!!!"

Chapter 37
A Blizzard Monday Morning

Joe, Blair and Isaac awoke early this morning because of reporting to work on their construction job as the result of a blizzard for Berg Construction Company. The last several days since Christmas have been cool and crisp even though they were not working those days due to the holidays. All of a sudden, on an impulse Joe opened the front door to retrieve the newspaper, which wasn't there, and was taken aback at the scene confronting him. A horrible wind had engulfed the city of Calgary, Canada. Their neighbor's trash receptacles are laying on their sides up and down the street and their small car has completely turned over upside down. The vampires have not taken their Christmas decorations down yet, so consequently, some of the cords with decorations and bulbs attached have been yanked loose from the trees by the ferocious wind storm. The sled, reindeer and Santa Claus are still intact for now. Not only that, a heavy snow is beginning to cloud the sky and surroundings with only minimum visibility for those that braved the elements. By now the streets, yards and sidewalks are completely covered by a blanket of snow with existing blizzard conditions prevailing. In the meantime, Joe called Berg Construction Company saying, "Isaac, Blair and I are unable to report for work this morning due to the inclement weather that has paralyzed the city of Calgary making transportation virtually impossible. I'm sorry about the inconvenience." Mr. Berg politely replied, "That's perfectly okay because you're not the first construction worker that excused themselves today. Even though you are working inside there is absolutely no way for you to report for work because of the existing conditions. Blair, Isaac and yourself are excused and "Thank you" for calling me." Joe courteously replied, "Thank you!" and hung up the phone. Since Joe, Isaac and Blair are excused from their construction work, indefinitely, they have no choice this afternoon but to don their winter attire and proceed to shovel heaps of snow on their property. Snow has accumulated on the street making driving hazardous and venturous. The porches, sidewalks and yards are laden with heavy snow and wind causing humongous tree branches to break off and topple to the ground while crippling the power lines in the process. Joe cautioned Isaac and Blair saying, "Please be aware of these falling power lines that are scattered all over the yard. They are treacherous wires that are capable of inflicting injury and possible death! Later on this afternoon I will report the fallen power lines to the city of Calgary to be disposed of as soon as possible." Blair and Isaac listened intently to Joe's informative remarks and said, "We will make sure that we are careful. Thank you!"

More Shoveling?

After Joe, Isaac and Blair acquired three hours of shoveling they were exceedingly sore, fatigued and chilled because of the cold, brisk, wind whipping at their backs. Eventually, they hustled indoors just in time for supper with Joe placing his telephone call to the city of Calgary in regards to the fallen power lines. Actually, several rooms in the house are without power for that reason. "Aggravating!" Joe and the vampires watched a movie after supper, occasionally, reversing to the weather channel with the announcer reporting, "There has been a cessation of snow for now with another accumulation of snowfall by morning. We have just received a report that the "city of Calgary is under a severe, city wide, weather alert. Please exercise caution when venturing outside! Thank you!" Ever since it started snowing, Joe, Isaac and Blair have been arising earlier than usual, 4:00 PM, due to the extra amount of shoveling the snowfall entails. After glancing outside noticing that it had snowed another three or four inches on top of the six inches that was already on the ground they decided to start shoveling right after breakfast. Again, the weather was brisk and chilly with light snowflakes draping the environment. They shoveled until dinnertime and resumed shoveling again after they had eaten. They shoveled off and on all afternoon taking breaks in between until it was time for supper. After supper they were not in a frame of mind to shovel again because of their sore backs, the cold and the constant snow drifting down.

Chapter 38
New Year's Day--2016

The snow has finally receded the last several days which eliminates the process of shoveling for Joe, Blair and Isaac. The city of Calgary, Canada was finally left with a grand total of seventeen inches when all was said and done. Lately, bright sunshine was peeking out between the clouds most of the day gradually melting the snow. Today is New Year's Day, January 1, 2016! The vampires are taking it easy today, lounging around in a lazy, relaxed atmosphere, watching television from the four couches that encompass the All Purpose Room in the basement, in other words, the television room. For breakfast, dinner and supper, today, the vampires can eat anything they want and watch any program on television they desire. The majority of the vampires agree, as a group, which movie they are interested in watching. They usually watch their favorite movies, accompanied by goblets of fresh, juicy, savory, thirst quenching, red blood and left over Christmas snacks. "Can you beat that for a lifestyle? Think about it!" Tomorrow everything reverts back to normal with Joe, Isaac and Blair returning to their inside construction job for Berg Construction Company. The remaining vampires will continue their household chores, as usual.

Confiscating Blood Again

Around Christmas time, 2015, Steve made a remark to the vampires one day saying, "At this point, we have not been able to make connections with anyone in regards to confiscating extra human blood to drink for our pleasure since this is what sustains a vampire's life. We found an extra case in the storage room we didn't know we had. Does anybody in our club have a vampire friend that is currently employed at the American Red Cross, The Calgary Memorial Hospital, a local mortuary here in Calgary, etc................. If so, would they be interested in donating cases of human blood for our cause? Please contact me here at the Vampire Club. Thank you!" Blair raised his hand and said, "I think I can be of some assistance in this situation. I currently have a vampire friend that is employed at the Calgary

Memorial Hospital on the late night shift that might be willing to oblige in this situation." Steve said, "That would be great, Blair! Are you able to make the connection, transaction, etc............... and relate the outcome back to me?" Blair said, "Hopefully, I can make the connection by telephone tonight and get back to you immediately."Later on this evening Blair called Steve saying, "I just got off the phone with my friend, Nolan, who works at the Calgary Memorial Hospital in the department that is affiliated with the hospital blood bank, the blood storage unit, etc................ Nolan is the only one in charge of the late night shift at the hospital, therefore , he has easy access to all the essentials on hand, including carts, keys to the back entrance, private rooms, etc................. You set the time and date and he will be expecting you." Steve said, "How about this coming Monday night at eleven o'clock at the back entrance?" Blair said, "That sounds great! I will tell him to be expecting you and the vampires Monday at the back entrance at eleven o'clock. Do you have any further questions before I confirm this appointment?" Steve said, "No, not that I can think of." Blair called Nolan immediately confirming the designated time for the confiscation of cases of blood from the Calgary Memorial Hospital.

Monday Night

Monday night has finally arrived for the confiscation of cases of bottled blood from the Calgary Memorial Hospital under the supervision of Nolan and Steve. Gilbert, Blair, Isaac and Roman assisted Steve in the transfer of the carts of bottled blood from the back entrance of the hospital to Joe's hearse parked by the door. Before they departed they thanked Nolan, wholeheartedly, for the transition of the bottled blood from the Calgary Memorial Hospital to their hearse. Steve said, "Nolan, if in any way, I can reciprocate the favor bestowed on us tonight please don't hesitate to call me." Nolan retorted, "I sure will. Also, after the bottled blood has been depleted and there is a need for more please call me in the evening, preferably, before 10:00 PM." Both parties thanked each other and went their respective ways. When Steve and the vampires arrived back at their house at 2125 Melbourne Street they transferred the cases of bottled blood into the storage room in the basement for further use. After the transferal was completed the vampires retired to their coffins early for a goodnight's rest because of arising early for their construction job the next morning. Berg Construction Company's owner, Mr. Adolph Berg, notified the vampires Joe, Blair and Isaac two weeks ago that their construction job would be completed in three months. They have made considerable progress inside the office building, besides, making preparations on the outside of the building for a complete renovation back to its original design.

Chapter 39
A Valentine's Haunt

Today is Valentine's Day, February 14th, 2016, with the vampires hurriedly exchanging Valentine cards and feasting on some Valentine chocolates to satisfy their craving for sweets. They are showering, shaving and dressing to the nines to present a more dapper appearance as they stroll in the back alleys of the Calgary business district to see whom they can victimize. It is rather cool and exceptionally dark this evening as they meander nonchalantly through the side streets, for a change, to possibly follow a person or two that is unfamiliar with the area. After they meandered through a certain side street, a time or two, they sidled after a middle aged man and woman who gave the impression they were unfamiliar with the environment. By now, they are only fifteen or twenty feet behind unbeknown to them. Suddenly, the man and woman picked up their pace with the vampires doing likewise. The vampires are edging considerably closer while grasping their dry, weathered, bony necks for a quick, thirst quenching blood sucking rendezvous in the dark shadows of the business buildings. The vampires continue their sucking rampage while the man and woman are screaming incessantly to be released from their grip. The vampires ignored their pleas until they had to eliminate their sucking sensation because of their uncomfortable, bloated stomachs. They were able to drag the man and woman back to the hearse and fling them in the back seat until they were ready to depart for their residence at 2125 Melbourne Street. They will fling them down the basement stairs where they will lie until 4:00 PM the next afternoon.

The Next Day

As Joe, Blair and Isaac leave for work in the hearse this morning they are aware of a heavy, misty film draping their windshield and surroundings. Joe said, "I hope it doesn't snow like it did the last time. Remember?" Blair and Isaac said, "Yes, we hope not because there was too much shoveling involved. Ha! Ha!" By this time, Joe is parking the hearse in a stall with another hard day's work ahead of him.

According to Mr. Berg they have about three months of work left and they will be terminated because the job will be completed. Joe, Blair and Isaac are planning on scouting around Calgary for employment again. Who knows? They might get lucky and find another job. They can also check the Want Ads in the newspaper for businesses that are seeking employees. In regards to the couple the vampires flung down the basement steps last night, they are both breathing but unable to walk or speak, similar to a comatose situation. The vampires transferred them to coffins and are monitoring them on a regular basis for an improvement in their condition. By now their breathing has become shallow and deteriorating close to the inevitable. Steve has been observing this incident as it becomes apparent that the couple are nearing the cessation of life. At this point, he approaches the vampires, "Everyone, please step up to both coffins. I became aware of a gurgling noise from both parties which is imminent as their life is in the last stages. I will post someone at the coffin periodically to keep a watchful eye as the condition progresses. Thank you!" The vampires immediately manned their posts at the coffin for a two hour stint until they expire. It also includes the nighttime hours around the clock. Finally, while Gilbert was taking his turn this morning at 7:00 AM he became aware of a cessation of breathing on either of the couple which indicated death. He notified Steve, Joe and the other vampires making them aware of the situation at hand. They instantly removed the bodies from the coffins and suspended them simultaneously, side by side, from the ceiling in the Death Chamber to be used at a later date. As usual, their bodies will be dissected into pieces to be served as the main entree' plus other additives, banquet style, for any upcoming, personal or social event the vampires are engaged in. The vampires are becoming increasingly fatigued today as a result of positioning themselves at the coffin periodically during the day and night. They viewed a three hour movie on television this evening retiring to their coffins immediately when it concluded. At 3:30 AM Steve was awakened with a spooky, eerie premonition that someone was in the proximity of his coffin. He automatically shifted to his side and was confronted by the deceased corpse of the man they suspended from the ceiling presumed dead. Oh no! That indicates that the woman is not dead either but alive and well. With his peripheral vision intact he got a glimpse of a woman in the process of sucking Joe's left, jugular vein to the point of Joe screaming, "Get away from me! You ugly creep! Get out of here!" In the meantime, a man grasped Steve by his neck and thrust his canine fangs into his left jugular vein to slurp an enormous amount of juicy, succulent, blood to his liking. After these abominable tasks were completed all the vampires were awake and inquiring. What happened?" In the meantime, Joe and Steve leaped out of their coffins grabbing the couple and escorting them up the basement stairs and flinging them violently out the back door screeching, "Don't ever come back or you might not live to tell about it. Get going! We don't ever want to see the likes of you again!" They both stumbled off into the darkness mumbling to themselves incoherently not looking back!Steve and Joe discussed the episode with the vampires as follows: "We misjudged the couple as being deceased, when in all retrospect, regarding past experiences they had ceased breathing for a while giving us the appearance of being presumably dead. We were overconfident in the breathing evaluation process. Let this be a lesson to us! Sorry! Thank you!" The vampires smiled, nodded their heads and returned to their coffins saying, "Thank you!"

Chapter 40
Let's Attack the Witches!

Lately, the vampires have been in a heated discussion with each other in regards to the whereabouts of their next vampire escapade. "Who are going to be the lucky victims? Ha! Ha! Guess?" Joe suggested, "Steve and I decided that we could impose on the witches, as a payback, for the blood sucking rendezvous they conducted on us in the middle of the night! Remember? What is your opinion on this suggestion?" Blair raised his hand and made the remark, "I think that is a great suggestion. Actually, I like the idea of the "payback" because they got by with murder! There was no counter attack or retribution on our part whatsoever. Set the time and date and we will be available at your beck and call." Joe said, "How about this Friday at 9:00 PM? Meet us at the hearse at 8:15 PM in the driveway." The vampires nodded and smiled acknowledging Joe's invitation, saying, "We'll be there!"Actually, Friday arrived sooner than usual it seems. The vampires met Steve and Joe at the hearse raring to go for a good old fashioned blood sucking rendezvous on the witches. They immediately left for 2429 Tyler Road which is several miles out of town. When they arrived at their residence everything had a dark, evil, eerie shadow enveloping the house kind of foreboding. It had a sinister, weird, ominous prediction of something that might take place. "Get the message? Too scary?" Several of the vampires approached the front door, expecting entrance, in spite of their last experience with the witches. They banged on all the doors repeatedly with no answer. On a sudden impulse, they decided to canvass the witch's property for clues as to their whereabouts. After roaming the area awhile they discovered an outside, underground, huge cellar in which they barged into with all the witches present conducting a séance, which is communicating with the spirits of the dead. Instantly, the vampires grabbed the witches by their dirt infested, swollen, greasy, vile necks sucking horrendously and greedily their juicy, tasty, succulent, savory blood, until their stomachs could contain no more. The witches were pleading and lamenting their plight, some in English, some in their native tongue and others not understandable at all. The vampires speedily dropped the witches on the cement cellar floor, screaming, to fend for themselves or die. They quickly exited up the stairs, out the door and into the hearse for the ride back to Calgary. On the way back Joe said, "Well, we got even with the witches today, our payback. We will never see them again! Never! Agreed?" The vampires nodded their heads, smiled and said, "Never! Agreed!"

Memorial Day, May 30, 2016

A free, Memorial Day recognition gathering is on the Vampire Club's agenda accompanied by patriotic music in the background for May 30, 2016 at Riley Park in the northeast section of Calgary. The vampires are scheduling the above mentioned in honor of the deceased, our fallen comrades, etc................... A patriotic poem will be recited by Isaac in their honor and a discourse will be delivered by Joe to the audience following prayers by Chaplain Carl. In the meantime, the vampires with Joe at the helm, are hastily assisting him in dissecting the body of a homeless man suspended in the Death Chamber for several months. The delectable, main entrée at the banquet will be roasted flesh, no barbecued chunks as in previous banquets, scalloped potatoes immersed in a bloody liquid, peas laced with dead bumble bees, bloody dinner rolls, a garden salad with dead spiders as an ingredient and filthy, rotted, dirty dishwater to be used for salad dressing. To complete the banquet how about homemade, Chocolate Chip ice cream laced with human vomit accompanied by goblets of scrumptious, flavorful, juicy, crimson blood? Do you want a free meal? Let's go! I'm starved now already!" The vampires arose early this morning, Memorial Day, to a sweltering, steamy, humid atmosphere surrounding them as they transported the banquet food that was prepared in advance yesterday to the hearse. It included paper plates, silverware, table cards, decorations, etc................... for the upcoming banquet in the four shelter houses. When they arrived in Riley Park Les Brown's Band of Renown was serenading the regular customers that were filteringinto Riley Park for the Memorial Day recognition program banquet.

The Memorial Day Recognition Program started at 10:00 AM, followed by the banquet at 11:30 AM, simultaneously with Les Brown's

Band. According to the customers everybody enjoyed the Memorial Day Recognition Program, Banquet and the background music in the band shell of The Les Brown Band of Renown. Evidently everybody left Riley Park with thoughts of loved ones and fallen comrades that have passed on and a full, bloated stomach while humming the classical music of the Les Brown Orchestra. I'm sure everyone enjoyed the afternoon as they thanked the vampires for all their time, labor and effort that was involved in today's Memorial Day event. The vampires acknowledged their remarks, shaking hands, smiling and saying, "Thank you!" At this time, the vampires were exceedingly fatigued, in regards to the labor that was involved in today's activities while transporting the remaining food, utensils and incidentals to the hearse for the trip back to Calgary. When they arrived back in the city in the sweltering heat they were practically overcome with exhaustion by this time as they transferred the supplies back into the house. The vampires ate a light meal while viewing television and then retired to their coffins for a goodnight's rest which they so readily deserved. "Sweet Dreams!"

Chapter 41
What Happened to Steve?

Joe and Steve decided to take a drive to Mohegan Cemetery because they hadn't been there for a while and it is staying light longer in the evenings past 9:00 PM. They would like to do some meditating on certain gravesites if they can locate them. They parked the hearse several blocks north of the Mohegan Cemetery and entered the cemetery gates. They strolled through the cemetery too hastily looking for the gravesites but couldn't find them. They decided to part ways each looking on their own. Joe discovered his uncle's gravesite he was looking for, kneeling on it and meditating. Steve also encountered the gravesite he had in mind (or thought he had) and proceeded to kneel down and meditate likewise at his friend's gravesite. All was good and well until the soil under Steve's knees began to move, rumble and spread wider and wider indicating an unknown force under the ground. By now, the movement and motion became increasingly larger causing Steve to topple sideways onto the gravesite. As he was lying there he sensed a mummy head beginning to protrude through the soil, reaching above ground, as his arms were flailing to grab Steve. He tried to avoid being snatched but he wasn't fast enough. The mummy had him in his clutches while Steve was trying to fight him off tooth and nail wrestling him every chance he got. Evidently, Steve didn't get enough chances because, eventually, the mummy overpowered him, yanking him underground to descend in a downward direction about twenty five feet. After they landed on the cement floor Steve was overcome with fear because he knew exactly where he was at. He was in the same area that Earl, Chris and Ryan had landed only they were engulfed by the soil while he was actually pulled by the mummy with his hands underground. "Oh! No! What will befall Steve now? Is there any way he can escape?" The length of time he has been underground in the company of the mummies I'm sure he has had very little to eat, besides, being at the mercy of them in regards to the violent, blood sucking encounters he has had to endure which have left him very weak and fatigued.

Searching for Steve

By now, Joe has been searching for Steve endlessly but to no avail! He has canvassed the complete Mohegan Cemetery but no sight of Steve. He thought to himself, "What happened to Steve? I can hardly believe this is happening! What will the vampire's reaction be?" He decided to leave the cemetery because it was totally dark and a filmy mist was beginning to envelope the tombstones. When he reached the house he immediately conveyed to the vampires what had transpired at the Mohegan Cemetery to Steve. They were appalled and aghast at the loss of the Steve which they didn't expect to happen. Most of the vampires were weeping because they knew what the end result would probably be. The vampires were lamenting their plight saying, "Oh no! What will we do now? We could always rely on Steve when certain issues had to be dealt with. There is no one that will be able to assist us now besides Joe." Joe was overcome with grief at the loss of his best friend, Steve. He related to the vampires, "What actually happened was Steve and I went our separate ways trying to locate the gravesites where our friends were buried. I discovered my friend's gravesite immediately and assumed Steve did the same. Well, Steve also found a gravesite presuming to be his best friend's which it wasn't. He wasn't aware of this and proceeded to kneel on the soil in private meditation in honor of his best friend because I got a glimpse of him from a distance. Since it is the same gravesite that engulfed Earl, Chris and Ryan I'm under the assumption the same misfortune befell Steve." He continued, "I will make arrangements tomorrow at the Ronton Mortuary for a private, memorial service to be held displaying his school album, etc..................in spite of the fact there will be no body in a casket for public viewing. Is everyone in agreement with this?" The vampires nodded their heads in accord while continuously shedding tears at the inevitable.

The Day After

Joe and the vampires were meticulously groomed, with every hair in place, fingernails perfectly manicured, flawless makeup, etc..................as they sat in mourner's row awaiting the beginning of the private memorial service for their friend Steve Stanley. Relatives and friends expressed their condolences as they filed past several of his school pictures, personal memorabilia on display, newspaper articles, etc………………The New Haven Baptist Church Minister, John Burton, conducted the private, memorial service for Steve at 4:00 PM, June 9, 2016, with a free meal to follow in the dining area of the church. There was an overflowing attendance at the meal in Steve's honor accompanied by the camaraderie of a wide circle of acquaintances, several, locally distinguished guests, relatives, friends, etc………………

Two Weeks Later

One evening after supper Joe asked the vampires, "It's been a while since any of us have frequented the Mohegan Cemetery in search of a good, old fashioned, blood sucking rendezvous preferably at the Mohegan Mausoleum. Is anybody interested in making the trip?" The vampires smiled and nodded indicating they were willing to make the trip. Blair spoke up saying, 'Set the time and date and we will be there!" Joe said, "How about this coming Friday night at 7:00 PM, June 13? My hearse will be parked in the driveway for your convenience." The vampires remarked, "We'll be there!" Friday night rolled around, "fast and furious" as the vampires were lined up at the hearse ready to make their entrance. They were making a trip to the Mohegan Cemetery, hopefully, for a thirst quenching, blood sucking episode in the Mohegan Mausoleum. They are equipped this evening with extra tools and equipment, in the event, the mausoleum door is locked and they can't gain entrance. They entered by way of the cemetery gates approaching the mausoleum door which opened with ease indicating, possibly, someone forgot to lock the door when they left. "How careless can you get? Really! Joe and the vampires entered the mausoleum approaching the caskets that were stacked on top of each other. They opened the first casket which was empty, the second casket was occupied by an older, embalmed man and the third casket was possessed by none other than Steve Stanley. He was not in mummy form like Earl, Chris and Ryan but his usual self. Evidently, he passed away in the meantime while being exposed to the mummies. Joe and the vampires went through a crying spell again as they viewed Steve once more knowing that might be the last time they will ever get to see him again! "You never know! What a shame!" After seeing Steve again the vampires were in a sad frame of mind and not interested in any blood sucking encounters of any sort. They exited the mausoleum with a depressed look on their countenance while positioning themselves in the hearse for their ride back to Calgary.

Chapter 42
Depressed?

Joe and the vampires are in a depressed, dejected, melancholy state of mind as the result of their vampire friend, Steve Stanley's, sudden exposure to a tribe of mummies infiltrating the Mohegan Cemetery. Steve's cessation of life evidently occurred while residing underground in the presence of the mummies. Joe reminded the vampires explicitly saying, "In the future, when we frequent any cemetery, especially, the Mohegan Cemetery I suggest we depart and return as a group. When we pass through the gates no one is allowed to deviate from our assembly but remain together as a whole because of what transpired with Steve. Not all of us are one hundred percent sure where the gravesite is located that engulfed Steve into a premature death. We don't want that to happen to anybody else. This is the fourth vampire in our group that has been subject to this, excluding Earl, Chris and Ryan, which supposedly, according to the mummies, have been reincarnated likewise. If anyone accidentally kneels or steps on the gravesite soil where Earl, Chris, Ryan, and Steve were engulfed I'm sure it will happen again! Please follow instructions specifically! Are there any questions? Please raise your hand!" No one raised their hand indicating they were in acceptance of Joe's orders. Joe continued, "While we're on the subject of cemeteries another cemetery came to my mind that I think we used to visit when Albert or Jean were still alive and that is the Poheta Cemetery. The vampires nodded their heads signifying the recognition of the name, Poheta Cemetery. Joe remarked, "Is anyone interested in a blood sucking rendezvous among the mourners that visit the cemetery on a regular basis? We are running low on suspended corpses in the Death Chamber for future banquets and events indicating a need to replenish our supply." The vampires exclaimed, "We're ready to go whenever you are! Just say the word! We're raring to go!" Joe said, "How about tomorrow night at 7:00 PM? Meet me at my hearse in the driveway." The vampires smiled and nodded their heads in agreement.

Poheta Cemetery

The vampires were gathered at Joe's hearse for a ride to Poheta Cemetery, east of Calgary, Canada about seven miles. It is another Indian Cemetery the same as the Mohegan Cemetery. They parked two blocks east of the cemetery walking the remainder of the distance. Everybody remained together, as a group as Joe suggested, strolling through the cemetery in hopes of acquiring a victim to feast their canine fangs on. Poheta Cemetery also has a mausoleum but the vampires forgot to bring their tools and equipment, in the event, the door would be locked so they are resorting to the few stragglers that are meditating at certain gravesites. Joe approached a middle aged man at a private gravesite at the farther end of the cemetery with the vampires observing. He thrust his gleaming, white fangs into the man's left jugular vein for a violent, blood sucking, thirst quenching episode as volumes of blood gushed forth. This left the victim weak and fatigued as he collapsed to the ground. Isaac managed to wrestle around with his eighty year old victim in the proximity of Joe's encounter with the middle aged man. As usual, according to Joe's instructions the vampires were observing. By this time Isaac overpowered his older victim thrusting his sharp pointed fangs into his victim's lily livered, withered, grimy, left, jugular vein. Isaac sucked his red, scrumptious, delectable, tasty blood violently with his victim screeching and screaming in full force saying, "Who are you? Leave me alone! Get away from me!" Isaac released his grip on his victim's neck, due to the fact, that he was unable to continue his sucking sensation because of his full, bloated stomach and his desire for blood has decreased. His victim slowly collapsed to the cemetery ground at Isaac's feet. The vampires were gathered in a group keeping a watchful eye on the day's activities at hand. By now, dusk is beginning to emerge as Joe and Isaac with the assistance of the vampires transported the two victims to the hearse for the trip back to Calgary. When they returned Joe and Isaac each flung their victims down the basement stairs to lie there until 4:00 PM the next afternoon after which they will monitor their condition for a day or two. Before everyone retired for the evening Joe asked the vampires, "Is anyone interested in going back to the Poheta Cemetery again sometime?" The vampires giggled with glee as they said, "We would enjoy going back to the Poheta Cemetery since there are more victims frequenting the gravesites than other cemeteries. As always, you set the date and time and we will be waiting by the hearse." Joe said, "How about this Thursday night at 7:00 PM?" The vampires remarked, "We're ready to go!"

Chapter 43
Poheta Cemetery Again?

As Joe and the vampires are strolling through the Poheta Cemetery they are also transporting their tools and equipment, in the event, they decide to enter the Poheta Mausoleum by choice. Actually, they have two mausoleums, side by side, and another mausoleum a short distance away. The cemetery is totally deserted this evening, not a soul in sight, as the vampires canvass the cemetery to make sure no one is in the proximity of the mausoleum. The vampires decided "on the spur of the moment" to try their luck at gaining entrance to the mausoleum of their own accord. Blair and several of the vampires clanged and banged on the lock incessantly while jerking the handle to and fro in hopes of releasing the lock. Finally, after their continuous effort they heard a sharp, screeching, shrill noise as the lock loosened and the door was ajar. It was firm and unyielding as the vampires slid stealthily inside to be greeted by a foul, rancid, rotten, offensive odor. A large variety of caskets were stacked on top of each other and some were side by side as the vampires glared at the corpses encased in the caskets. Joe made the remark, "Well, we'll just have to take a chance on their left, jugular vein since we don't know if they have been embalmed or not." Joe thrust his gleaming, white fangs into the young man's left, jugular vein with volumes of delicious, crimson, delectable, fresh blood erupting from the corpses' swollen veins. This indicates there was still a vast amount of blood concealed in his veins. Joe gulped the yummy liquid until his stomach was swollen, very uncomfortable and he was left with a nauseous, loathing, vomiting feeling. Since there was still plenty of fluid enclosed in his left, jugular vein Isaac decided to follow in Joe's footsteps for the immeasurable pleasure at his beck and call. After Isaac had quenched his blood sucking thirst he handed the corpse in the casket over to Blair since there was still some blood flowing freely from the young man's left, jugular vein. Every one of the vampires took their turn at the corpses' in the casket since most of them were not embalmed so it was a simple matter. After everybody had completed their blood sucking rendezvous Joe said, "Well, I guess we might as well leave since we accomplished what we came here for." The vampires smiled and said, "That's right! We're ready to leave!" On the way back to Calgary Joe remarked, "Since we had such good luck tonight, because most of the corpses' were not embalmed, we can consider frequenting this Poheta Mausoleum oftener. What do you think?" The vampires nodded and smiled saying, "You're the boss! Whatever you say goes!"

A Swimming Escapade, July 4, 2016

Joe decided to bypass the July 4, 2016 Banquet and Fireworks display similar to past years treating the vampires to a "free for all" swimming escapade at the Calgary Swimming Pool sometime this week. He approached the vampires asking them, "Would anyone be interested in a swimming rendezvous at our local swimming pool some night this week since the weather is getting increasingly hotter day by day? Please raise your hand." Everybody's hand was raised indicating they were all thrilled at the idea of bashing and splashing in the cool, refreshing Calgary Swimming Pool with each other and their friends. Joe remarked, "Good, that's settled! I will make the necessary arrangements and give you the date and time." He immediately stepped to a phone in the hallway to make the arrangements with the Calgary Swimming Pool for this coming Friday, July 4th, 2016, from 7:OO PM to 1O:OO PM. He related the message to the vampires and everything was in accordance with their wishes. Friday was a broiling, steamy day with the thermometer reaching 105 degrees as Joe and the vampires dived into the cold, sparkling water to soothe their overheated, moist, clammy skin. They were splashing around in the frothy, foamy bubbles of water, besides, racing each other back and forth from one end of the swimming pool to the other end. Joe was winning most of the time because of the exertion the vampires had to put themselves through. They took a break for a refreshing container of soda to quench their thirst and a sandwich to satisfy their craving for food. After they finished their snack they leaped back into the crisp, clear water, minus most of the swimmers that had left they practically had the pool to themselves with the exception of two, lone, young women. Several of the vampires encountered the two women about three feet ahead of them. They hastily came closer, snatching them by their lily white, streamlined, left jugular vein as they ranted and raved saying, "Leave us alone, you creeps! Who are you anyway? We've never seen you here before! Get away from us!" By this time, the vampires were satisfying their craving for blood while sucking horrendously every drop they could muster hunched over in a darkened corner of the pool. At this point, they were the only swimmers left in the Calgary Swimming Pool. They hurriedly transferred their bodies to the hearse after they collapsed at their feet. When they reached the house they flung them both down the basement stairs to lie there until 4:00 PM the next afternoon. If they are still alive they will be shifted to a coffin. If they are deceased they will be suspended in the Death Chamber until a future date after which they will be dissected for holiday banquets, events etc............... That has been the standard procedure dating back to Albert's existence.

Chapter 44
The Poheta Cemetery Once More?

Joe must be anticipating another blood sucking rendezvous at the Poheta Cemetery because of their short excursion there two weeks ago that met their expectations. "Remember, the thirst quenching episode in the mausoleum? Doesn't that tell you something? It does me!" By this time, Joe had access to the vampires asking them, "Is anyone interested in frequenting the Poheta Cemetery again like we did a couple of weeks ago?" They smiled, nodding their heads, saying, "We're raring to go! You set the date and we'll be at the hearse at the appointed time." Joe remarked, "How about this coming Wednesday night at 9:00 PM? Please meet me at the hearse. The vampires said, "We'll be there with flying colors! Ha! Ha!"Another Blood Sucking Rendezvous

Wednesday night, 9:00 PM, rolled around as usual with Joe and the vampires meandering through the Poheta Cemetery once again. Tonight they are not interested in frequenting the Poheta Mausoleum, as they thought, but excavating a gravesite with their tools and equipment on hand. Since there is no one in the cemetery at the present moment Joe posted a vampire to watch for intruders. Joe and the vampires are hastily digging the top of a gravesite in the farther end of the cemetery. One of their friends not associated with the Vampire Club, Arthur Belton, was buried there, not embalmed, this past year. Joe and the vampires decided to unearth his gravesite for a thirst quenching rendezvous and a strong possibility of transporting his corpse back to Calgary with them. Joe and the vampires are still frantically digging anticipating the exposure of the vault and casket before their eyes. Suddenly, Blair yells, "My shovel hit a sharp object with a thud," which the other vampires were aware of. They continued digging when all of a sudden they were confronted by a vault and enclosed casket. They banged and clanged on the casket, eventually, releasing the lock with the lid rising automatically to reveal, Arthur Belton, his appearance the same as the day they buried him. Joe grabbed his limp, lifeless corpse by his neck, jerking his left, jugular vein within distance of his gleaming, white, canine fangs. He immediately thrust them into his vein releasing volumes of red, succulent, juicy, delectable blood much to his morbid pleasure. Joe sucked the red fluid voraciously while licking his slimy, red lips practically begging for more. Blood continued to flow freely with Joe sucking violently until his bloated stomach could not contain the overflow. At this point, Joe released his grip on Arthur slackening his pace due to a superfluous amount of blood. Joe suggested to the vampires, "Start taking your turn whoever is next in line. Help yourselves!" The vampires stepped up to the casket underground each taking their turn at a blood sucking rendezvous on Arthur Belton. Joe asked the vampire posted at the gravesite, "Are you aware of any intruders, meditators, night stalkers etc………………..in the cemetery the length of time you have been posted out there?" The vampire said, "So far this evening there has been no one frequenting the cemetery." Joe remarked, Good! Please retain your post until we depart." Since it was very dark and misty by this time Joe and the vampires decided to confiscate the corpse from the grave transferring it to the Death Chamber in Calgary. It will be suspended from the ceiling for dissection purposes in the near future for holiday banquets, events etc……………... After the vampires completed their sucking sensation Joe posted three vampires at the top of the grave. He and two other vampires managed to maneuver or hoist Arthur's casket to the top of the grave with Arthur contained. They hurriedly transported Arthur's casket to the hearse for the ride back to Calgary. When they arrived back they deposited the casket in the spare room with the other caskets. Arthur's corpse was instantly suspended from the ceiling in the Death Chamber. Joe made the remark, "This was a splendid idea bringing Arthur back with us and suspending him from the ceiling. Besides, everyone was the recipient of a thirst quenching, bloody escapade at no one's expense. That was a good deal! It won't be long and we'll be back at the Poheta Cemetery for another bloody feast. I can think of several, personal friends of mine that were buried within the last two years, not embalmed, according to Earl, Chris and Ryan when they were still employed at the Ronton Mortuary. We might as well set the date now for our next Poheta Cemetery outing. How about next week Friday at 9:00 PM again the same as tonight?" The vampires were ecstatic at the idea of another bloody feast that would be awaiting them. They were grinning from ear to ear at the prospect of another bloody encounter with a non-embalmed corpse at the Poheta Cemetery again. Joe is planning on confiscating another corpse from the cemetery again the same as this last time.

Chapter 45
Confiscating Another Corpse!

Joe and the vampires are on the road again to Poheta Cemetery to confiscate another non embalmed corpse, a personal friend of Joe and his family that was interred at the cemetery several years ago. At this point, they are taking a leisurely stroll through the cemetery since Joe is an authority on the whereabouts of his friend Victor Burg's gravesite. Within a few minutes they arrived at the intended gravesite with tools and equipment on hand to excavate the burial space for this specified purpose. Joe posted Blair and Gilbert at the grave in the event that homeless, destitute, stragglers might be frequenting the cemetery at any given time. The vampires continued shoveling and scraping until George yelled, "My shovel struck a metal frame which I think is the vault and casket." He kept shoveling until he uncovered the vault and casket as he predicted. Immediately, George yanked Victor's emaciated frame towards him while sinking his vampire fangs into Victor's left, jugular vein for a juicy, blood curdling episode to his liking. George sucked voraciously every drop of blood he could muster until he was overcome by the bloody fluid and almost collapsed in the process. The other vampires stepped up to the casket, single file, in order to partake of the crimson, juicy, delectable, tasty blood that was erupting from Victor's left, jugular vein. Joe was last in line with volumes of blood still gushing out of Victor's vein in spite of the vampire's blood sucking rendezvous. As soon as the blood ebbed away, Joe repositioned Victor in the casket, sealed the lid and hoisted him up the walls of the grave. Blair and Gilbert transferred the body to the hearse for the ride back to Calgary. When they came back they suspended Victor's corpse from the ceiling in the Death Chamber and placed the casket in the adjoining room with a variety of other caskets. Some of the caskets contain corpses' while others are recovering from blood sucking rendezvous,' severe attacks, comas, etc................... The vampires that are recuperating will remain confined in their caskets until they are up and about mixing and mingling with the other vampires. The ones that are deceased and suspended from the ceiling will be dissected eventually and used for holiday banquets, festivals, events, etc……………..

Back to the Calgary Swimming Pool? August 5, 2016

Since summer is gradually fading away Joe decided this would be a good time to make another trip to the Calgary Swimming Pool since the pool will be closing on Labor Day, September 4, 2016. He asked the vampires, "Is anyone interested in going to the Calgary Swimming Pool again since it will be closing next month? Please raise your hand." The vampires were thrilled at the prospect of frequenting the pool again because the heat is becoming very intense and overwhelming, up to 105 degrees. All the vampires raised their hands indicating they were more than happy to spend an evening in the cool, refreshing water at the Calgary Swimming Pool. Joe mentioned, "How about this coming Friday night at 7:00 PM? Please bring a towel and meet me at my hearse at 6:15 PM. It's possible we will get as lucky as the last time with the two young women we transported back. They passed away after they were confined to the coffin for two days, then suspended from the ceiling and used consecutively in the dissection process for banquets, festivities, multiple meals, etc…………….. The vampires continued smiling and saying, "We'll be at the hearse this coming Friday night at the appointed time of 6:15 PM. Thank you!"

Friday Night!

As usual, Friday night rolled around sooner than expected as the vampires were showering, shaving and donning their swimming trunks. They groomed their hair meticulously with manicured nails and flawless makeup. They were waiting with their towels at 6:15 PM for Joe at the hearse. When he arrived and saw the vampires lined up and raring to go he said, "Good! Rather too soon than too late! Right?"When they arrived at the Calgary Swimming Pool they checked in and immediately jumped off the diving board into the cool, clear, crisp water enclosing their hot, steamy bodies. They raced each other the length of the pool and back while mingling with their past friends and acquaintances. As the evening progressed a large amount of people exited the swimming pool with the exception of Joe and the vampires and two young men in their forties. The vampires approached them as they were swimming towards a darkened area of the pool. Blair and Isaac hastily grabbed their slimy, swollen, bronzed left, jugular vein and sucked violently and voraciously the red, tasty, succulent fluid that erupted and continuously flowed. They were sucking insatiably every drop they could muster in spite of their bloated, distended stomachs. Eventually, they could not keep up with the overflow of blood, causing it to move freely in the water, giving it the appearance of a red river. They discontinued their incessant sucking and decided to drag the two men to the hearse for the ride back since they were parked close to the pool. On the way back Joe remarked, "Well, that was worth the trip tonight. We're coming back with two extra bodies more than we had before." The vampires smiled and nodded saying, "This was our lucky night!"

Chapter 46
A Labor Day Celebration

September 8, 2016

Labor Day is fast approaching as Joe and the vampires are making their preparations in advance. They are sponsoring a free meal in Riley Park accompanied by the Les Brown, Band of Renown, besides, a free dance after the holiday banquet. Joe and the vampires are dissecting the body of one of the two women that passed away due to a blood sucking confrontation in the Calgary Swimming Pool. The dissection of the body into bite sized, cubed chunks of flesh is for the sole purpose of cooking stew for the main entrée. The stew will be accompanied by scalloped potatoes burned to a crisp, corn on the cob with earth worms crawling on every ear, a vegetable salad with dishwater for dressing, blood bread, vomit vanilla ice cream and goblets of delectable, bloody fluid to quench their insatiable thirst and hunger.

A Free Meal

Today is Monday, September 8th, 2016, Labor Day, with numerous people filing into Riley Park, with the Les Brown, Band of Renown, serenading them in the background. They are seating themselves at the picnic tables to partake of the scrumptious meal in their midst. Everybody was anxious to taste the cubed sized chunks of flesh that Joe had so meticulously prepared besides the remainder of the meal. A lot of people went back for seconds since it was very tasty and appealing to everyone. After everyone had finished their scrumptious meal, dessert and goblets of blood, they were anxious to get on the dance floor and cut a rug! Ha! Ha! The dance floor is beginning to get packed with many people trying their hand at dancing once again. How about for "Old Time's Sake!" Les Brown's Band starts with an old time polka, "The Beer Barrel Polka!" Also, some Elvis Presley tunes and several polkas again. And on and on and on into the night! As soon as the vampire waiters finished cleaning the tables, etc................ they hastily snatched one of their lady friends and twirled them around the dance floor. Everyone feasted on a cold drink and snack before proceeding to dance with their partner most of the night. The vampires enjoyed the dancing vowing to incorporate dancing again the next time they engage in a free meal! The weather was very accommodating and the evening was a few degrees cooler. A nice temperature to be outside. "Right?"

"A Blood Sucking Rendezvous Tonight?"

The general public was preparing to leave Riley Park this evening, thanking Joe and the vampires for the meal and dance because ominous, storm clouds were gathering on the horizon. Claps of thunder could be heard resonating in the background while fingers of lightening were inevitable. By this time, a violent wind was rustling the pines as everybody was hurriedly exiting the park for their cars. It has grown increasingly darker because of the change in the weather as the vampires gather their personal effects transporting them to the hearse. Gilbert and Blair decided to make a last ditch attempt to snag a couple of women behind the band shell where it was completely dark by this time. Unnoticed Blair and Gilbert were ten or fifteen feet behind them as they were meandering behind the band shell awaiting their ride. They hastily grabbed them, pulling both ladies into the thicket and brush, near the back entrance. They gallantly and leisurely thrust their canine fangs into their lily white necks, causing volumes of blood to erupt at any given time. They continued sucking until their bloated stomachs could not contain the overflow any longer. At this point, the two, young ladies are lying at Brian and Gilbert's feet, due to the fact, they collapsed during the blood sucking rendezvous. They transferred them to the hearse where they will lie in repose until Joe and the vampires arrive back in Calgary. By now, a violent rainstorm is inundating the city as they pull into the driveway. They are waiting a few minutes until the rain subsides before they make their entrance into the house while flinging the two, young women down the basement stairs to lie there until the next afternoon at 4:00 PM.

A Day Later

The next day at 4:00 PM Blair and Gilbert checked on the two women that they victimized earlier the day before. They were both in fairly good shape, alert, speaking and conducting themselves properly. The women ate their meals together, not with the vampires, watching television in another area of the basement. There was no interaction between the vampires and the women. "That's good!" Later in the evening, the women retired to their coffins earlier, supposedly, for a good night's rest in a private room because they had a hectic day the night before. Eventually, the vampires retired for the evening around 11:00 PM after watching the Calgary News and Weather Report. Within a half an hour all the vampires were sleeping and snoring "to beat the band." They were fatigued and worn out from assisting at the meal site, plus dancing, which they aren't acclimated to. This was probably the first time the vampires had danced in years! "Really! Maybe they need to dance oftener! Ha! Ha!" The two, young women were wide awake waiting their chance to escape from their surroundings. It was as silent as a tomb in the basement, other than the snoring, as they hurriedly picked up their personal effects departing up the basement stairs softly and quietly, out into the night. The weather was accommodating as they headed towards the downtown area to the closest phone to call for a ride.

Chapter 47
Where are the Victims?

Joe, Blair and Isaac are still dutifully employed at the Berg Construction Company in downtown Calgary due to a tornado that ravaged the city several months ago. They have been inundated with work, because of the damage inflicted on businesses and private residences within the city of Calgary. Since Joe, Blair and Isaac are running late this morning due to their hectic schedule the last couple of days they are hurriedly eating breakfast and dashing out the door oblivious of anything that is amiss. The remainder of the vampires continue to sleep on until 4:00 PM this afternoon after which they will arise and meet the day. Just by chance, Gilbert happened to leave his coffin earlier than usual this morning for no particular reason. As he was meandering around the basement he became aware of the fact that the two, young women were missing from their coffins. He started searching the basement and calling for them but to no avail. They must have escaped from the vampires during the night when everybody was sleeping and snoring. Gilbert thought to himself, "Well, they had one heck of a nerve escaping during the night. They really took a chance that one of us could have accidentally awakened while they were on their way out. How about, possibly, hearing the basement door close?" Gilbert instantly woke the vampires up saying, "The vampires were amazed the two women victims that we transferred back to the house escaped during the night before our very eyes as we were sleeping and snoring. What do you think of that?" The vampires were amazed and shocked when Gilbert related the news to them. Several of the vampires said, "We thought we heard something similar to a whisper and strange, rustling noises but we were too tired to get up. This is the first time we've had a victim or victims leave the premises after we transferred them back to the house. That's unusual!" Gilbert said, "I thought I heard the basement door softly close during the night but then I fell asleep again." He asked, "Did anybody else hear anything strange or unusual during the night?" Arthur said, "I was the last vampire to retire for the night and I didn't hear anything at all. We're probably better off without them." When Joe, Blair and

Isaac arrived home from their construction jobs this evening Arthur and the vampires related the news to them. They were totally shocked at the outcome of their escapade in Riley Park. This is the first time in the history of the vampires living at 2125 Melbourne Street that victims they brought back actually escaped during the night. "You never know! Some people will attempt anything! How about this old saying, Good riddance, bad rubbish!"

A Drive in Theater

Joe suggested the following for this weekend, "Do you any of you remember the Drive in Movies from the 1950's and 1960's? Please raise your hand!" Everybody's hand shot up as their faces smiled gleefully! Joe said, "There are only a few Drive in Movies in existence around Calgary. Who is interested in attending one this weekend?" All the vampires were equally fascinated at the thought of attending a Drive in Movie as opposed to sitting in a stuffy theater or in the basement watching commercials all night. Joe continued, "How about that Vampire movie at the Calgary Drive in that they are advertising all week long? It will be coming Saturday night at 8:00 PM." The vampires were "all in game" for the movie using the hearse and two other cars available by two vampires to accompany everyone.

Once again, Saturday night has finally arrived with the vampires patiently waiting at 7:30 PM at Joe's hearse in the driveway. By now, they are merrily on their way to the Calgary Drive in to view a new movie that has recently been released, titled "Vampires Galore." After they enter the concession stand, purchasing their cold drink and popcorn, they are settled in all three vehicles for a night of fun and relaxation." Not so with Joe! His mind is on a different track tonight! I guess he's a little derailed! Ha! Ha!" Joe has, inconspicuously, parked the hearse beside an unknown couple awaiting the beginning of the movie while munching on popcorn and devouring their cold drink. Joe and the vampires were doing likewise, sheepishly glancing at the couple sideways trying to determine the most convenient time to confront them before the movie begins. All of a sudden, Joe said, "Now is the perfect time! Let's go!" Joe and several of the vampires hurriedly leaped out of the hearse, opened the back door of their car and slid inside while grabbing the necks of the couple. Their canine fangs flashed in the dark as they thrust them into their left jugular vein, sucking horrendously the juicy, crimson, savory, delicious volumes of blood that erupted from their vessels. After their sucking rendezvous was completed and everybody's attention was directed towards the movie screen Joe and the vampires quickly transferred the unconscious couple to the hearse for the ride back to Calgary. The movie, "Vampires Galore" was very interesting, humorous and beneficial while keeping the vampires on their toes. They immediately exited the drive in when the movie was over for their ride back to Calgary. When they arrived at 2125 Melbourne Street Joe cast the two bodies down the basement stairs to lie there until 4:00 PM the next afternoon after which they will be evaluated.

Chapter 48
"Last Day at Work"

As they were eating breakfast this morning Blair made the remark, "Well, this is our last day of work for Berg Construction Company. Our work is completed." Joe and Isaac nodded their heads in agreement saying, "I can't believe how fast the time went by after that tornado. We might be in for a long vacation with no work. We're well aware of that!"After the remainder of the vampires arose at 4:00 PM this afternoon they did a routine check on the couple that Joe cast down the basement steps. That's strange! Both of them are still unconscious since last night. Did they strike their head on a hard object as they careened down the stairs? The vampires went about their household duties assigned to them the rest of the day, keeping a periodic watch on the couple for any signs of consciousness or gradual recovery. "If this evening doesn't bring any further results, Joe was saying, we can assume they are in a coma and death is imminent."The next day at 4:00 PM the vampires did a check on the couple again lying in their respective caskets with no response and no breathing. "What happened? Did they have a cessation of life?" Joe checked their vital sign since he was employed as a male nurse in a hospital years ago before his present lifestyle. Joe declared, "Both of them passed away sometime during the night which we were not aware of. We will suspend them from the ceiling in the Death Chamber until further notice." The vampires nodded in somber silence and respect indicating they were aware of the upcoming problem.

Joe's Birthday September 20, 2016

Joe's birthday is coming up September 20, 2016 and the vampires are going to celebrate the occasion with a meal for the vampires only. Joe will be conducting the dissection process the night before in the Death Chamber of all places. The male corpse' body from the incident at the Calgary Drive In will remain suspended from the ceiling as Joe and the vampires start dissecting the body from the toes upward. Joe will be the main dissector, slicing fleshy chunk after fleshy chunk onward to the thighs, stomach, on up. Organs that will not be used will either be frozen or discarded in a trash receptacle. The fleshy chunks will be used for barbecued beef stew. Since the above mentioned procedure has been completed, the vampires are busy preparing the remainder of the meal for tomorrow's birthday celebration in Joe's honor. He will be fifty years old by today's standards. "Right?" September 20, 2016 arrived bright and early for Joe and the vampires since Joe is already preparing the beef stew in the basement kitchen. The remainder of the vampires are equally busy collaborating with each other while making all the meal preparations for the festive meal they will be partaking in. The balance of the meal will consist of mashed potatoes laced with slimy, dishwater gravy, fresh vegetables from the vampires backyard garden, soaked in rotten vinegar as opposed to fresh salad dressing, frozen blood bread, vomit chocolate chip pudding and goblets of icy, smooth, red, delicious blood to complete the meal. After everything was completed each of the vampires presented Joe with a birthday card and gift, money, etc………………The vampires furnished soothing music in the background for everyone's pleasure, plus, a video on the screen of Joe's past life prior to becoming a vampire. Joe thanked everyone saying, "I want to thank everyone present this evening for the fabulous meal, cards, gifts, music, video, etc…………….. I appreciated it wholeheartedly! Thank you!" The vampires smiled, nodded their heads and clapped their hands, plus, a standing ovation. "Wow!!!" After the celebration came to a close everybody retired to their coffins early because they arose at dawn this morning. Besides, a light rain is beginning to fall on the roof and windows with claps of thunder resonating in the background and streaks of lightening spiraling through the night sky. At this point, the velocity of the night wind is reaching a violent crescendo.

Chapter 49
A Delayed Vacation

Joe was visiting with the vampires at random this afternoon making a casual remark, "An idea entered my mind in regards to the next blood sucking rendezvous that will be relatively new. As far as I'm aware of since I have been associated with our Vampire Club we have never been on a vacation, as a group, to a resort, island, etc.................. Does anyone care to make a comment on that?" Gilbert raised his hand and declared, "You are absolutely correct, Joe. Since I have been with the Vampire Club when Albert was president there was never a time that I recall that we were on a vacation to some remote area. Does anybody care to add their input to this discussion?" Blair raised his hand saying, "I have also been associated with this Vampire Club since Albert was in charge and I don't ever remember our club going on a vacation at any time to my knowledge." After listening to the comments Joe made the following remark, "Well, I guess it's time we went on a vacation for a couple of weeks while the weather is still accommodating. What does everyone think about that?" The vampires were smiling, as usual, and nodding their heads in agreement asking, "Where will we go? Are we going to some resort? How about an island? Will we be water bound? That sounds great! When are we leaving? We're ready to leave now! Ha! Ha!" Everybody was eager to have the afore mentioned questions answered. Joe said, "I suggest we conduct an informal meeting tomorrow night at 7:00 PM in the Conference Room in the basement since it is completely renovated now.

An Informal Meeting

The vampires are slowly filing into the Conference Room in the basement to discuss the details of their upcoming vacation that was brought to their attention during a discussion yesterday. Joe made a duplicate presentation today saying, "Yesterday I suggested that we spend a few weeks on vacation, as a group, possibly to some resort island or some remote area with numerous vacationing prospects.

I will be doing some research this week on possible vacationing destinations in the Calgary, Canada area and beyond. Does anybody have any suggestions at this point? Please raise your hand," Gilbert said, "None of us have ever really done any personal investigating, for our gratification, in regards to a cross country vacation incorporating the Pacific Ocean, etc................ I guess we never expected to be confronted with a vacation of this distance and nature. The vampires smiled and nodded their heads in regards to Gilbert's statement while commenting, "It sounds like something we would all be interested in!" Blair asked Joe, "When will be taking this vacation, may I ask?" Joe said, "Soon, probably next week before the fall weather sets in. In three days we will have another informal meeting to determine where our vacation spot will be. If possible, please bring some maps, pictures, etc.............for us to review to make our final decision that day. The vampires said, "We are in agreement with the detailed discussion on the upcoming vacation that we will be experiencing in about a week or two. We will be bringing maps and a variety of literature advertising vacation areas in and around Calgary, Canada and beyond." Joe said, "That sounds good! We'll be looking forward to reviewing them for an actual happening."

Three Days Later

The vampires are filing into the Conference Room in the basement this afternoon to get into a heated discussion in regards to their final vacation destination. Joe and the vampires reviewed the books, maps, magazines, etc................... and finally set their sights on Vancouver Island about five hundred miles straight west of Calgary, Canada. Actually, Vancouver Island is adjacent to the Pacific Ocean. According to some of the more prominent vacation islands Vancouver Island is listed as No. 3 on the charts. Since the vampires have decided on Vancouver Island Joe immediately said, "I will place a call this evening to reserve lodging for all of us in a reputable resort to our liking on Vancouver Island. We will be leaving next week Monday, September 27, 2016, while the weather is still warm at 10:00 AM in the morning. Please launder your clothes and pack your luggage this weekend and be ready to go Monday morning. We will need two extra vehicles to accommodate all of us. Are there any vehicles available?" Gilbert and Blair raised their hands and offered to use their vehicles and driving capabilities for the extended trip to Vancouver Island. This is a two day trip so the vampires are in for a long haul! Right?"

Chapter 50
Vacation Time

Monday morning rose bright and early as the vampires hurriedly showered, dressed, ate breakfast, checked their luggage and focused on last minute incidentals. They left at 10:00 AM sharp, headed west on Highway 14 with their destination Kamloops, Canada for an overnight stay at a motel of their choice. They stayed in Motel 6 for one night and continued on the next morning reaching Vancouver Island that same night at 9:00 PM. They checked into the Vancouver Motel, ate supper very late while watching television and retired early because of extreme travelers fatigue.

A Schedule of Events

The next morning after breakfast Joe and the vampires received a "list" of events they could witness or participate in for their sheer pleasure. Joe said, "It even includes a large, ferry ride in the Pacific Ocean, closer to the shore, where it is safe for anyone involved in a ferry excursion." The vampires also have their choice of visiting the amusement park, playing golf, going fishing off the pier, swimming and snorkeling in the ocean, plus rafting for those that are brave enough to make an attempt, just to mention a few things to do. Tourists can also take a complete tour of Vancouver Island, by day light, to view the huge, outdoor skating rink for everyone's delight. It is situated near an outdoor swimming pool for those that are hesitant about immersing themselves in the Pacific Ocean. "Ha! Ha! As far as I'm concerned, "It's nothing deeper than the bathtub for me! How about you?"

Vancouver Island Tour

Joe and the vampires toured Vancouver Island at 9:00 AM this morning to their ultimate gratification and pleasure, witnessing the thrills of outdoor skating, swimming and snorkeling in the cool, crisp, clear water of the ocean, close to the shore, an outdoor swimming pool for those that aren't brave enough to step into the Pacific Ocean etc……………..fishing off the pier or golfing. On the way back in the touring bus Joe said, "Well, what shall we attempt to try first? The amusement park, the outdoor skating rink, fishing off the pier? Too close to the water?" The vampires smiled and nodded their heads since none of them were familiar with swimming off shore in the Pacific Ocean. Blair raised his hand and said, "We would all be interested in the outdoor swimming pool some evening. You name the day." Joe made the remark, "How about tomorrow, towards evening around 6:00 PM, to avoid the heat?" Blair said, "That sounds good! We'll meet you at the hearse around 5:15 PM to give us allowable time to arrive at the Vancouver Swimming Pool. Thank you!"

Vancouver Swimming Pool

Joe and the vampires arrived at the Vancouver Swimming Pool earlier and checked in immediately upon the staff's request. Their first impulse was to jump off the diving board which was the best swimming experience of all. They got an exhilarating thrill diving through the air at breakneck speed to land in the clear, cool, refreshing water of the Vancouver Swimming Pool. They are bashing and splashing while frolicking to and fro besides racing each other back and forth from one end of the pool to the opposite end to see who could outswim who! Most of the vampires are good swimmers, in spite of the fact, they are not at a swimming pool every day like some adults because it is virtually impossible. They have other numerous activities that require their time and effort. They are also tirelessly swimming around the pool sharing their camaraderie among new friends they have just become acquainted with during their night at the pool. By now they are in the process of taking a break for a light lunch before proceeding into the water again. Joe and the vampires are eating a cold sandwich while sipping a cool, refreshing soda to quench their thirst in this 95 degree heat today. At this point in time, the vampires are ready to dive into the cold, streaming water again to revitalize their energy and vitality for the days ahead. "There doing a good job, aren't they? I think so!" The vampires managed to rent a ball the size of a basketball to play catch with in the swimming pool for fun and relaxation. They said, "If anyone drops the ball I'm sure it will stay afloat. "What do you think?"Not only are they having a fun and relaxing evening they are also on the "lookout" for one or two isolated individuals that may be meandering in the pool in no particular direction. Possibly several persons with no particular course in their life. The vampires are interested in approaching individuals of this nature for a, hopefully, blood sucking rendezvous while they are on vacation on Vancouver Island. The approach needs to be consistent with the last several days they will be on the island since the bodies will be in storage in the trunk of their car.

Chapter 51
A Variety of Activities

Today, the vampires are interested in fishing off pier 57 overlooking the Pacific Ocean since the weather is a balmy 75 degrees, very accommodating, with a slight breeze rustling in the background. They brought their fishing poles and other incidentals, associated with fishing, etc............... to supplement anything they are lacking. They also came supplied with sandwiches, chips and cold drinks to sustain themselves the length of time they would be fishing. They have been fishing for about an hour with nary a nibble on their line so they proceeded to eat their lunch and cold drink while continuing to cast their fishing line out into the off shore waters of the Pacific Ocean. Finally, Blair noticed a constant jerk on his line, besides, getting a glimpse of the twelve inch fish on the other end. He withdrew his pole from the water, removed the catfish, placing it in a container and cast his line into the off shore waters again for more of the same. By this time Joe came from the other side of Pier 57 with a string of catfish, basically five, caught within the last hour. "Maybe it depends on what side of the pier you are fishing from?"Suddenly, Gilbert sitting next to Blair, became aware of a repetitive twisting on his fishing line indicating a pulling sensation by a much larger fish than he surmised. "He couldn't have been more accurate." He, instantly, yanked the pole towards him while sprouting a fifteen inch catfish hooked on the end of his line. Since the remainder of the vampires were unable to catch anything the length of time they were fishing they decided to terminate their expedition for the day. The Vancouver Motel does not allow fish of any sort to be brought into the motel or stored outside of the motel at any given time, therefore, the vampires had no choice but to sell their fish on the Vancouver Island boardwalk or to a fish nursery.

Roller Skating Anyone?

The vampires awoke to another fun filled day this morning according to their plans while they are still on vacation the rest of the week. They are going to go on an afternoon of roller skating with personal participation on their part since they have not roller skated for months in Calgary, Canada. Joe, Isaac and Blair are permanently unemployed from the Berg Construction Company and in the process of scouting around for another job that will last indefinitely with no change in sight. The aforementioned is hard to come by with no jobs available. This is why the vampire's vacation has been reduced to one week because of Joe, Isaac and Blair exploring for new jobs. "Too bad!"At present, the vampires are thoroughly enjoying themselves on the Vancouver Roller Rink this afternoon in spite of very few in attendance. The outdoor skating rink is accommodated by a balmy temperature of 75 degrees and not a cloud in the sky. "Actually, it is shirt sleeve weather so they say!" They are skating single file, in a circle, racing each other around the roller rink to the sound of music. They have taken a break for a snack and have gone back to the art of skating again full speed ahead. The vampires have made quite a few acquaintances with their friendly antics and sharing their camaraderie with less fortunate people. They have exchanged numerous telephone numbers with friends from outlying states to be used in the future.

Vancouver Swimming Pool

Besides frequenting the Fishing Pier 57, Vancouver Roller Rink, Billon's Bowling Alley Barton's Billiard Parlor, the Vancouver Golf Club and the Vancouver Swimming Pool, they decided to go back to the swimming pool one more time before they left in the morning. They made up their minds to swim from 6:00 PM till 10:00 PM and then retire for the night. There were quite a few swimmers at the pool this evening considering a storm was brewing, as dark, ominous clouds were gathering on the horizon. A large amount of people started departing from the swimming pool for their cars as loud claps of thunder and fingers of lightening streaked across the night sky. The vampires were still bashing and splashing at great lengths with only a few couples remaining plus two college girls swimming the length of the pool for their delight. Isaac and Blair were keeping a watchful eye on the two college girls not letting them out of their sight. The sky was turning increasingly darker as the college girls swam in front of Isaac and Blair giggling to themselves as they entered a dark, secluded corner of the swimming pool. Blair and Isaac yanked the college girl's pale, thin, necks forward, thrusting their gleaming, white, canine fangs into their left, jugular vein while sucking their red, thick, delicious blood voraciously. Finally, their screaming subsided and they collapsed into the swimming pool leaving bloody rivulets of water flowing randomly in the pool. By now, everybody had exited the pool except the vampires and the college girls. The staff was nowhere to be seen which was very unusual. Blair and Isaac hurriedly dragged the college girls to a dark, secluded area outside of the pool while Joe backed the hearse, unseen, behind a building where they quickly transferred the two bodies to the trunk. Since it is now totally dark Joe said, "We will check on the bodies when we reach the Vancouver Motel to make sure everything is satisfactory."Joe slid the key into the trunk and the lid rose immediately exposing the two college girls. Joe spoke a few words saying, "What are your names? Where are you from?" There was no response, no eye interaction, nothing of any sort, indicating cessation of life was imminent. Their bodies were stored in the trunk because they are departing for Calgary, Canada in the morning.

Chapter 52
Back in Calgary, Canada

On the way back to Calgary, Canada Joe and the vampires stayed at Kamloops, Canada at Motel 6 where they stayed on the way to Vancouver, Canada. When they opened the trunk of the hearse the college girl's reaction was the same, nothing! Evidently, they had passed away in the swimming pool from sheer shock, loss of vital blood, fright, etc…………….. Could both of them possibly have had a heart attack? "Oh no!!! What a shame!" Joe told the vampires, "We will cart them back to Calgary, Canada to be suspended in The Death Chamber for upcoming events regarding holiday banquets, etc……………..

A Two Week Break!

Joe approached the vampires today saying, "I decided to take a two week break after our vacation from Vancouver Islanddoing thorough household chores from top to bottom, including renovation, painting, menial, work related jobs outside, wherever anything is required. In this respect, we will have our residence spotless and shining, for the upcoming Halloween Holiday which we are anticipating, as usual." Starting this morning some of the vampires are doing a thorough job of cleaning every nook and cranny available while some of them are painting certain areas in the house that are in dire need. Several others are in the process of renovating areas upstairs and downstairs while making more rooms ready to be used immediately. In the evenings all of the vampires have been congregating outside cutting grass, pulling weeds, tending the garden while a couple of vampires have been doing touch up painting on the house which was needing it pretty badly. Everybody is eating supper at a different time because of their fluctuating work schedule. Since it is the season of fall and getting dark sooner everyone has eaten and is seated around the television set awaiting the beginning of the 7:00 PM movie. By now, the vampires have completed the cleaning, renovation and painting process besides all of the combined outside work that was on the agenda.

Having completed the abovementioned for the upcoming holidays of Halloween, Thanksgiving and Christmas the vampires can sit back and relax for several days having accomplished quite a feat. In a couple of days they will be ready to stroll through the downtown back alleys in search of victims such as the homeless, derelicts, stragglers, vagrants, mentally challenged, social outcasts, etc…………….. whomever is available. Actually, the downtown haunts are the vampire's favorites because they usually get lucky victimizing a variety of the above mentioned alleyways at any given time. Besides that, they frequently transfer them back to the house for future reference in regard to dissecting them for public, holiday banquets for the people to partake of such as Thanksgiving and Christmas. As Blair was saying one day, "We also enjoy frequenting the New Haven Cemetery, Mohegan Cemetery and the Poheta Cemetery. We enjoy vandalizing the graves and transporting the corpses' to the house to be suspended from the ceiling in the Death Chamber for the dissection process before a holiday banquet. We also utilize our expertise in areas victimizing people in swimming pools and we are good at conniving new ideas to solicit the general public in response to them.

Strolling the Back Alley Haunts

For a change Roy, Blair and Gilbert are meandering through the back alleys, behind the businesses downtown, in search of the usual homeless, derelicts, vagrants, etc……………that frequent the area. Some of them are awaiting the disposal of food from local restaurants that they can salvage for their own personal use. "What a shame!"Since it is two weeks before Halloween the evenings are turning colder with a circle of homeless people around a fire, with their arms outstretched, to warm their frozen hands. Roy, Blair and Gilbert stroll on by, oblivious of their actions as Blair said, "Since we are interested, solely, in victimizing the living creatures we are familiar with we prefer to subject our victims to an onslaught in a darkened, secluded area of the back alleys or in between business buildings with no one in the immediate area." They continue strolling, glancing wildly to and fro making sure they haven't missed anybody, since it is even darker than when they came. Joe said, "A heavy mist is beginning to cloud the surroundings as a variety of night people are deviating the back alleys because of, possible, inclement weather on the horizon." Finally, Roy, Blair and Gilbert encountered two middle aged men, partially intoxicated, stumbling ten feet ahead of them on their way in between two business buildings headed towards the main thoroughfare. They hurriedly stepped up behind them grabbing their thick, greasy, stubbly necks while protruding their canine fangs into their left, jugular vein. They sucked their crimson, blood horrendously and voraciously with the men screeching, screaming and pleading with them (to release them of their restraint). Eventually, they were unable to keep up their "bloody antics" any longer so they let their bodies collapse in an unconscious stupor on the cement pavement which by now is totally wet. At this point, a light rain is filtering down as Roy, Blair and Gilbert drag the two men out of a private entrance to their car which was parked in proximity of the attack. They flung the two men in the backseat of the hearse and left the downtown area. When they arrived at the house they cast the two men's bodies down the basement steps to lie there until the next afternoon at 4:00 PM.

Chapter 53
Partially Intoxicated

    This afternoon after the vampires arose at 4:00 PM they immediately checked on the two men that Joe, Blair and Gilbert cast down the basement steps last night. Naturally, Joe, Blair and Gilbert were the first vampires on the scene examining them and evaluating their condition. Joe brought them some food which they ate hungrily. By now, they were sober managing to partly open their eyes, but they were still groggy from their encounter with Joe, Blair and Gilbert. Roy asked them, "What are your names and they replied, "Dean Jones and Paul Bentley." Joe continued, "Where are you from?" They said, "We're from Calgary, Canada." "Joe asked them again, "Are you employed in Calgary somewhere?" They said, "No, we have been homeless for several years now. Why are you asking us all these questions?" Joe said, "Just curious." After Joe was through interviewing them he led them both to a coffin for the night saying, "If either of you needs anything during the night please call someone by the name of Blair, Gilbert or Joe," that's me," and one of us will come to your assistance. Is that understood?" Dean and Paul replied, "Yes. Thank you! Goodnight!"

The Next Day

    Since the vampires hadn't heard from Dean and Paul during the night, they assumed everything was okay. When they arose at 4:00 PM they were watching television with Dean saying, "We woke up at 1:00 PM and decided to watch television for a while. We hope you don't mind!" Joe said, "No, that's fine! Do you care to eat something?" They said, "Yes, we're getting hungry." After they finished their meal Joe remarked, "I would like to discuss the following issues with you first hand. Before we get started, "Do you have any questions you would like to have answered?" Paul said, "Yes, we would like to know what type of people you are? Who would bite us on our necks repeatedly while sucking blood from our veins viciously? In spite of being homeless, while living in the back alleys downtown and eating out of trash receptacles to keep alive, we have never been confronted by anything of this nature. Never! Please explain this to us." Joe commented, "Yes, I'll be glad to forward the following information to you which it sounds like you're not aware of at the present moment. You definitely need to be updated in regards to whom we are. We are live corpses, in other words, vampires that have risen from the grave at some point in time to suck the blood of living people. Since we have drawn blood from your veins, which we thrive on to stay alive, you have become vampires, also, and will be required to do the same in order to stay in existence. You are now a part of our vampire household going on nightly haunts and rendezvous to supplement your blood sucking cravings. Is that clearly understood? Any other questions?" Dean and Paul nodded their heads saying, "We are in total agreement regarding your explanation and are willing to conform to the vampire's lifestyle. If we are amiss with anything please draw this to our attention. Thank you!" Joe said, "Thank you!" likewise, which completed the conversation for the time being because various issues always arise in the future.

A Cemetery Rendezvous

Joe was carrying on a conversation with the vampires at supper last night saying, "We haven't been to the Poheta Cemetery for quite a while in search of meditators at the tombstones, stragglers, intruders, etc............... Is anyone interested in frequenting the Poheta Cemetery tomorrow night besides training our new vampires in the art of a blood sucking rendezvous?" All the vampires were giddy with glee, including Dean and Paul saying, "We're raring to go! Give us the time and we will be lined up at the hearse!" Joe replied, "How about 6:00 PM tomorrow night because it will be totally dark by then and rather chilly. "Please bring a jacket!" The vampires smiled indicating they are in accordance with Joe's instructions.

By now, the vampires, including Paul and Dean, were waiting patiently at the hearse for Joe to make his appearance. Here he comes, jacket and all to transfer them to the Poheta Cemetery, in the hope of encountering a few people to practice their blood sucking antics on! Paul and Dean are anticipating the trip since they are in the process of familiarizing themselves with the blood sucking procedure that is required of them. They will be observing prior to attempting the procedure themselves at first. As they are passing through the cemetery gates the vampires are becoming aware of a constant snickering and giggling as they start strolling through the cemetery grounds in search of anyone at this time of the evening. Suddenly, they spied several witches gathered around a tombstone whispering and laughing while continuously shoveling and scraping the top layer of soil on the gravesite.

Witches at the Cemetery

For some reason, unknown, the vampires have always detested the witches since the beginning of time. Because of this they have not had anything to do with each other ever since their first encounter. In regards to the witches the feeling is "likewise." Because of their dislike of the witches the vampires have decided to really frighten the witches with a vicious, horrendous, blood sucking rendezvous this evening. They decided to slowly creep up behind them while they were shoveling the gravesite hoping to gain entrance to the bottom of the grave. They were unaware the vampires were behind them as they kept giggling and snickering while shoveling away. Suddenly, Joe, Blair and Gilbert jerked the witch's necks towards them so they could suck their left, jugular vein in a menacing, terroristic style. They sunk their white, gleaming, canine fangs extra deep into their veins so they would feel the lasting effect. There was no talking, screeching or screaming, nothing! Momentarily, there was a soft moan several times and then complete silence as the witches collapsed immediately at the vampire's feet. Instantly, the vampires left the scene of the ferocious, bloodthirsty rendezvous for the safety of the house.

Chapter 54
Dead Witches

After the vampires arrived at the house they were not in a frame of mind to visit because of the excitement at the prospect of their onslaught on the witches so they decided to view the 10:00 PM news of the evening. The first announcement by the news forecaster was "A news item has just been handed to me in regards to three dead bodies that were retrieved from the Poheta Cemetery within the last hour. If anybody has any information about the three deaths at the cemetery please call the Calgary Police Department at 1-649-260-2902. Thank you!"Joe and the vampires were shocked and flabbergasted at the outcome of the three witch's deaths that transpired while they were at the gravesite in the process of a vicious onslaught on their person. Blair made the following remark, "I'm not concerned about the witches three deaths being related to us since we were long gone by the time the Calgary Police Department entered upon the scene." Joe made a similar remark, "Blair is absolutely correct! I remember glancing around the cemetery and there was no one else in sight while we were victimizing the three witches so there is no cause for concern." Dean also said, "Paul and I kept a close eye on the surroundings while you were in the process of your encounter with the three witches." By this time, the vampires were rather fatigued and overwhelmed at the whole procedure so they decided to retire for the night. Goodnight!

Halloween, October 31, 2016

Halloween is fast approaching and the vampires have begun decorating the house inside and outside with Halloween decorations for a festive holiday that is imminent. The most intriguing décor that caught everyone's eye was an actual dead corpse suspended on a pole in the front yard of the vampire's house. "Talk about scary! Everyone that trick or treats at the vampire's house has to pass by the corpse. How would you like that? I wouldn't!"Tonight is Halloween night, October 31, 2016, and the vampires are dressing in their Halloween attire besides answering the door to all the ghosts, goblets and vampires that approach them. "Trick or Treat! Give us something good to eat!" This was the common phrase that was heard all over Calgary, Canada and still heard today. The vampires threw a few pieces of candy into each Halloween bucket with all the trick or treaters and their parents commenting on the dead corpse suspended in the front yard on a pole for everyone's delight. After the trick or treaters subsided Joe and the vampires decided to go trick or treating themselves to see what they could accomplish. Most of the vampires went door to door solely to see whom they could lure into their trap. But to no avail! Finally, Joe approached a front door, rang the doorbell and said, "Trick or treat! Give me something good to eat!" An older lady answered the door slowly while Joe swiftly yanked her neck, sucking her left jugular vein, hungrily and greedily, while the older woman screeched, screamed and lamented in pain. She sluggishly collapsed to the floor while Joe grabbed a handful of candy heading back to the house. None of the other vampires got even as lucky as Joe. After all the vampires arrived back at the house they examined the different varieties of candy they were presented. They viewed a Halloween movie incorporating vampires, zombies etc................, while nibbling on their Halloween candy. After the movie ended everybody was tired, especially Joe, after the wild, sucking rampage he was involved in. They all retired to their coffins at 11:00 PM with a heavy rain pelting the rooftop and windows accompanied by fingers of lightening on the horizon.

The Calgary Library

Joe approached the vampires the other day asking them, "Are any of you interested in going to the Calgary Library sometime soon? We haven't been there for a long spell. Since it is the beginning of fall it is a perfect time to do some reading when there isn't anything interesting on television to watch." The vampires were all fired up as Blair said, "Yes, I think we would all be interested in going to the library because it's probably been several years since we've been there. I feel like I can speak for the remainder of the vampires today when I make that remark." The vampires smiled and nodded in acknowledgement at an upcoming trip to the Calgary Library soon. Joe mentioned, "How about going tomorrow afternoon? Please be at my hearse at 1:00 PM."

The vampires smiled and said wholeheartedly, "We'll be there at 1:00 PM. Thank you!"The vampires have been standing by the hearse since 12:30 PM waiting for Joe to transport them to the Calgary Library. Joe arrived at 1:00 PM with the vampires smiling and nodding their heads saying, "We're ready to go!" with Joe saying, "Boy, I can see that!"When they arrived at the Calgary Library everybody took off in a different direction to a department of their choice. Most of the vampires are interested in Vampire books, magazines, encyclopedias, a variety of other books and photographs incorporating Germany, Russia and countries beyond etc…………… All the vampires were sitting at two library tables reviewing the different books they were interested in checking out. After they presented their library card and checked their books out Joe transported everybody back to the house. After eating their supper the vampires relaxed in the All Purpose Room in the basement. They reviewed the Vampire books, magazines, encyclopedias and books with images of major, foreign countries and beyond, such as Russia, Germany etc………….. The vampires could relate to the various lifestyles depicted in the Vampire books plus the enjoyment they derived leafing through their favorite newspapers, magazines, informative encyclopedias and photographic books consisting of other countries, regions and nations. When everybody was through reviewing all the books etc………… they exchanged them with other vampires' books they had never seen before. "Smart idea, right?"Everybody took a break for a late night snack of a can of soda and peanut butter cookies. "Sounds yummy!" After they finished their snack they resumed leafing through and glancing quickly at an article or picture that sparked their interest!By now, it is getting later and later as the vampires are yawning and forcing themselves to keep their eyelids open. They have retired to their coffins for a peaceful night's rest. "Goodnight!"

Chapter 55
Another Vampire Meeting

November 5, 2016

Joe is busy posting signs on the stairwell about the upcoming Vampire meeting, November 5, 2016 in the All Purpose Room in the basement at 7:00 PM. As is customary, the vampires filed in at 6:45 PM and took their respective seats next to their best friends, naturally, to partake of the meeting and voice their unbiased opinion. Joe brings the meeting to order introducing Blair as the secretary and Gilbert as his co- secretary. The secretaries have reviewed the events, banquets, dances and haunts the vampires have sponsored in the last several months not to mention the profit they have amassed in the meantime. This evening Joe made the following statement saying, "The main reason I have brought this meeting to order tonight is the lack of corpses in their coffins and suspended from the ceiling in the Death Chamber to accommodate the banquets etc……………..that we sponsor. Our nightly downtown haunts, the cemeteries, roller rinks, Halloween and other such incidentals etc…………… does not bring in enough corpses to sustain us when we provide the holiday meal. We are going to have to bring an extra corpse home from now on when we leave on a haunt, a trip to the cemetery, a night at the roller rink etc………………..Joe also said, "Incidentally, I don't know if any of you are aware of this but a new cemetery called "The Rest in Peace Cemetery" is going to be dedicated next week Monday morning at 10:00 AM, located at 2174 Noland Road, three miles east of the New Haven Cemetery. I strongly suggest that everyone attend the dedication of the "Rest in Peace" cemetery for personal reasons. Our hearse is leaving at 9:15 AM for anyone that is interested in attending the dedication. Please be at the hearse at the appointed time. Are there any questions at the moment? Please raise your hand." Brandon raised his hand asking, "How long will the dedication last?" Joe said, "About an hour." Joe also mentioned, "There will be a free community dinner at the Community Center on Brinkley Street for those that wish to attend. I just received this extra dinner notice the other day because it had not been planned in advance. Are there any other questions before we dismiss this meeting tonight?" The vampires shook their heads indicating No!

A Subway Encounter

While Joe and the vampires were eating supper he brought another important issue up that never entered the vampires mind. Joe made the remark, "I recalled years ago when Jean was still living that we all went on a "Subway Snatching Haunt" in one of the subways in downtown Calgary. I remember several of us loitering around in the dark, isolated areas of the subway tunnel awaiting the appearance of homeless stragglers, derelicts, people that slept on the subway all night, etc...............After we completed our "Subway Snatching Haunt" Jean conveniently parked her car in an undisclosed, limited area near the subway tunnel to facilitate the transfer of the body or bodies to the car. As I recollect this was a onetime only "Subway Snatching Haunt" because we never frequented the subway again. Why, I don't know. Probably, because we had too many other haunts to take care of is my understanding. "Have any of you ever heard of an encounter of this nature by any chance? Please raise your hand." No hands were raised so Joe assumed this was an unusual encounter. Nevertheless, he is still interested in conducting a "Subway Snatching Haunt" in the main subway in downtown Calgary, Canada for everyone's benefit. He asked the vampires, "Would all of you be interested in a "Subway Snatching Haunt" this coming Friday night?" All the vampires smiled, nodded their heads and said emphatically, "Yes." Joe said, "Meet me at the hearse at 6:00 PM," to which they replied, "We'll be there!"By this time supper is completed and the vampires are attending to their own duties.

A Subway Snatching Haunt

A light snow is drifting through the air, while the vampires are patiently waiting for Joe to make his appearance at 7:00 PM to transport the vampires to the main Calgary Subway Tunnel for their "subway rendezvous" this evening. Finally, Joe appears around the corner, all smiles, asking "Are we ready to go "Subway Snatching" this evening?" The vampires smiled as they said, "We're raring to go!" Everybody positioned themselves in the hearse anticipating a "lucky night" this evening. As they arrived the vampires indicated the area to Joe where it would be the least inconspicuous place to park the hearse. He parked the hearse accordingly with everybody exiting for their trek through the subway tunnel. As they approached the subway they noticed a steady stream of homeless people, transients, nondescript outcasts, etc…………..filtering into the subway for a lengthy nap on the train. The majority of them are isolated in the dimly lit areas of the subway either sleeping or staring subconsciously into space. The vampires positioned themselves in the immediate area keeping a watchful eye on the nondescript individuals in their presence. Suddenly, the subway train came to a halt with numerous people dispersing in different directions to their destination. By this time there were even less people in the subway train with nondescript individuals still occupying the dark, secluded area of the subway. Since no one was seated in the proximity of the homeless people toward the back of the subway the vampires grabbed the transients by the neck while sucking their left, jugular vein of its delicious, savory, scrumptious, sweet, distinctive flavor. By now I'm sure their left, jugular veins are void of any blood etc………… After the vampires completed their bloody feast, unnoticed by anyone, they left the subway train with three extra victims they approached that were able to walk on their own. I guess this was their lucky night! All the vampires, including the three victims, crawled into Joe's hearse for the ride back to the house where they will be cast down the basement stairs to lie there until 4:00 PM the next afternoon. They will then be evaluated and dealt with accordingly.

Chapter 56
"Rest in Peace" Cemetery

November 10, 2016

All the vampires are waiting to depart in Joe's hearse for the "Rest in Peace" Cemetery dedication at 10:00 AM this morning. The cemetery is located at 2174 Nolan Road three miles east of the New Haven Cemetery. A large variety of people have congregated at the "Rest in Peace" Cemetery for the official dedication conducted by the Rev. Michael Jones of the "Rest in Peace" church in Calgary, Canada. The dedication consisted of a sermon, prayers and singing by the "Rest in Peace" choir. After the service was completed Rev. Jones made the remark, "I am going to lead a guided tour of the "Rest in Peace" Cemetery for those of you that are not familiar with the environment. Please follow me since I am starting now. Thank you!"Again, a light snow is beginning to cloud the sky with flakes accumulating on the cemetery grounds and the mausoleum roofs. While Rev. Jones was leading the guided tour he mentioned, "There will be a free, community dinner at the Community Center on Brinkley Street after this tour is over. Please plan to attend. Thank you!" Joe and the vampires did not attend the Community Dinner today because they had prior commitments that required their attention. Although they did not attend the guided tour by Rev. Jones the vampires observed that burials have already taken place and tombstones erected besides bodies preserved in the three, newly built mausoleums. Joe and the vampires are already conjuring ideas in their minds regarding the mausoleums.

A Free Thanksgiving Banquet and Dance

Thanksgiving is coming fast and the vampires are already making preparations well in advance because they are sponsoring a complete banquet with all the trimmings besides a free dance for all. Joe stated, "We still have several left over bodies in the Death Chamber which we will be using for the Thanksgiving Banquet. Joe and the vampires are busy dissecting the female corpse in the Death Chamber that is suspended from the ceiling. They are dissecting from the toes upward to the top of the head. Any organ that does not conform to their dissection process will be eliminated in the trash receptacle. Small sections and chunks of flesh will be baked in ovens, similar to that of turkey, accompanied by rotted, slimy mashed potatoes, green, spoiled gravy, fresh carrots laced with moldy, dish detergent, blood bread with fresh blood draining out of the bread itself, Chocolate, vomit ice cream, a combination salad with several, tiny, live lizards slithering through the bottom of the salad and goblets of red, delicious, scrumptious blood to top the meal. "How about that?"

A Scrumptious Meal

By this time, the general public has started filing into the Community Center where the free Thanksgiving meal and public dance will take place. A delicious aroma wafts through the air as people are seated, conversing with each other, while waiting for the vampire waiters to supply them with plates of food for their immediate consumption. Numerous goblets of red, succulent, flavorful, savory blood were served to accommodate the meal. This will quench their thirst after consuming such an enormous, scrumptious meal with no expense involved. To top the meal bowls of chocolate, vomit ice cream were served to everyone's delight. If second helpings were indicated the vampire waiters were more than happy to oblige. "How nice can the vampires get? Really!" After the meal was completed the vampires cleared the tables from the dining area while Les Brown's Band of Renown Orchestra positioned itself to start serenading the public with their variety of musical entertainment. After the dancing got in full swing the vampires said, "Now that we are finished with our banquet chores let's try our style of dancing like we did before. Remember?" Everybody remembered the incident nodding their heads and laughing at the fun they had. The vampires danced the night away with the general public following suit. Their dancing was interrupted at 10:00 PM for a snack break which was enjoyed by all and resumed again. The dance ended at 12:00 AM, midnight, with everyone gathering their personal effects and exiting the Community Center. The vampires made the remark, "We know a good meal and dance was had by everybody and we are always glad to oblige with our free service to the city of Calgary, Canada since they have been good to us."

Chapter 57
Rest in Peace Cemetery

December 3, 2016

Gilbert approached the vampires the other day with the following question, "Would any of you be interested in frequenting the "Rest in Peace Cemetery" since they have just recently opened the cemetery to the general public?" The vampires said, "Yes, we would be anxious to go. You name the date and time and we will be at the hearse waiting." Gilbert said, "How about this Thursday night at 5:30 PM, just after dusk, when most of the meditators have left the cemetery?" The vampires said, "That sounds great! We'll be there at the appointed time!"

Thursday Night

Naturally the vampires were waiting again at the hearse ready to leave for the Rest in Peace Cemetery. As they were driving Gilbert said, "I forgot to mention the other day that I, most recently, had a friend underground at the Rest in Peace Cemetery two weeks ago. He was not embalmed, therefore, I brought shovels and tools, in the event, I have to pry the casket lid open while we are in the complete process of violating the vault and casket itself. Is that clearly understood?" The vampires nodded and smiled while saying, "We clearly understand! We're at your beck and call."At this time, Gilbert and the vampires have arrived at the "Rest in Peace" Cemetery, strolling through the gates with Gilbert leading the way to his friend's grave. Now that it was getting darker it was easier to work hurriedly at the newly constructed gravesite. The vampires started shoveling from the top of the grave straight down to the vault and casket in hopes of forcing the casket lid open. When they couldn't release the lock they used their tools to pry it open so they could gain access to the corpse. "That worked!" Since Gilbert was first in line he had access to his friend, the corpse, sucking violently his emaciated left, jugular vein, with crimson, thick, juicy, savory blood spewing forth. He sucked the red, thick fluid until nothing spilled out of his veins anymore. After Gilbert's bloated stomach could not contain the excess blood any longer he handed the corpse over to Blair and down the line. "It seems like all the vampires got a taste of the corpse's blood."After the blood sucking rendezvous was completed the vampires shoveled the soil back on to the casket and vault. Then they escalated to the top of the grave by means of a ladder and shoveled the remainder of the grave closed. They exited the gravesite and were transferred back to the house by Joe's hearse.

Christmas Decorations, December 3, 2016

Christmas Day will be approaching soon so the vampires are eagerly anticipating all the Christmas trees they will be displaying in different areas of the house upstairs and downstairs plus outside. They brought the trees from the storage room in the basement where they are stored after the holidays until the next year. The vampires are putting the Christmas trees in full view for themselves and the general public to observe for their holiday delight. They decorated the trees with lights, balls and decorations to enliven the atmosphere generally speaking. After completing the inside of the house they have started decorating the large Christmas trees outside plus the house itself. They are in the process of hauling the Santa Claus sled to the front yard, reindeer and all, to be on display from today, December 3, 2016 until January 2, 2017. A large Christmas wreath adorns the gates that encompass the complete property at 2125 Melbourne Street. The gates were added earlier this year to keep the homeless, vagrants, derelicts and social outcasts from invading their real estate. The vampires are getting an earlier start this year with their Christmas shopping since they are going to visit the stores tonight from 7:00 PM until 10:00 PM in downtown Calgary. Some of the stores will be featuring special sales in certain departments for the interest of the local consumers looking for a certain item. The vampires are leaving at 5:30 PM this evening, well in advance, so they will be one of the first consumers in the store to take advantage of the sale items on display. They exchanged names for the gift exchange with a limit of $15.00 to be spent individually on each person that is participating. At present they are sitting in the hearse in front of Dwight's Department Store waiting for the front doors to open at 7:00 PM until 10:00 PM. "Here we go!" The saleslady unlocked the doors allowing access to Dwight's Department Store smiling and saying, "First come, first served." Joe and the vampires were first in line to enter the department store and consequently be served first. The vampires have certain sale items that they are purchasing while feasting their eyes on other items of interest in other areas of the store. By now there was an influx of people streaming into the department store at breakneck speed to take advantage of the sale items advertised in the Calgary Gazette Newspaper recently. Consumers are pushing and shoving each other in the aisles reaching for the same articles as the vampires only to fall short of their article, dropping it on the floor, etc............... Actually, the vampires were able to purchase every sale item they desired. "Good for them!"Joe and the vampires stayed in the different department stores until 10:00 PM which was closing time with Joe saying, "I guess it's time we leave for this evening. If everyone is like myself you have not completed your Christmas shopping yet. Is that correct?" The vampires shook their heads emphatically, indicating No, because of the swarm of consumers inundating the department stores. Joe said, "We will be back later this week since the sales will be continuing. Thank you!" Joe and the vampires exited the department stores climbing into the hearse with their packages headed for 2125 Melbourne Street.

Chapter 58
Some More Christmas Shopping?

Several days have passed and Joe decided to approach the vampires again saying, "Who is interested in going Christmas shopping again tonight? Please raise your hand." All the vampires raised their hands signifying they are raring to go Christmas shopping again tonight because none of the vampires had completed their personal shopping. Joe announced, "We will be leaving at 5:30 PM tonight even though the doors don't open until 7:00 PM. Is that clearly understood again?" The vampires nodded, "Yes!" The weather is quite chilly this evening, with a heavy snow beginning to drape the rooftops of the business buildings downtown. The streets are very dangerous and perilous to drive on tonight so Joe will need to reduce his speed considerably. The vampires were waiting to board the hearse tonight at 5:30 PM for the remainder of their Christmas shopping that was left to be done. The existing sales from last week are still in effect with new items on display daily because of the tremendous amount of consumers filtering through the displays for items of their choice. According to Joe everyone has completed their Christmas shopping for the time being unless extra gifts are inevitable. Joe made the statement, "We will be coming back one more time to the department store of your choice before Christmas Eve. Is everybody in agreement with that?" The vampires said, "That sounds great! A few of us are not completely finished, therefore, an extra trip to the department stores will come in handy."

Christmas Eve, December 24, 2016

Tonight is Christmas Eve. The vampires are accumulated in the All Purpose Room in the basement to celebrate this joyous holiday. They are in the process of exchanging gifts, thanking each other amidst munching on Christmas delicacies while being serenaded by Christmas music in the background. The vampire's camaraderie is very evident in their household since they enjoy each other's company which is consistent in their lifestyle. After the gift exchange, snacks, camaraderie and music came to an end the vampires retired to their private coffins for a peaceful night's sleep. Tomorrow they will help Joe prepare the fleshly chunks to be barbecued for the private Christmas banquet they will partake in. Joe and the vampires dissected a corpse suspended in the Death Chamber two weeks ago in preparation for the Christmas banquet. The meal will be accompanied by slimy, mushy, baked potatoes, a cucumber salad with small beetles and black spiders climbing within, blood bread, with fresh blood oozing out of the bread, a fresh, garden salad with fresh blood used as a salad dressing, vomit peanut butter ice cream and goblets of fresh, delicious, insatiable, savory blood to top the banquet off. "How does that sound? Delicious?"Joe and the vampires enjoyed the Christmas banquet immensely after which they watched a Christmas story on television for their private, relaxation time. It was a wonderful, holiday movie which held everybody spellbound for the evening. Eventually, the vampires were fatigued and ready to settle into their coffins for a good night's rest.

January 1, 2017

Today is New Year's Day, January 1, 2017. Joe and the vampires are extremely fatigued due to the physical and mental strain with which they have taxed their bodies. As Joe was saying, "I'm sure we can each prepare our own meal for dinner instead of an elaborate banquet since there are many leftovers in the refrigerator from the Christmas banquet we had for ourselves. After that we can relax in front of the television set to watch a special New Year's Day Parade and movie they have been advertising for weeks titled, "It's a New Year!" The vampires were in game with the inevitable saying, "That's what our poor, old bodies need! Several hours in front of the television set accompanied by a long nap! How about that?" They all agreed saying, "It sounds like a great idea! We're all for it!"The vampires started watching the New Year's Day Parade and then the movie at 2:00 PM. By 3:00 PM Joe was the only vampire watching the movie. The rest of the vampires have been sleeping since 2:30 PM. "I guess they really were fatigued like they claimed."According to the weather report this evening Joe mentioned, "A fierce snow storm is scheduled to infiltrate the city of

Calgary, Canada tonight and sometime tomorrow with approximately twenty to twenty five inches of snow on our sidewalks and streets. More than likely, some of our main streets will be barricaded due to the onslaught of weather that is specifically geared for Calgary, Canada. I guess we better get our snow shovels ready! This year we will all be shoveling in teams of three, for two hours at a time, because the temperature will be a blustery fifteen degrees above zero without the wind chill factor. If anybody happens to arise during the night please take a glance at the oncoming weather outside.

Chapter 59
The Onslaught of the Storm

When the vampires arose at 4:00 PM this afternoon they were confronted with several feet of snow piled up in the yard, driveways, streets, sidewalks, etc………………The wind was blowing fiercely without control while snow was continually drifting and draping the entire surroundings. Traffic is at a standstill while stranded motorists evacuated their cars for higher ground while it is still available. At the present time there is no one on the city streets, in cars etc……………. only the Calgary Police Department canvassing the main thoroughfares for people encountering traffic problems. Three of the vampires are shoveling mounds of snow as they are bundled up with furry hats, gloves and snow boots to complete their winter attire. Since it is growing increasingly darker and slicker the vampires are headed for the warmth of the house and a hot meal because they are very hungry. Joe and the remaining vampires prepared a huge pot roast for everyone for supper including potatoes, carrots and celery for the main entrée. It was accompanied by a vegetable salad, vanilla ice cream and goblets of flavorful, red, juicy, succulent, fresh blood to their liking. "Sounds delicious, doesn't it?" After they consumed their meal they settled down in front of the television set discussing the day's activities while trying to focus on the movie that is airing on the local KIBX station in Calgary. According to the Calgary Weather Report several days of snow are forecast for Calgary, Canada with wind up to fifty miles an hour.

Calgary Ski Resort

Joe approached the vampires while they were eating supper last night asking them, "Since we are embarking in the upcoming, snowy season of the year I have a question that I would like to present to you." The vampires displayed a strange, quizzical look on their faces unsure of the nature of the question. Joe continued, "Would any of you be interested in sledding at the Calgary Ski Resort like you participated in when Albert was still president of your Vampire

Club?" All the vampire's faces lit up tremendously as they laughed and shouted out with glee, "That's the most fun we've ever had in our lives!" In a couple of days when it stops snowing, the streets are passable and the weather subsides, will be the perfect time to venture on a snow sledding expedition like we are familiar with. As usual, you set the day and time and we will be waiting by the hearse, sleds and all!" Joe laughed at the reception he received from the vampires at his suggestion saying, "I will make an appointment for a snow sledding experience for a day next week and update everyone. How does that sound?" The vampires were in agreement with the aforesaid saying, "That sounds great! Thank you!" Several days later Joe said, "The snow sledding fun is scheduled for next week Wednesday at 11:00 AM which will include your meal and an afternoon of fun on your sleds. How does that appeal to all of you?" The vampires laughed, clapped their hands and said, "We're so anxious to go we can hardly wait because it's been years since we have been snow sledding. Thank you so much!" Joe laughed and said, "No problem!"

Wednesday Afternoon

Wednesday rolled around sooner than expected with the vampires making preparations for their upcoming trip today to the Calgary Ski Resort for an afternoon of snow sledding, a meal and more snow sledding to come. They will be accompanied by their immediate vampire friend plus old and new acquaintances they will be making while in the process of expanding their camaraderie. The vampires were waiting, excitedly, at Joe's hearse for their trip to the Calgary Ski Resort for a fun filled day of snow sledding and racing with their friends. "Here comes Joe! All ready to go!" The vampires hurriedly positioned themselves in the hearse for the trip to the Calgary Ski Resort this morning with their sleds in tow. Actually, they came just in time for their 11:00 AM meal comprised of their favorite dishes on the menu. After they finished their meal they chose to race each other to the bottom of the hill to see who will be the winner. Joe and Isaac were seated on one sled while Blair and Anton were seated on the other sled awaiting their signal to take off. The signal was activated and both sleds started racing, spiraling downward toward the base of the hill, with Joe and Isaac proclaimed the winners. The remainder of the afternoon was spent in repeat performances of racing each other down the snowy slopes in their final quest to become victorious. After all, since the vampires have taken their turns repeatedly on their sleds at breakneck speed on the slippery slopes their skiing rendezvous has come to an end because of the time frame. The vampires bid "farewell" to their old friends and new acquaintances until they meet again. Before they departed Joe made the arrangements for another skiing rendezvous two weeks from today to everybody's delight.

Chapter 60
Whatever Happened at the Mohegan Cemetery?

At the present time, the mummies have kept a low profile in regards to haunts at the Mohegan Cemetery, desecrating the graves and mausoleums, rendezvous in the back alleys of the Calgary business district downtown etc.................. Tonight, for a change they have decided to infiltrate the Mohegan Cemetery for a blood sucking rendezvous on whomever they encounter. Whether it will be underground, above ground, in the mausoleum, wherever and whatever! Earl, Chris and Ryan will also be part of the entourage! As you read this, the mummies are stumbling and mumbling around Mohegan Cemetery in search of the inevitable. All at once, they heard a clamoring noise which is indicative of the witches as they snicker, giggle and snarl their way to a tombstone of their liking. At present, they are positioning their black cauldron on top of the soil covering a gravesite. They are boiling and stirring a concoction to their liking while laughing to themselves and each other. The mummies slowly ambled up behind them, including Ryan, Earl and Chris, while grabbing their filthy, slimy, dirt infested left, jugular vein for a blood sucking rendezvous. All of a sudden, the witches splashed the scalding concoction they have been boiling onto the mummies faces that were uncovered at this time. The mummies screamed continuously while trying to wipe the slimy mess off of their faces mumbling something incoherent to themselves. Ryan, Earl and Chris were also in the process of cleaning their faces after the incident occurred.

Earl, Ryan and Chris?

Since Joe and the vampires have no contact, whatsoever, with the mummies they aren't the least bit concerned about them. Especially, since they chased them out of the basement months ago and told them, "Don't ever come back!" They scampered up the basement stairs sniveling and whimpering and have never come back. "Good riddance!"This evening since it is a clear, cold night in January with all the snow shoveled and everything in place Joe and the vampires decided to watch a 7:00 PM movie titled, "The Forgotten War." At one point in time, during a commercial Silven decided to glance outside for a look at the weather since they were forecasting snow again for the city of Calgary. While the door was ajar Silven started to say, "It sure is beginning to snow heavily right now. Not only that there are three people walking from the north carrying suitcases headed towards our area." Joe asked, "How many blocks away are they?" Silven replied, "About two blocks, that's all." He closed the door and continued watching the movie. Suddenly, a continuous knocking sound could be heard on the upstairs basement door. Silven quickly answered the door recognizing the three people with their suitcases asking, "May we speak to the head of the household?" Silven said, "Of course" and proceeded to call Joe. He came to the door recognizing Earl, Ryan and Chris. Silven did not recognize Earl, Ryan and Chris because he had only been living in the vampire household one month. Joe said, "Earl, what brings Chris, Ryan and yourself out on a night like this? Earl said, "Well, there's a story connected with this encounter we had with the witches several days ago at the Mohegan Cemetery. A small group of mummies, incorporating Chris, Ryan and myself, went to the Mohegan Cemetery for a blood sucking rendezvous. When our mummies discovered the witches boiling a concoction in a cauldron on the top soil of a gravesite they grabbed the ugly, old witches by their yellow, withered necks for a blood sucking encounter. They instantly splashed the boiled substance on our face for us to fend for ourselves. We finally managed to rid ourselves of the scalding, lathering concoction while walking back to our underground residence. After several days, Ryan, Chris and I began to notice that we do not possess the qualities, standards and characteristics of mummies anymore. The lathering concoction must have had an impact on our mummy characteristics. Therefore, we have resorted back to our lives as vampires again. "Joe said, "Since I see that you have your personal effects with you I'm assuming you are willing to move back into our household again?" Earl said, "Yes, if you will have us we will be happy to be a part of your household again! Thank you!" Joe said, "Thank you and welcome back!" Silven escorted Earl, Chris and Ryan to extra coffins the vampires kept in reserve. Tomorrow they will pay a visit to the Ronton Mortuary to inquire about getting reinstated with their mortician jobs again. Silven happened to glance outside again at the oncoming weather consisting of heavy snow forecast for the Calgary, Canada area tonight and tomorrow.

Chapter 61
A Valentine Party

February 14, 2017

Joe and the vampires are sponsoring a Valentine Party, February 14, 2017, at 7:00 PM in the basement for their relatives, friends and old and new acquaintances, especially, those they met at the Calgary Ski Resort. After hours they are busy sending out party invitations to the aforementioned plus information about the card and gift exchange. There will also be a display of Valentine cakes, candy, cupcakes, etc................ besides all the goblets of red, insatiable, succulent, juicy blood anyone can devour! The party people will be serenaded to the music of Bert Heinz and his fabulous orchestra complete with dancing to follow.

A Valentine Party and Dance

Today is the day of the Valentine Party and Dance at 7:00 PM in the basement of the vampire's home at 2125 Melbourne Street. Couples can be seen filtering in to the basement carrying cards and gifts, sampling the Valentine goodies and desserts while extending their camaraderie to their fellowmen. A variety of people are partaking of the red, juicy, delectable goblets of blood that are on display for their savory pleasure. After the Valentine goodies and desserts were consumed, the vampires reorganized the dining area to allow extra room for all those interested in taking their partner on a twirl on the dance floor. And many there were! There was barely enough room to accommodate the dancers once they all stepped out on the dance floor with their partner.Before everyone departed for the evening there was a sign up and raffle with several monetary door prizes given away. As they exited out the door everybody said, "Thank you for the delicious snacks, goodies and scrumptious goblets of fresh blood you supplied us with to accommodate our eating pleasure." Another lady mentioned, "Also, thank you for the background music presented by Bert Heinz and his fabulous orchestra and dance that followed. They sounded absolutely great!" Another couple strolled out the door with the man commenting, "I believe this is the nicest Valentine Party my wife and I have attended in years. Thank you so much! I hope one of us can reciprocate the favor next year." The vampires smiled and were very pleased at the astounding comments that were related to them in the course of the evening. They said, "Thank you!" likewise.

A Resting Weekend

Since the Valentine Party and Dance are over the vampires are settling down in front of the television set Friday and Saturday night to watch some interesting rerun movies they have seen years ago for their viewing pleasure. They are western and murder mystery movies to their liking. "Sounds like fun, doesn't it?" Besides watching television, the vampires are also touching up the porch, sidewalks and driveway with their shovels, because of the trampled snow that accumulated the night of the Valentine Party and Dance. Even though today is Saturday, Earl, Ryan and Chris are working as morticians at the Ronton Mortuary since they were hired again. They explained the situation to the presiding manager of the mortuary with Mr. Ronton saying, "We are more than happy to have you back again! Welcome!" Earl, Ryan and Chris smiled saying, "Thank you! You don't realize how good it is to be back!"

Calgary Ski Resort?—Wednesday

Joe and the vampires, including Earl, Chris and Ryan, because they are not employed at the Ronton Mortuary on Wednesdays are positioned in Joe's hearse for their ride to the Calgary Ski Resort for an afternoon of fun and relaxation. Their sleds are in back of the hearse since the vampires are preparing for a swift descent down the slippery slope trying to outdo their friends to the base of the hill. The vampires have been taking their turn repeatedly, but so far, they have not been able to outsmart them and win a race yet! "I guess they are not getting a "fast enough" start. What do you think?" At this point in time, the vampires are saying, "We are going to eat dinner now. Please excuse us. We will see you later!" Their friends said, "Sure, we'll be around!" After they were finished eating dinner they looked around for their sled racing friends but they were nowhere to be found. "Maybe they went home sooner?" The vampires kept racing each other down the steep, snowy descent until they finally started winning some races for their own pleasure. Before they departed from the Calgary Ski Resort Joe reserved another appointment for the vampires for March 6, 2017 to display their snow sledding expertise to their families, friends, and to each other. "What a fun way to end the day! Right?" On the way back to Calgary the vampires expressed their interest and personal pleasure to Joe in regards to their snow sledding experience besides a profound "Thank you!"

Chapter 62
Another Rendezvous

Ryan approached the vampires the other day about a blood thirsty rendezvous at the "Rest in Peace" Cemetery, newly opened, and dedicated several weeks ago. He made the remark, "Is anyone interested in frequenting the 'Rest in Peace" Cemetery some night, after hours, since some of the corpses are not embalmed? Preferably on a Wednesday when Earl, Chris and myself are not employed on that day at the Ronton Mortuary as morticians?" The vampires said, "Yes, all of us would be excited and looking forward to frequenting the "Rest in Peace" Cemetery since we have only been there for a dedication and a bloody escapade. We are "tickled pink" at the thought of frequenting the "Rest in Peace" Cemetery again! We remember we had an enjoyable evening the last time we were there. You set the date and time and we will be waiting by the hearse, tools and equipment, etc............... Ryan said, "That sounds great! The date is March 1, 2017 at 5:00 PM."

Rest in Peace Cemetery

This evening is the long awaited night the vampires were looking forward to in regards to a fresh, bloody encounter on several of the vampires that are not embalmed and friends of Joe. Since spring is not far away the weather has become unseasonably warm for this time of the year but an accommodating time for the task that lies ahead! They approached the gravesite, one at a time, as they started unearthing the soil, going deeper and deeper, while getting closer to the vault. The casket is encased in the vault sometimes making access to the casket lid extremely difficult. Most of the time a lot of banging and clanging are involved in the process of releasing a corpse for the inevitable. The vampires worked incessantly with their tools and equipment trying to pry the lock on the casket lid open. Finally, after maneuvering the lock various ways it started to budge with the lid gradually rising to expose the male corpse inside. Since the aforementioned are friends of Joe he had first access to the blood sucking escapade with the male corpse. Joe jerked the corpse by his withered, yellowed, scabby neck forcing him to face Joe, eyes closed, while Joe thrust his gleaming, white, canine fangs into the corpse's neck. Volumes of crimson, succulent, fresh, scrumptious blood flowed freely with Joe trying to swallow every drop that came spewing forth! Eventually, the volume decreased with Joe still sucking violently but to no avail. Joe dropped his friend, Jake Baker, back into the casket saying, "If anyone of you can manage to extract another drop of blood from my friend, help yourself." None of the vampires took the chance since Joe, himself, couldn't draw another ounce of blood out of his friend, Jake. About this time the vampires slammed the casket lid and scampered up the walls of cold earth to the top of the grave shoveling the soil till the gravesite was sealed. By now, they are proceeding to the next gravesite, several feet away, for the same procedure on another one of Joe's friends, Caleb Kenyon. The procedure was the same only now a light snow is beginning to fall covering the tombstones with a white, cloudy film that nothing can outshine. Several of the vampires sucked themselves into a frenzy with volumes of blood gushing forth until their swollen stomachs could not tolerate anymore. They hurriedly shoveled the gravesite closed and continued onto the third excavation site. The vampires started digging the outer layer of soil quickly as they gradually descended farther into the walls of the earth. Suddenly, one of the vampires, Heston, yelled, "My shovel struck a metal object, so I'm sure in a few minutes, we will be unearthing the vault, casket, etc............. He couldn't have been more accurate! Eventually the casket was exposed with the exception of the lid, as usual, was locked solid. Heston and the vampires started banging and clanging on the lid while trying to maneuver the lock to no avail. Once again they decided to moisten the lock while manipulating it with a different tool. Finally a slow, creaking sound could be heard emanating from the casket as the lid gradually elevated to expose the body of a young, teenage boy at rest with a smile etching his face. Naturally, Heston was the first vampire to practice the art of blood sucking on his corpse victim at this point. He yanked the boy's neck towards his face while vehemently sucking every drop of blood his body could muster. After he sucked ferociously, at length, he slowly reneged on his sucking encounter because of his extended stomach due to an overwhelming desire for blood. Heston relaxed his hold on the boy, thereby, letting him fall back into the casket. Joe stepped up to try his expertise in his sucking escapade which netted him quite an amount of blood in such a short time. Jake also came forward trying to muster enough strength to complete his blood thirsty rendezvous on such short notice also. He managed to withdraw a sizeable amount of blood for his sucking pleasure. Gradually, everybody was on their way back to 2125 Melbourne Street, their private home, for a relaxing night viewing a movie on television besides a peaceful evening's rest in their coffin. "Naturally, NO SUPPER!"

Chapter 63
Calgary Ski Resort

March 6, 2017

Joe asked the vampires last night, "Is everybody ready to go on a snow sledding excursion tomorrow?" The vampires said, "Yes, we are looking forward to our snow sledding experience because this will be our last outing for this season. Is that correct?" Joe said, "That's correct!" The vampires asked Joe, "What time are we leaving tomorrow morning?" Joe said, "At 10:15 AM. Please be at the hearse at the appointed time. Thank you!" The vampires said, "We'll be there!"Everybody was up bright and early this morning for the last snow sledding outing of the season at the Calgary Ski Resort. The vampires ate a hearty breakfast in the event they would be eating a late dinner. When they arrived at the Ski Resort some of their friends and former acquaintances were already there saying, "Welcome back to the Calgary Ski Resort! How have you been?" The vampires replied, "Fine! This will be our last snow sledding outing for the season!" Their friends replied, "The same for us so we better have a good time today!" The vampires replied, "Don't worry! We will!" By now, the vampires are positioning themselves on the sled with their friendly competitors doing likewise as they spiral downward on the steep, hilly slope for their destination which is the base of the hill. "The vampires won their first race against their friends but how many more will they win?"The vampires, friends and acquaintances enjoyed their snow sledding racing immensely today because this was the last race until 2018. Actually the vampires and their friends won about the same amount of races apiece. After the last race the vampires bid everyone "Goodbye and we hope to see you again next year." Their friends said, "Thank you! We also hope to see you in the coming year of 2018." Before they departed they exchanged telephone numbers, in the event, they call each other. Joe pulled up in the hearse while the vampires positioned themselves within, snow sleds in tow and all, for the ride back to Calgary.

The Calgary Restaurant

It's been years since the vampires have frequented a restaurant as a group or individually. While they were attending their meeting in the basement last night Joe asked them, "Would any of you be interested in going to a local restaurant of your choice, for a change instead of eating here all the time?" The vampires said, "Yes, we would enjoy eating at a local restaurant of our choice for a change, namely, The Calgary Restaurant." Joe said, "Fine! I'm in agreement with that! Calgary Restaurant is an exceptionally good restaurant by today's standards. How about this coming Friday night? We will be leaving at 5:00 PM. Please meet me at the hearse in the driveway. The vampires said, "We'll be there!"Friday night was here before they knew it! The vampires showered, shaved, dressed to the nines, their hair immaculately styled, their fingernails manicured, their makeup flawless, minus their capes for fear of getting recognized by the general public or the Calgary Police Department.

The Menu

Joe and the vampires entered the Calgary Restaurant at the appointed time, being ushered to several booths, while taking their respective seats accordingly. The male waiter presented them with a menu for their selection of meals to accommodate their appetite. Since they were all exceedingly hungry for dinner very little time was spent browsing through the menu. Everybody had their choice of a meal selected before they even walked into the Calgary Restaurant. Basically, everyone was interested in a meal that consisted of meat, potatoes, gravy, vegetables, bread, salad, dessert and coffee, tea or soda of their choice. "A regular Sunday dinner!" After everybody had completed their meal, while being serenaded by background music, the vampires were mingling with each other on a camaraderie basis. Sometimes the vampires get out of touch with one another so this is a good time to renew those friendships again! "Right?"Joe suggested, "Is anyone interested in a nightly haunt this evening in downtown Calgary since we are in the proximity of the alleyways incorporating the vagrants, derelicts, homeless, etc……….. The vampires said,

"We're not interested in a nightly haunt this evening because of the heavy meal that we consumed at the Calgary Restaurant. Thank you!" After the vampires made this statement everyone took their place in the hearse for their ride back to their residence at 2125 Melbourne Street.

Chapter 64
Barnum and Bailey Circus

Numerous businesses are posting signs inside and out advertising the Barnum and Bailey Circus that will be presented in entertainment form in the city of Calgary, Canada the week of May 8, 2017. The vampires are anxiously awaiting the day to partake in their form of entertainment which includes the Ferris wheel, Roller Coaster rides, the Merry Go Round, the Flying Airplanes etc............. Included in the edible fun are ice cold drinks, ice cream cones, popcorn, taffy, etc............... Besides the rides and snacks to amuse oneself the gypsies are infiltrating the circus grounds with their variety of tents to accommodate those that are interested in having their fortune told. "Are you interested? Neither am I!" Also on display are a variety of jungle animals for those of you that enjoy zebras, lions, tigers, jungle snakes, giraffes, monkeys or anything with four legs. They are trained and will come up to the fence, within petting distance, if that is your intention. "What do you have in mind?"

Barnum and Bailey Circus, May 8, 2017

Joe and the vampires arose early this morning to participate in the different rides, food, and the variety of jungle animals to observe after hours for their nocturnal pleasure. There were also an assortment of tents on display housing different games for the general public to try their luck on. Before the vampires left the circus they decided to spend some time in the darkened, outer areas of the grounds. They might even encounter a homeless person, straggler or someone in an unknown area at the wrong time. Silven and Gilbert were nonchalantly traipsing behind the tents in search of anybody or anything they could feast their white, gleaming fangs on. As luck would have it two older women were walking a ways ahead of them while visiting with each other at random giggling and laughing all the way. Silven and Gilbert picked up the speed, in excess, until they were only several yards behind them without being noticed. They continued bantering and joking as they approached several tents in a dark, secluded area. Silven and Gilbert sporadically twisted their frail, spindly, weathered necks, forcing them to face each other in the process. The older women repeated, "Who are you? Are you vampires? Please let us go!" While they were pleading and lamenting their plight Silven and Gilbert were thrusting their canine fangs into their delicate, weak, left, jugular vein, at this point, exposing gallons of scrumptious, delicious, crimson blood while sucking horrendously and vehemently every last drop of blood they could muster to avoid an overflow. Eventually, when Gilbert and Silven could not contain their sucking sensation any longer they released their grip on the two, older women with them collapsing to the cement pavement behind the carnival tents. Joe pulled their hearse closer to the darkened area while Silven and Gilbert lugged the two, older women to the hearse. They flung them in the back seat until they were ready to depart the Barnum and Bailey Carnival Grounds. Later on after they arrived back they flung them down the basement steps to lie on the cement floor until 4:00 PM tomorrow afternoon.

The Next Afternoon

At 4:00 PM Joe and the vampires could hear the two, older women conscious, screeching and screaming, wondering where they were and what happened to them since last night? Have they been exposed to a den of thieves, kidnapped, or even worse are they in the hands of murderers? "Oh no! What's happening? What's going on?"The two, older women started asking questions again such as, "Do you live here? What kind of people are you? You look kind of weird!" When Joe and the vampires heard this they became agitated and upset snarling at them, "You might wish you hadn't said that by the time we're done with you! You'll be sorry! Hah!" The two, older women started crying saying, "Please don't hurt us! Please! We didn't mean anything by that statement!" The vampires said, "You'd better not repeat that again!" They said, "We won't!" At present both of the older women were transferred to their coffins because their shallow, irregular breathing was very imminent. The vampires will check their condition throughout the night since their pulse is also very weak due to their emaciated frame.

During the Night

The vampires took their turn during the evening with no indication of any response or sound from them since their eyelids are sealed shut and their pulse has practically stopped beating. Joe awoke the vampires saying, "I think they have reached their cessation of life. There is no response from either of them and almost no pulse. This indicates the inevitable. What do you think?" The vampires said, "We all agree, Joe!" Joe said, "After they have passed on we will remove their bodies from the caskets and suspend them from the ceiling in the Death Chamber to be used for upcoming events. What do you think?" The vampires said, "That sounds great! There's plenty of room in the Death Chamber!" The vampires left the two, older women in their coffins until they passed away peacefully at 4:00 AM the next morning. After that they suspended their bodies from the ceiling in the Death Chamber until they can be used on further notice.

Chapter 65
Memorial Day

May 30, 2017

Memorial Day is fast approaching with the vampires planning a free banquet in Riley Park for the general public as is the custom for these past years. Prior to the free banquet everyone attended a Memorial Day Program for our fallen comrades in Riley Park adjacent to the free banquet. Numerous people attended the Memorial Day Program which consisted of the "Pledge of Allegiance," a Poetry reading, prayers by Chaplain Streen, a speech given by Corporal Bolton, a gun and bugle salute etc……………..In the meantime, Joe and several vampires dissected one of the older women they transferred home from the Barnum and Bailey Circus that passed away in her coffin the other morning. They dissected her body into bite sized chunks to replace the beef in pot roast. The meal will be complemented by gravy, baked, rotted, slimy potatoes, salad prepared a month ago, broiled carrots infested with worms, moldy, frozen bread and strawberry vomit ice cream. The meal was supplemented by goblets of red, scrumptious, flavorful, savory blood. Everybody was overwhelmed at the marvelous, excellent banquet that was presented before them considering the labor and effort involved. Besides that the vampires also organized the Memorial Day Program for their fallen comrades out of personal respect. Everybody exclaimed, "It was such a wonderful program and delicious banquet with the camaraderie outstanding. As the general public departed they stood single file shaking hands with the vampires (since most of them were vampires themselves) remarking, "We appreciate the time and effort incorporated into the banquet and program involved. Thank you!" The vampires smiled at the outpouring of good will and cheer saying, "Thank you!"

A Fishing Expedition, June, 2017

Gilbert has been harboring a wild idea in his mind the past several days but has yet to mention it to the vampires. Finally, on an impulse, he said, "Is anyone interested in going on a fishing expedition to

Haney Lake, north of Calgary, about fifteen miles? It is a huge lake with a lot of depth which encompasses a width and length of nearly half a mile. Are there any questions so far?" Joe asked, "Are there boats available for those of us that would be interested in boating?" Gilbert answered, "Yes, boats have been available for years." Joe said, "I think most of us would be interested in trying our hand at fishing again because we haven't been fishing since we were on vacation at Vancouver Island last summer. We sure had a wonderful time there! Is everybody agreed?" Everybody nodded and grinned from ear to ear saying, "We had a marvelous time! We're ready to go again!" Gilbert said, "Does it make any difference what day we decide to go? How about Wednesday when Earl, Ryan and Chris aren't employed and are available?" The vampires said, "That sounds great! You set the date and time and we will be waiting by the hearse." Gilbert said, "Then it's settled! Next week, Wednesday, June 21. We will be leaving at 12:00 PM. Please have your fishing poles, bait, beverages etc................. with you when we depart."

"What Happened to Gilbert?"

As is the custom an expedition day always comes sooner than expected! "Right?" Joe, Gilbert and the vampires arose bright and early eating a healthy and hearty breakfast consisting of bacon, eggs, a sweet roll, hot chocolate etc................... to carry them over until dinner. Gilbert transported the vampires in the hearse while two of the other vampires furnished their own cars for the benefit of the remaining. They arrived at Haney Lake close to 1:00 PM with the vampires hurriedly gathering their personal effects. It included their fishing poles, bait, beverage coolers etc............ for their trek to Pier 1 where they will be displaying their fishing expertise. As they tromped through the sand in the proximity of Haney Lake they could get a clear cut view of the fresh, blue, water incorporating the outlying areas. A variety of swimmers were out on the lake, bashing, splashing, snorkeling, water skiing etc............... Various fisherman can be seen on the shore casting their poles toward the water in the hope of snatching a fish unexpectedly. "Good Luck!" By now more people are beginning to frequent Haney Lake since the weather is unseasonably warm today which creates an influx of visitors and tourists to the Lakeside Resort. People are streaming towards the lake accompanied by boats on the shore. Gilbert decided to rent a fishing boat for a short outing close to the lake's edge to improvise his style of fishing on such short, quick notice. Gilbert asked, "Does anyone want to go on a fishing excursion with me from my boat this afternoon for a while?" The vampires gave Gilbert a strange, quizzical look indicating their fear of being exposed to a large body of water, in the event, something might happen. Silven said, "It doesn't look like anyone is interested in going out on a boat today, Gilbert! I guess they would rather fish off the shore, myself included. I hope you aren't offended?" Gilbert made the remark, "Of course not! I was just curious. I'll go out by myself, staying close to the shore, for a short outing of fishing. Maybe I'll catch a fish or two! I see various people in their boats, by themselves, with the same intentions as mine." The vampires yelled, "Good Luck!"

At this point in time, Gilbert is still in the process of making preparations for his short, fishing outing, close to the shore, since his counterparts are doing likewise. In the meantime the vampires are beginning to notice a slight rustle of wind picking up and unfurling the waves on the lake a distance from the shoreline. Suddenly, the rustle of wind subsided and the lake was left with a cool, calming, tranquil effect.By this time, Gilbert can be seen maneuvering his boat into Haney Lake while casting his fishing pole into the outer water to catch a fish or two. Several boaters managed to latch onto a few fish since they can be heard screaming, "Hah! We got lucky! We caught several fish!" Their friends could be heard yelling and laughing saying, "It's about time!"

Chapter 66
Gilbert Drowned

At present, Gilbert is still fishing close to the sandy shore while intermittently sailing a distance away void of anything or anyone in sight. Without warning a sudden wind escalated to a high velocity twisting Gilbert's boat to and fro while he sat helpless at the mercy of Mother Nature. He is equipped with a seat belt but still unable to swim. By this time the boat is rocking back and forth with Gilbert pleading and lamenting his plight. "Help me! Help me! Someone, please save me! I will drown! Help!" As Joe and the vampires were staring towards Gilbert, Joe screamed, "We have called the lifeguards and personnel to come to your assistance! Stay hunkered down in the boat!" Eventually, smoky, ominous, threatening clouds started casting dark shadows on Haney Lake with violent, tornadic winds engulfing the atmosphere. All of a sudden, a swift downpour of rain enclosed the immediate area with Gilbert's boat capsizing into the lake. Gilbert could be seen by the vampires overwhelmed and suffocating in the water. The lifeguards and personnel are on their way to the scene of the accident as they transport Gilbert's body back to the shore. Immediate resuscitation is administered but to no avail. The lifeguard said, "Gilbert died from drowning about forty five minutes ago. I'm sorry!" Joe and the vampires were overwhelmed with grief at the outcome of the fishing excursion that was, supposedly, to be an enjoyable time had by all. They were huddled in a group at Pier 1 shedding tears of sorrow and regret because they decided to go along on the fishing excursion. The vampires remember Gilbert asking them, "Does anyone want to go on a fishing outing with me on my boat this afternoon for a while?" They also remember giving Gilbert a strange, quizzical look indicating their fear of being exposed to a large body of water, in the event, something might happen. Silven told Gilbert, "It looks like no one is interested in going boat fishing today, Gilbert!" Gilbert made the remark, "I was just curious. I'll go out by myself, staying close to the shore, for a short outing of fishing. Maybe I'll catch a fish or two. I see various people in their boats, by themselves, with the same intentions as mine." The vampires remember yelling,

'Good Luck!" The last conversation they had with Gilbert was his pleading and lamenting his plight screaming, "Help me! Help me! Someone, please save me! I will drown! Help!" Joe answered, "We have called the lifeguards and personnel to come to your assistance! Stay hunkered down in the boat!"By this time, ominous, storm clouds and violent, winds engulfed their surroundings with a fierce deluge of rain incorporating the immediate area. In the meantime Gilbert's boat capsized into Haney Lake. The vampires caught their final glimpse of Gilbert overwhelmed and drowning in the water. Gilbert's body was transported by the lifeguards and personnel back to the shore with resuscitation administered and no response. The inevitable was at hand!

Gilbert's Viewing

Gilbert's body was transferred to the Ronton Mortuary where Earl, Ryan and Chris are employed as morticians. They are assisting in the preparation of Gilbert's body to be displayed for a general public viewing tomorrow night from 7:00 PM till 9:00 PM.The vampires have filed in and taken their respective seats while glancing at Gilbert periodically with tears of sorrow clouding their eyes at the onset of these fatal consequences. Gilbert was a 54 year old male, short, dark brown hair, clad in a dark blue suit and necktie, white shirt etc............. A slight smile is creeping across his face as he rests in peaceful sleep. A large variety of people are filtering into the Ronton Mortuary's Viewing Room to pay their final respects to Gilbert Evans. Throughout the evening Chaplain Jones conducted several prayers in honor of Gilbert. Before everyone departed he announced, "Tomorrow morning at 10:00 AM there will be a funeral service here at the mortuary in honor of Gilbert Evans for anyone that cares to attend. Interment will be at New Haven Cemetery following the funeral service.

Gilbert's Funeral

Joe, the vampires and the general public have started taking their respective seats while glancing at Gilbert for the last time. Chaplain

Jones is conducting the funeral in a timely manner accompanied by organ music in the background. He is also in the process of delivering a eulogy in regards to Gilbert and the untimely death he had to endure. Tears welled up again in the vampires eyes as Chaplain Jones touched upon the subject. As the funeral service came to a close Joe and the vampires followed the casket to the hearse accompanied by "Amazing Grace." When they arrived at the New Haven Cemetery six of the vampires were pallbearers transferring the casket to the gravesite while standing at attention until the service was concluded. Before everyone departed Chaplain Jones said, "There will be a free meal for everyone gathered here today at 12:30 PM at the Star Restaurant in downtown Calgary. We'll see you all there! Thank you!"

Chapter 67
In Honor of Gilbert!

Joe and the vampires have acquired an "attitude of prayer" in regards to the dilemma that inflicted Gilbert at Haney Lake. Lately every evening before bedtime they are in the habit of kneeling in a circle before God reciting a variety of prayers for the benefit of their deceased vampires and beyond. They have also subdued their extracurricular activities for a couple of weeks due to the inevitable. The vampires have been keeping a "low profile" regarding their lifestyle routinely updating their household chores, yard maintenance etc……………..Since they have been living in a secluded lifestyle for the past two weeks Joe has decided as he said, "We will be resuming our vampire activities this coming Friday evening for anyone that wants to frequent the "Rest in Peace" Cemetery. We all had an enjoyable time when we visited the "Rest in Peace" Cemetery some time ago. Remember?" The vampires smiled and nodded their heads saying, "We remember our encounter at the "Rest in Peace" Cemetery. It sure met our expectations and we expect the same this time!" Joe made the remark, "I'm sure it will be! We will be leaving this coming Friday night at 6:00 PM. Please meet me at the hearse at the appointed time equipped with tools etc……………. At this point in time I am not expecting anyone in the "Rest in Peace" Cemetery because of the isolated environment, it is relatively new and the most outlying, remote cemetery in the immediate area compared to the others. Thank you!"

Friday Night, June 29, 2017

Friday night rolled around, as usual, with the vampires waiting at the hearse prior to 6:00 PM for their ride to "Rest in Peace" Cemetery. They were anticipating another encounter with corpses that might have been overlooked the last time. Their equipment and tools are in tow, beside their person, ready to go. Joe is behind the wheel and the remaining vampires are in position headed for the "Rest in Peace" Cemetery. The weather is very accommodating, a clear, blue sky, not a cloud in sight, and a balmy 75 degrees. When they approached the "Rest in Peace" Cemetery Joe was correct, not a single person anywhere. They proceeded to the gravesites and started digging downward, six feet, until they reached the vault with their shovels. They were able to maneuver the vault exposing the casket which was still sealed from their last escapade. Since he was Joe's close friend he made the first attempt at yanking Jake Baker's cold, scaly, decrepit, yellow neck toward him. He sucked his left, jugular vein repeatedly for the red, scrumptious blood that still encased Jake's vein until it ceased to spew forth blood any longer. By now the vampires started scampering up the cold, earthen walls to the top of the grave. They, instantly, started shoveling soil sealing the gravesite as to go unnoticed. They automatically proceeded to an unknown grave when Earl, Chris and Ryan said, "This corpse is a young woman, Maria Rale, because Ronton Mortuary made the preparations and we assisted, therefore, we know that she is not embalmed." They started shoveling again to the bottom of the grave till they reached the vault proceeding to the casket itself. The procedure for opening the casket lid was more difficult, than otherwise, requiring more time and effort. Eventually, the lid creaked open emanating a foul, rancid odor permeating the complete gravesite and its surroundings. Heston decided to try a blood sucking rendezvous on the young woman because he had not eaten dinner. He jerked her thick, swollen, slimy neck towards his lips, thrusting his white, gleaming, canine fangs into the folds of her neck while volumes of red, delicious, savory blood came gushing forth. Heston sucked ravenously and hungrily till every morsel of blood was depleted. The vampires hurriedly shoveled the soil back into the gravesite smoothing it over to give it the appearance of never being touched. The vampires happen to have time for one more gravesite to unearth which is one of Joe's friends, Caleb Kenyon, which they proceeded with the last time. They shoveled six feet down into the grave working on the vault, while preparing to open the casket lid. "Oh no!!! What happened?" They lifted the casket lid and were shocked and taken aback that Caleb Kenyon's corpse is missing. The last time they visited Caleb's grave was March 1, 2016 for a blood sucking rendezvous involving several of the vampires. Joe said, "I'm wondering how long Caleb has been missing from his grave? That's strange! Is he digging himself in and out?" Heston made the remark, "That's a good question! He might be prowling through the back alleys at night on a vampiric haunt similar to us. Not only that he could be loitering in various parks, cemeteries, mausoleums etc……………. to see whom he can encounter in a blood sucking rampage." Joe and the vampires agreed saying, "Anything's possible! We don't doubt anything for a minute! There might even be a remote possibility that Caleb Kenyon might visit us, after hours, at 2125 Melbourne Street! It wouldn't surprise me!"

Chapter 68
How About the Mausoleum?

Before departing the "Rest in Peace" Cemetery the vampires decided to visit the only mausoleum available at the time. The door lock was relatively new so they had a difficult time disengaging the lock to gain entrance into the mausoleum. Since a special tool was brought along for the lock it was opened in no time exposing layers of caskets most of them empty while a few of them contained corpses! Several of the vampires tried their luck at opening the casket lock with the special tool in their possession releasing the lock immediately after it had been disengaged for some time. Since Earl, Chris and Ryan were participating in tonight's escapade at the "Rest in Peace" Cemetery Earl remarked, "We know for a fact that the corpses in these caskets have not been embalmed because preparations were made at the Ronton Mortuary, therefore, they are at your disposal for a thirst, quenching rendezvous." Earl, Chris, Ryan, Blair and Joe each took their turn sucking their left, jugular vein, savagely and repeatedly, with volumes of red, juicy, succulent, savory blood flowing forth. After everybody had completed their rendezvous they flung their corpse victim back into the casket, slammed the lid shut and exited the mausoleum. They rode back with Joe and the remainder of the vampires saying, "We sure got lucky tonight considering the corpses in the mausoleum were not embalmed. It couldn't have gone any smoother!"A News Report

When the vampires reached 2125 Melbourne Street they exited the hearse keeping a "low profile," for fear of the neighbors. They entered the basement reclining in front of the television to watch the KIBX News for their comfort and relaxation. The first item on the news agenda the announcer proclaimed was, "Several gravesites at the "Rest in Peace" Cemetery have been dug six feet downward and the caskets and corpses have been violated. The mausoleum door has been broken into, therefore, incorporating much damage hereto. Forthcoming news will be made available as soon as we are aware of it. Anybody with any information in regards to this matter please call the Calgary Police Department at 1-649-260-2902. Thank you!"The vampires said, "We hope no one at the "Rest in Peace" Cemetery got a glimpse of us, possibly, standing behind a tombstone, a tree, the mausoleum, walking on the road, etc………. even though several of us were posted outside observing in case of invaders or intruders desecrating private property."

A Public Dance, July 4th

The vampires are getting ready to go out "on a night on the town" like they used to say! Tonight is the 4th of July with everyone shaving, bathing, attired in their black suits and white shirts and no capes for fear of being recognized by the Calgary Police Department. Their hair are immaculately coiffed, flawless makeup and their fingernails are perfectly manicured. "What more could you want?" Tonight, instead of catering a free meal to the general public and providing a free fireworks display they decided to cater a meal to themselves at the Calgary Restaurant downtown and a public dance at the Calgary Dance Hall open to the general public for a mere pittance. 'Something different for a change!"The vampires walked into the Calgary Restaurant, in regards to the aforementioned, and had the lady waiter usher them to their respective seats, presenting them with a menu for their culinary pleasure. The vampires knew, in advance, what they were interested in ordering. They said, "It will consist of rib eye steak, a baked potato, a vegetable, garden salad, bread, butter brickle, vomit ice cream, coffee, soda or tea. They enjoyed their meal immensely while being serenaded with a live orchestra's background music. The vampires are enjoying each other's camaraderie once again, as usual, since some of them eat at different times due to unusual circumstances. Besides enjoying the public dance this evening the vampires also have intentions, during intermission, of slinking around outside of the Calgary Dance Hall to see if they can encounter a stray victim or two that meets their expectations. In the meantime, the vampires have been dancing every chance they get whomever will dance with them. They are dancing the Polka, Two Step, Waltzes, Jitterbug, etc…………. any type of music the Les Brown Band of Renown can furnish. Since it is intermission time they are enjoying a refreshing snack to their liking the same as everyone else. By now they are headed outdoors in the dark to loiter next to the back of the dance hall close to their car, in the event, they approach someone to their liking. At this point Bryan and Heston are following two, young men several yards behind while slowly gaining speed they snatch their filthy, slimly, burnt necks in an attempt to reach their left, jugular vein. It worked! Heston and Bryan sucked their left, jugular vein overflowing with crimson, savory, succulent, juicy blood. Their male victims screeched and lamented their distressing circumstance begging to be left alone, saying, "Who are you? We've seen you somewhere before! But where?" Eventually, by the time their sucking sensation ebbed the two, young men collapsed to the ground forcing Heston and Bryan to transfer them to the back of the hearse. They immediately left the Calgary Dance Hall for 2125 Melbourne Street and the safety of their house. They transported them to the top of the stairs and flung them to the basement floor where they will lie until tomorrow afternoon at 4:00 PM. In the meantime, Bryan and Heston are worn out from the day's activities and decided to go to their coffins to relax and sleep earlier than usual. Their bodies were transferred the next afternoon to their coffins for several days of rest and recuperation.

Chapter 69
A Vampire Meeting

This morning Joe can be seen posting meeting signs on the stairway down to the basement indicating a tri-monthly assembly of the vampires in regards to various issues that have arisen on the agenda. Discussion was held on the following subjects: The confiscation of two, older women from the Barnum and Bailey Circus resulting in their deaths a day later. A Memorial Day dinner on May 30, 2017 resulting in a large crowd of people representing the Calgary Community commenting on the superb Memorial Day program and banquet. Gilbert Evan's death at Haney Lake and the outpouring of cards, monetary gifts and comments with the conclusion of a free meal at the Star Restaurant in downtown Calgary. The vampires lived an isolated lifestyle for the past several weeks in honor of the passing of Gilbert Evans. A resumption of their vampire activities began Friday evening for anyone that wanted to frequent the "Rest in Peace" Cemetery. A blood sucking rendezvous transpired in regards to Jake Baker and Marla Rale. Caleb Kenyon's corpse was missing from the casket at this time. A news report was announced on television in regards to the violation of caskets and corpses incorporating much damage hereto. Also, the mausoleum door has been broken into and anyone with any information in regards to this matter please call the Calgary Police Department at 1-649-260-2902. Thank you!" The vampires attended a July 4th meal at the Calgary Restaurant followed by a public dance at the Calgary Dance Hall to complement the evening. They devoured a scrumptious, holiday meal while being accompanied by Les Brown's Band of Renown. At intermission time they loitered in the back of the dance hall following two, young men whom they snatched sucking their left, jugular vein until they collapsed. After the discussion was completed on the aforementioned Joe terminated the meeting saying, "This meeting is drawing to a close for this evening. Our next meeting will be October 10th, 2017. Thank you for your attendance. Good evening!" The vampires said, "Thank you" and were dismissed. Since it was getting quite late because of the lengthy discussion it entailed everyone was ready to retire early for the evening. "Goodnight, everybody!"

A Night Visitor, July 20, 2017

Everything seems to be back to normal in regards to the vampires daily schedule of household chores, yard maintenance, etc............... Lately their evenings have been spent watching old rerun television movies for their viewing pleasure accompanied by a snack and a bottle of red, juicy, delicious, blood to accommodate their taste buds. Occasionally, they play cards or a game of billiards in the billiard parlor to pass the time during the evening hours. Now and then they will erect a movie screen on the basement wall with slides of pictures from years gone by of various vampires in different stages of their lives. It usually creates a roar of laughter for the "good old days! Ha! Ha! Ha!"Most of the time the vampires are making their nightly preparations in regards to retiring in their coffins about 10:O0 PM after their television movie has ended. Tonight was no different than any other night. At present they are reclining in their coffins, some snoring, while others are breathing heavily in a deep, sound sleep. In the stillness of the night, several of the vampires are dreaming and mumbling to themselves in their sleep. Suddenly, Ryan woke up with a start exclaiming, ""I have been hearing a soft, rattling noise on the outside basement door upstairs. Has anyone else been hearing this?" By this time, most of the vampires are totally awake shaking their heads indicating "No!" Ryan made the remark, "Very well! Maybe it was the wind rustling the leaves in the trees or my imagination." Heston said, "Maybe you were dreaming again!" Ryan remarked, "Not that I can remember!"Within a few minutes, all the vampires, including Ryan, were sound asleep and off to dreamland. All of a sudden, a slow, creaking noise can be heard at the top of the stairs signifying the presence of someone else in the house besides the vampires. But the vampires continue to sleep in their coffins. Soft footsteps can be heard creeping stealthily down the basement stairs in search of a vampire to feed on! Since Ryan's coffin was in proximity of the basement stairs the unknown assailant hurriedly yanked Ryan's frail, spider veined neck towards his face. He then started sucking his left, jugular vein with all the strength he could muster. Immediately Ryan recognized Joe's friend, Caleb Kenyon that was missing from his casket at the "Rest in Peace" Cemetery on June 29, 2016. By this time, all the vampires were awake observing the horrific, bloody encounter that ensued in their presence. Finally Caleb released his grip on Ryan's neck with Ryan screaming and screeching saying, "Get away from me, Caleb! I recognize you! Get out of here! How did you happen to find us?" Caleb mumbled, "Arg! Arg! Arg! Besides trying to repeat some words. Instantly, Ryan jumped out of his coffin chasing Caleb Kenyon up the basement stairs and out the door yelling, "Don't ever come back!" Caleb continued mumbling and grumbling as he traipsed north towards the "Rest in Peace" Cemetery. Ryan mentioned to the vampires, "I was absolutely correct when I heard a soft, rattling noise at the top of the stairs. Remember?" The vampires nodded their heads saying, "Yes, we remember and are sorry this happened!" Since it was Joe's friend, Caleb Kenyon, he was shocked at the outcome and said, "I'm sorry this encounter transpired, likewise." Even though it's almost 5:00 AM and the vampires were awakened twice during the night they crawled back into their coffins once more to sleep until 4:00 PM.

Chapter 70

Mummies on Patrol

August 10, 2017

It's been several weeks since Joe, Blair and the vampires have been on a nightly haunt in the back alleys of downtown Calgary. They are always in search of disconnected, homeless vagrants to accommodate their blood sucking antics. "What a life!" Joe, Blair and the vampires are all slicked up tonight! They shaved, bathed, dressed to the nines in their black suits, white shirts, sporting a black tie, with no capes because of getting recognized by the Calgary Police Department. Their hair was immaculately groomed, with flawless makeup and manicured fingernails. They are strolling nonchalantly behind the main thoroughfare in search of victims they have never encountered before for their blood sucking pleasure. Since the heat has subsided storm clouds can be seen clouding the atmosphere with an occasional rumble of thunder and fingers of lightening scraping the sky. By now the vampires are not strolling nonchalantly anymore but shifting and stumbling haphazardly through the alley in search of anyone or anything that has a left, jugular vein. "Sounds like their desperate tonight! What do you think?""All of a sudden the vampires have become bombarded by a group of blood sucking mummies. The vampires are still upset from their last encounter with the mummies when the soil on the gravesite swallowed Earl, Chris and Ryan at the New Haven Cemetery and they were not seen for months after that. In the meantime, the vampires are living a carefree lifestyle visiting and laughing while sharing their camaraderie and good will with their special friends they associate with on a daily basis. Many of the vampires and mummies are out in today's heat to take advantage of the weather while it lasts! The vampires have decided to stroll along the path between the two business buildings that face the main thoroughfare. Suddenly, they are imposed upon by the zombie's full force. Several of the mummies have jerked the vampire's necks to their red, bloody lips while gorging themselves with the succulent, savory, scrumptious blood that spewed forth. Several of the vampires screeched and screamed in pain saying, "Let us go! Please! Leave us alone!" The mummies kept on an endless, sucking rampage with Joe and Ryan's bodies slowly descending and then total collapse. In the meantime, the remainder of the mummies are chasing the vampires through the alley ways on one pretext or another pretending to catch them. The vampires hurriedly left in the hearse knowing that Joe and Ryan are at the mercy of the mummies. They said, "We are sorrowed at the outcome of this haunt. Joe and Ryan are completely under the power of the mummies at this point. What will happen to them? Will they come back to us several months from now like Earl, Chris and Ryan? This is the second time this has happened to Ryan! Oh no!!!" Blair and the remainder of the vampires were also overcome with grief and mental distress at the thought of the loss of Joe and Ryan to the mummies. Blair made the comment, "I hope and pray that Joe and Ryan will be as lucky as Earl, Chris and Ryan were since they were only gone about three months. What a shame! But we were lucky to get them back! Right?" The vampires smiled in spite of their grief and nodded saying, "Most definitely!"

No Word from Joe or Ryan!

Several weeks have passed since Joe and Ryan were abducted by the mummies in the alley ways of downtown Calgary, Canada adjacent to the main thoroughfare. An emergency meeting was conducted by Earl, Chris and the vampires in regards to Joe and Ryan's situation being at the mercy and power of the mummies. Earl made the remark, "Now that Chris and I think about our encounter and abduction with the mummies we feel like we are at liberty to reveal the circumstances and lifestyle involved. Would anyone be interested in the following?" The vampires said, "Yes, we would be very interested in hearing your story!" Earl narrated the events as they unfolded: "While the other vampires were meditating Chris, Ryan and I were investigating the gravesite for any unusual circumstances that might lead to the inevitable. While they were retrieving the remainder of the tools and equipment, Chris, Ryan and I stepped on the actual gravesite where the mummy corpse protruded out of the soil the week before. Immediately, the soil opened up into a gaping hole and swallowed Chris, Ryan and myself. Eventually the hole started filling in with more soil until the gravesite was filled up and smoothed over. Paul raised his hand and asked, "How deep did you fall? Earl answered, "Probably close to fifty feet, by today's standards! Paul continued, "What was your living lifestyle like?" Earl laughed and said, "Well, I can assure you it wasn't the "Grand Hotel" by any means! Chris, Ryan and I spent three months in solitary confinement similar to a jail cell, bars and all. Occasionally we would be included in a cemetery haunt or a blood sucking rampage etc................ The interior of the chamber consisted of floors of solid earth, plus, we were barely existing because of the minimum amount of food at our disposal. Basically, we were very restricted in regards to bathing, clean clothing etc................ I'm sure Joe and Ryan are experiencing this same lifestyle again!" Dean asked, "How and where did you sleep at night?" Earl replied, "Chris, Ryan and I slept in flatbed boxes with a carved mummy design accompanied by a lid. None of us slept too well since we weren't adjusted to these strange, sleeping arrangements." Earl asked, "Are there any more questions in regards to Chris, Ryan and myself for the length of time we were confined with the mummies?" The vampires remarked, "No, thank you!"At this point, the meeting was dismissed with each of the vampires going to their respective coffins for a peaceful night's rest.

Chapter 71
One More Swimming Escapade?

According to Earl relating to the vampires, "The Calgary Swimming Pool is closing in two weeks so I thought we could possibly go on one more swimming outing before summer is over. Is anyone interested? Please raise your hands!" All hands were raised, plus, smiles and giggles galore! Earl said, "How about this coming Friday night from 6:00 PM to 10:00 PM?" The vampires yelled, "Yes, we'll be waiting by the hearse!" Earl said, "Good, then it's all settled! Meet me at the hearse at 5:15 PM. Do not forget your beach towels!" As always Friday is here before we know it. The vampires ate an early supper, assembled their personal effects and were waiting by the hearse before 5:15 PM. They're pretty fast! Right? By the time Earl and the rest of the vampires arrived at the Calgary Swimming Pool it was exactly 6:00 PM. They immediately jumped into the pool from the diving board, bashing and splashing to their heart's content! Some of their friends they met before happened to be at the pool this evening joining in the fun and relaxation. The vampires raced their friends the length of the swimming pool and back to determine the winner several times. Everyone is swimming to and fro in the cool, clear, crisp water with a heat index of 99 degrees, not a cloud in the sky, only the blazing sun overhead. "It paints a pretty picture, doesn't it?" It's time for a snack break as the vampires crawl out of the swimming pool headed for the snack bar. After they purchased their cold drink and several cookies they are relaxing at several tables within the proximity of the Calgary Swimming Pool. They are getting reacquainted with their friends and sharing their camaraderie with them. At present, it is 8:30 PM with the vampires and their friends diving into the swimming pool from the highest diving board available. Once again, they are greeted by the moderately, cool, refreshing, brisk, water that invigorates their bodies giving them strength and vitality. Most of the swimmers left earlier, including the vampires friends leaving a handful of people. Basically, there were two women and three men, plus the vampires, cavorting in the swimming pool by themselves. By now dusk is fast approaching and trees are encompassing the swimming pool casting dark shadows in the immediate area. The vampires are vigorously swimming in the darkened, isolated areas of the Calgary Swimming Pool in the proximity of several, young men and women in the prime of their lives. They are swimming several yards behind both parties while gradually gaining speed with them oblivious of anyone following. Hastily the vampires yank their thin, firm, tanned necks exposing their left, jugular vein for their succulent pleasure. The vampires opened their mouths with their gleaming, white, canine fangs protruding while thrusting them into their victim's left, jugular vein. Earl, Chris and Dean sucked horrendously with volumes of red, juicy, succulent blood bursting forth. They gulped greedily as blood started pouring onto their victims and into the swimming pool causing red, bloody rivulets to float in the water. There were no attendants or life guards on hand to witness the inevitable since the victims succumbed to the vampire's bloody antics. Earl said nervously, "I will hurry and get the hearse and park it close to the pool so we don't have to transfer them so far." Chris and the rest of the vampires said, "We will be waiting in the darkened area on the other side of the pool with our victims since no one is around this evening." Earl hurriedly brought the hearse transferring the bodies while the vampires positioned themselves for the ride back to their house at 2125 Melbourne Street.

Visiting the Different Cemeteries?

For a change Chris asked the vampires, "Would any of you be interested in frequenting all the cemeteries in the immediate area, such as, the New Haven Cemetery, the Poheta Cemetery or the Mohegan Cemetery?" The vampires said, "Yes, we would be interested in going. Especially, three cemeteries in one evening." Chris also said, "If we frequent all three cemeteries in one night we might have a better chance of encountering victims. Possibly, those that are meditating at the gravesites, strolling through the cemetery at random or stragglers and disconnected people at loose ends. You never know whom you might approach in this day and age!" Chris continued, "We will be leaving this coming Wednesday evening at 4:30 PM to cover the three cemeteries. Is everyone available for the time and date? Please meet me at the hearse at the appointed time."As usual, the vampires completed their household chores, yard work etc……………… Monday, Tuesday and Wednesday, with the expectation of visiting three cemeteries in one evening. They were waiting patiently at the hearse for their ride at 4:30 PM with beautiful, balmy weather in the forecast. They visited the New Haven Cemetery first since it was the closest. They meditated at the gravesites of several of their vampire friends besides visiting the mausoleums and strolling through the cemetery for new plots, victims or other ideas or objects of interest. Since there was nothing in particular to intrigue them they proceeded on. By now they are visiting the Poheta Cemetery with the same intentions as the New Haven Cemetery. The Poheta Cemetery is a relatively newer and smaller burial area thus incorporating smaller burial plots as mostly recognized. Once again, they visited the few gravesites on hand and the Poheta Mausoleum while traipsing tiredly through the cemetery looking for victims etc…………… There were no victims, stragglers or intruders available so Chris and the vampires moved on to the Mohegan Cemetery, or Indian Cemetery since it was first established in the 1800"s. As they were approaching the Mohegan Cemetery a group of mourners were departing leaving in their vehicles for Calgary, Canada. Possibly, an interment for a loved one had taken place prior to the vampire's entrance. They trudged through the cemetery grounds taking note of the freshly, spaded cemetery plot while observing numerous tombstones that had gone unnoticed before. They also visited the mausoleum besides keeping a watchful eye for anyone that might be lurking behind a tombstone, tree, etc…………….. There were no homeless, intruders or vagrants in the Mohegan Cemetery this evening.

Chapter 72
A Broken Down Hearse

Since there were no victims to encounter this evening in the three cemeteries the vampires decided to call it a night and head back for Calgary. As they were driving along Chris made the remark, "Well, we didn't have any luck in any of the three cemeteries today. Better luck next time!" The remaining vampires agreed saying, "That's right! You never know which evening is the right time to go. Dean said, "Maybe we should have gone when it was completely dark?" Heston remarked, "I don't think that would have made much difference!" All of a sudden, while they were driving along the vampires started hearing a strange, hissing sound emanating from the motor of the hearse. By now, it is sputtering incessantly and on the verge of deteriorating. This has prompted a reduced speed with a burning odor encompassing the inside of the vehicle. Smoke can be seen billowing from underneath the front hood as it gradually fizzles to a complete stop. Chris managed to park the hearse on the side of the road while the vampires exited and lifted the hood for further inspection. Clouds of vapor are released into the air as the hood is further extended with the motor creating an intense heat. At this point oil and transmission fluid are draining from the hearse onto the road. Chris said, "What happened to this hearse? This is the first time we have had any trouble with it. It has always served us faithfully for the several years it has been in our possession. Something must have gone wrong!" Heston remarked, "We have been checking the hearse every couple of months for anything faulty and everything's been fine. We also replenished the hearse periodically with oil and transmission fluid to keep it in motion and it did the job." Dean commented, "I thought it sounded a little different on the way to the three cemeteries with a hesitating movement in progress. It didn't really phase me, therefore, I didn't comment on it."

"Let's Start Hitchhiking!"

Earl replied, "Well, I guess we don't have any choice, except to start hitchhiking a ride back to Calgary since it will be dark quite soon!" The vampires stood at a distance from the hearse displaying the hitchhiking sign towards the city of Calgary, Canada. A variety of vehicles passed them, honking, but no one offered them a ride or even bothered to slow down. Not only that the weather has changed dramatically with the vampires huddled together in a group braving the elements. Finally, an older couple pulled up beside them asking, "Do you need a ride?" Chris said, "Yes, our hearse broke down and we would appreciate a ride back to Calgary. Can you accommodate all four of us?" The man said, "Certainly! Please take your respective seats."While they were driving and conversing with each other Chris reached forward, yanking the older man's neck, forcing his wife to pull to the side for a complete stop. Chris sucked the older man's left, jugular vein, sporadically, with volumes of red, succulent, savory blood gushing forth. In the meantime, Heston drained the older woman's left, jugular vein, likewise, with a sizeable amount of blood spurting from her vein. The older man and woman screamed, "Leave us alone! Get away from us! Help! Help! The vampires repositioned the older couple in their car, thus, transporting them to their house at 2125 Melbourne Street. When they arrived Chris flung them down the basement steps to lie there until 4:00 PM the next afternoon.

Death before Life

After Chris and the vampires checked on the older couple that picked them up when they were hitchhiking on the way back from the Mohegan Cemetery they noticed they were still and lifeless. Evidently, they had passed away sometime during the night unbeknown to Earl, Chris and the vampires. The vampires immediately suspended their bodies from the ceiling in the Death Chamber to be used for future reference.

A Labor Day Celebration, September 3, 2017

Earl, Chris and the vampires decided to have a free, Labor Day Celebration, Music accompaniment and Bingo. Earl dissected the older woman the day before Labor Day to be prepared in the form of roasted flesh(roast beef) slimy, rotted mashed potatoes, beetle juice gravy, frozen bread, burnt, black, crock pot corn, a vegetable salad floating in water, cherry, vomit ice cream laced with worm infested cherries and goblets of tasty, crimson, savory blood. The Labor Day meal will be free and open to the public starting at 11:30 AM. The vampires posted signs in the downtown Calgary stores and businesses indicating the time and location of the meal which will be in Riley Park with the Les brown Band of Renown on the center stage.   After the meal is completed there will be free Bingo games for the general public to participate in. Prizes will be awarded in monetary form or gifts. "Sounds like fun, doesn't it? Let's line up to eat! Hurry!"As 11:30 AM rolled around a superfluous amount of people filtered into Riley Park for the free meal, music and bingo. Extra picnic tables had to be transferred to the park to accommodate the masses of people that accumulated for the above mentioned. Approximately, six hundred people attended the free meal with the music accompaniment of Les Brown's Band of Renown. The general public was in a jovial, ecstatic mood as they enjoyed the good company of their family, relatives and friends. They were sharing their camaraderie with everyone at their table, plus, anyone they came in contact with. By now, the tables have been cleared and everyone is anxious for the Bingo games to begin. Heston won the first Bingo game and was awarded $15.OO in the process. Earl won the second game and was also awarded $15. OO. A variety of people, plus children, won gifts to their delight. In the meantime, Les Brown's Band of Renown is performing a variety of popular, classical music for their era of time. The Bingo games ended when all the money and gifts had been depleted. By this time the general public is tired and ready to leave thanking Earl and the vampires for a free, enjoyable meal, music and Bingo plus a chance to share their camaraderie once again. After the general public and Les Brown's Band of Renown departed the vampires cleaned the tables and deposited their extra banquet food in the hearse and proceeded to drive back to Calgary for a good night's rest. While the vampires were driving back to Calgary a light mist is beginning to form on the windshield of the hearse. "Well, I guess any kind of weather is possible for September 3, 2017! Right?"

Chapter 73
Calgary State Fair

The Calgary State Fair will be held in Calgary, Canada, September 10 to September 15, 2017 which the vampires are getting anxious to attend since this will be their first time. The first activity on the agenda this year will be the annual Calgary State Fair Parade on September 10, 2017 at 5:00 PM on the main boulevard in downtown Calgary. Earl said, "I would like to enter our hearse and ourselves in the Calgary State Fair Parade this year since this will be our first time. What do you think?" Heston raised his hand saying, "I think it's a great idea! How about the rest of you?" Dean spoke up saying, "It sounds like a lot of fun! I'm all for it!" Chris made a remark, "We can also walk beside the hearse and hand out candy to the kids! How about that?" Sherman said, "I say, let's go for it!" That caused immediate laughter to break out among the vampires. Earl said, "In a few days we will have to start getting our hearse prepared for the parade since September 10, 2017 is next week Wednesday already. Anyone that is interested in helping decorate the hearse please meet in the driveway next week Tuesday afternoon at 1:00 PM. Thank you!"

Tuesday Afternoon

Today is perfect weather for the Calgary State Fair Parade. It is a balmy 75 degrees not a cloud in the sky and a great forecast. The vampire's entry number is 62 which puts them towards the end of the parade. The vampires gave the hearse a good cleaning, besides, posting signs on either side of the door for the viewer's pleasure. The vampires are up extra early this morning due to the fact that the Calgary State Fair Parade starts at 10:00 AM on the main boulevard in downtown Calgary. Lineup begins at 8:30 AM because of the numerous amount of entries that are expected. Earl and the vampires hurriedly ate breakfast, showered, shaved, dressed to the nines, flawless makeup, hair groomed to perfection, fresh manicures, etc…………..no capes are worn because of, possibly, being recognized by the Calgary Police Department. They can't afford to take that chance! The vampires also brought sacks of candy to be handed out to the children and general public while two of them are walking beside the hearse. At this point, the parade is slowly advancing down Main Street in Calgary with masses of people lining the thoroughfare for a glimpse of their favorite float. Numerous floats are preceding Earl and the vampire's hearse, since they are number 62, which is to the back of the parade. Earl and the vampires are waving, smiling and distributing candy to the throngs of onlookers viewing the parade site. By now, the vampire's hearse float is cruising in the business district of downtown Calgary where even larger crowds of parade watchers are congregated. The people are screaming, waving and smiling as the hearse passes by with Earl at the helm and Heston and Dean passing out candy to the public for their eating pleasure. Eventually, the parade route has reached the end of the floats, including the vampire's hearse, and all are dispersing in different directions.

The Ferris wheel Rides!

Tonight, for a change, Earl and the vampires parked the hearse at 2125 Melbourne Street and proceeded to the Calgary State Fair Grounds with several of their private cars. They ambled nonchalantly through the fairgrounds viewing the different booths while sampling eating delicacies to their desire and pleasure. Suddenly, Earl made a remark, "Who wants to take a ride on the Ferris wheel or Roller coaster? Speak up because I'm raring to go on both of them!" The vampires looked at each other, then at Earl, laughing and saying, "We're also raring to go! You pick the ride!" Everybody decided they would like to ride the Ferris wheel first and then the Roller Coaster! "Which ride did you say you would like to go on? Ha! Ha!" The vampires are hurriedly buying their Ferris wheel tickets for the next upcoming ride. The Ferris wheel is coming to a temporary halt as the passengers vacate their seats to let the vampires and the general public occupy them for the next ride. The vampires have positioned themselves in their Ferris wheel seats and are anxiously awaiting for their ride to begin. All of a sudden, they are smiling and saying, "Here we go! Wow! This is fun! How about a little faster?

C'mon!" While the Ferris wheel was twirling the vampires round and round accommodating music could be heard in the background for the rider's delight.

Chapter 74
Roller Coaster Rides

Finally the Ferris wheel is coming to a temporary halt again as the vampires and general public exit their seats for the next available passengers to occupy. The vampires are scampering to a smaller Roller Coaster ride which is located in a huge, open field adjacent to the Calgary State Fair grounds. They are quickly purchasing their tickets for the next available ride to come their way. At present the Roller Coaster is coming to a screeching halt as the passengers file out and the vampires file in adjusting their seat belts in the process. They can feel the movement of the Roller Coaster as it gains speed with the sound of music in the background again. The vampires are screaming, yelling and laughing as the Roller Coaster is going through the motions, at breakneck speed, much to the delight of the vampires. They are screeching, "Faster! Faster! Faster! Wow! This is the first time I've ever been in a Roller Coaster in my life!" Gradually, the Roller Coaster reduces its speed as it comes to a slow halt and eventually to a complete stop. The vampires leave the Roller Coaster as new passengers take their seat for an exhilarating ride much to their delight. The vampires and other people seem a little wobbly as they exit the Roller Coaster due to the impact of such a whirlwind ride only to regain their composure in a few minutes!

Fortune Tellers

As the vampires were strolling through the Calgary State Fair Grounds they decided on an impulse to have their fortune told by a group of gypsies that were labeled "fortune tellers." These are not the same "witches" that reside in the country outside of Calgary, Canada that the vampires were involved with. These are gypsies or fortune tellers that travel with the Calgary State Fair. The vampires approached the fortune tellers, one by one, handed them the money and proceeded to have their fortune told. As Dean was saying, "I was told, by looking at the palm of my hand, good luck is coming to me soon and I should wait patiently for the inevitable. How about the rest of you?" Heston said, "I was told the total opposite! I will have bad luck befall me sometime in the near future if I continue my present lifestyle as a vampire!" Earl said, "I was told I will eventually get married, father three children and discontinue my present lifestyle." Blair made the remark, "The fortune teller with the long, black, hair looked at the palm of my right hand and said, "I have bad news! You will experience a short life from the present time till the end. I'm sorry!" Chris also added to the conversation saying, "I was told I will experience a lifespan of several months before I succumb at the hands of strangers." The remainder of the vampires also had their fortunes told at the hands of gypsies with the same foreboding premonition. "What is your opinion? Have you ever been to a fortune teller? I haven't and I'm not ever going either!"By now, Earl and the vampires are worried sick at the outcome of the fortune teller's prediction. Heston said, "I wish I would never have had my fortune told! How accurate or inaccurate can the gypsies be?" The vampires continued touring the Calgary State Fair Grounds, as a group, but their heart wasn't in it. They all had a worried, depressed look on their facial countenance indicating the inevitable according to the gypsy fortune tellers. It is getting considerably darker and later as the hour nears 12:00 midnight prompting Earl and the vampires, plus Chris and Heston's cars, to transport the extra vampires back to their home at 2125 Melbourne Street. Actually, Earl and the vampires were also interested in, possibly, snatching a victim or two behind the fair tent as it grew darker and later in the evening. The vampires were not in the mood after their harrowing experience with the gypsy fortune tellers. At the present, they are all in their coffins, hopefully, for a good night's rest.

Back to the Calgary State Fair Grounds!

Since the State Fair will only be in Calgary for several more days Earl and the vampires decided to frequent the grounds one more time before they dismantle the rides, tents, etc…………… Also they will definitely keep their distance from the gypsy fortune tellers! As the vampires approached the Ferris wheel ticket booth they were told, "All tickets to the rides are two for the price of one" which suited the vampires just fine. Everybody took advantage of the slash in the prices saving them money to spend on other items such as games, food, etc............. Before they left the Calgary State Fair grounds for the evening they traipsed in the darker areas, namely, behind the variety of tents that were constructed for different activities for the pleasure of the general public. They immediately encountered a couple of middle aged men prowling in the area also while the vampires gave the impression of meandering nonchalantly behind the tents for no particular reason. Suddenly, they quickened their pace behind the middle aged men while grabbing them by their dirt infested, thick, weather beaten, necks. They ravenously and voraciously sucked their left, jugular vein, depleting it of volumes of crimson, savory, succulent blood to their heart's content. When Earl witnessed the inevitable he said, "I will quickly bring the hearse to the back of the tent to load the two stragglers you encountered since it is time to leave anyway." The vampires hurriedly loaded the two, disconnected stragglers into the hearse for the ride back to their home at 2125 Melbourne Street. "Well, at least they gained two more individuals to add to their household! Right?"

Chapter 75
Two New Stragglers

The vampires checked the two stragglers that they flung to the bottom of the stairs to lie there until 4:00 PM today. Evidently, they are still alive since they have been transported to their coffins where they will be monitored periodically. They have been in their respective coffins for several days now but will soon be emerging to join the vampire household. Their names are Richard Poller and Benjamin Crole. They joined the household for supper this evening, revealing their identity, plus their birthplace which is Calgary, Canada. Richard is 45, unmarried and a construction worker by trade. Benjamin is 43, unmarried and "jack of all trades." Earl asked, "Where have you, basically, been living all these years?" They replied, "On the streets. We have been eating discarded food out of restaurant receptacles for years and sleeping in parked cars in the winter. In the summer we sleep on the park benches and in the doorways of businesses in the back alleys. Once in a while we might meet another derelict that occupies a cheap apartment with a little money on hand but no desire to work and lead a productive life. Those types of people will invite us to their apartment to get cleaned up besides sharing a meal with them." Earl asked them, "Have either of you ever considered getting a job, pooling your money and, possibly, purchasing a cheap car to go back and forth to work?" They replied, "No, not really! We're happy and contented with the way everything is at the present moment." Earl asked them, "Are you willing to live the lifestyle that we are accustomed to which is the life of a vampire?" Richard and Benjamin were familiar with the lifestyle, by word of mouth, that Earl was referring to. They said, "Yes, we can try and blend in with your lifestyle and if things don't work out we can always revert to our old lifestyle. Right?" Earl replied, "That's absolutely correct!"

Poheta Cemetery Again?

Earl approached the vampires asking them, "Would any of you be interested in frequenting the Poheta Cemetery, in the event, there are intruders, stragglers or homeless people invading the cemetery?" All the vampires, plus Richard and Benjamin said, "Yes, we haven't been to Poheta Cemetery for about a month now and we are definitely interested in going back! Earl said, "Meet me at the hearse tomorrow night in the driveway at 5: 00 PM. The vampires said, "We'll be there!" The vampires are anxiously awaiting Earl's presence since he is the chauffeur of the hearse. At the present, they are entering the Poheta Cemetery Gates while strolling through the hallowed grounds in search of unwelcome visitors at this time of the day. They encountered four or five people in the cemetery at certain gravesites, meditating, oblivious of anyone around. The vampires approached two women, yanking their spindly, tanned, dirt infested necks to reach their left, jugular vein. They started sucking greedily and ravenously the crimson, savory, succulent blood that gushed forth volumes in the process. The women started screeching and screaming, "Please leave us alone! Who are you? Get away from us!" Richard and Benjamin also took their turn sucking the insatiable, fresh, flavorful, red blood saying, "This tastes better than I thought!" In the meantime, the two women continue lamenting their plight while spitting saliva into each vampire's face, hair and mouth that confronted them. Several vampires are sporting bloody, slimy spit dripping from the inevitable. At this point, Earl and the vampires have decided to take the two women back to their home with them at 2125 MelbourneStreet. Earl made the remark, "If these two women don't survive the impact of this horrendous attack on their person they will probably pass on. We will automatically suspend their corpses in the Death Chamber for reference at a later date. How does that sound?" The vampires said, "It sounds fine to us!"When they reached 2125 Melbourne Street they flung the two women's bodies to the bottom of the basement stairs to lie there until 4:00 PM the next afternoon. After both women were monitored the day after they were incoherent, unable to open their eyes, with a shallow breathing and very slow pulse. Earl said, "We will monitor both of them periodically as to their condition in the next several days."Three or four days passed with the cessation of life as it occurred on the fourth day when the vampires monitored their vital signs indicating no response, no breathing, etc............ no manifestation of life. The vampires immediately transferred their corpses to the Death Chamber where they were suspended from the ceiling to be used at a later date. A variety of corpses are suspended from the ceiling, at this point, but the coffins are totally empty. "What does this mean?" Even though fall and winter are soon approaching the vampires will need to transfer more bodies to their home for future holiday meals, private meals and birthdays etc…………..

Chapter 76
The Witches Return?

Chris decided to go on a vampire escapade in downtown Calgary this evening so he was asking, "Is anyone interested in frequenting the alleyways in the lower part of Calgary tonight since there aren't any interesting movies on television this evening?" The vampires were all smiles when they heard this saying, "We're raring to go! You name the time and we'll be waiting by the hearse!" Chris said, "How about 7:00 PM tonight?" The vampires said, "That sounds great! We'll see you then!"The vampires immediately started bathing, shaving, coiffuring their hair, dressing in their immaculate black suits, white shirts and black neck ties, no capes for fear of being recognized by the Calgary Police Department and their perfectly manicured, elongated fingernails. By this time Chris and the vampires have parked their vehicles in the reserved parking area adjacent to the downtown alleyways and are taking a slow, tedious walk towards the area. As the vampires are traipsing nonchalantly through the back alleys of the downtown business district they are observing a wide variety of homeless people, transients, vagrants, derelicts, etc............. They are frequenting the back alleys and loitering in between business buildings in search of a half smoked cigarette or several swallows of cheap wine. "What a life! Really!" By now, the evening was getting darker and darker as the vampires were meandering through the side streets while transients were rummaging through the trash receptacles in the back of the restaurants, fast food cafes, etc............ All of a sudden, the vampires decided to stroll in between the business buildings which they rarely do in search of anyone that meets their expectations. Instantly, they heard certain sounds they could associate with like a shrill, gibberish speech and a screeching, harsh form of laughter reminiscent of gypsies they encountered in the past. As they glanced down the cement path between the business buildings they caught a glimpse of a band of gypsies walking towards them with a devilish, daring look clouding their countenance. As they came closer Chris said, "There is no way we are going to get away from these gypsies. What are we going to do?" Dean said, "Possibly, we can try and squeeze past them, with luck, ignoring them in the process! Let's give it a try and hope it works!" At present, the vampires and gypsies are at eye level, glaring at each other, with the gypsies reaching for the vampire's necks of Chris and Dean. They are trying to embattle the gypsies, but to no avail, because they have the upper hand. The remainder of the vampires quickly scurried away while the gypsies sucked the left, jugular veins of Chris and Dean insatiably and horrendously until their bloated stomach's erupted spewing forth volumes of succulent, flavorful blood. There is no way the vampires can approach the gypsies because they will receive the same form of treatment. Since there is no way they could retrieve Chris and Dean the vampires left the scene departing in the hearse and private vehicles for their home at 2125 Melbourne Street. Another Loss?

At the present moment the vampires are privately lamenting and grieving the loss of Chris and Dean to the abduction of the gypsies. "What a shame! Can you imagine living with a band of gypsies?! Oh No!!! Maybe Chris and Dean can escape their clutches somehow! Let's keep them in our prayers. Right?"In the meantime, the remainder of the vampires are conniving and conspiring a plot, thereby, an attempt at rescuing Chris and Dean from the gypsy's entrapment. Got any suggestions?" Heston suggested, "Due to a former encounter with the gypsies is there a possibility we can raid their home in an attempt to release Chris and Dean from their captivity? Does anybody have any other suggestion? Please speak up! Time is of the essence!" Richard came forward expressing his opinion saying, "Another proposal would be to shackle the gypsies ankles or handcuff their wrists, therefore, making them unable to walk and move as readily. I observed a box of shackles and handcuffs in the storage room in the basement ready for disposal. While the gypsies are shackled and handcuffed we can free Chris and Dean! Any other ideas that have not crossed our minds?" Benjamin had another suggestion, "What would happen if we reported this abduction to the Calgary Police Department that our friends are being held hostage against their own will?" Heston, immediately, made the remark, 'The gypsies would probably report us to the Calgary Police Department as vampires and we would be arrested instantly!" All the vampires nodded their heads, simultaneously, in agreement with Heston's remark.Evidently, Earl will be the deciding factor in the aforementioned in regards to the encounter release of Chris and Dean from the grip of the gypsy's snare. He made the following statement, "I am interested in raiding the gypsy's residence out in the country some evening this week after dark. Is anyone willing to accommodate me on this trip? Please raise your hand." All the vampire's hands were raised in accord with Earl's proposal. He suggested leaving Wednesday evening at 6:00 PM, equipped with shackles and handcuffs if needed. Once again the vampires were in agreement with the date and time saying, "We'll be at the hearse at 6:00 PM." Earl laughed and said, "Thank you! I knew I could rely on all of you!"

Chapter 77
The Encounter Release

As usual, Wednesday night was a stone's throw away as the vampires waited patiently equipped with shackles and handcuffs, if necessary. The hearse will be accompanied by several of the vampire's private vehicles at their disposal. They arrived at the gypsies home in the hilly country, north of Calgary, Canada, parking in the darkened shadows of their residence. They coasted into the shadows with their vehicles, barely visible and audible as not to be heard by the gypsies. They instantly walked to the door banging and clanging, completely demolishing it, with boards and splinters scattered around loosely. The gypsies were screeching, screaming and crying in terror voicing gibberish words that were difficult to decipher as the vampires approached them with full force. They yanked them to and fro by their long hair while shackling their ankles and handcuffing their wrists in the process. After they had completed the inevitable they flung the gypsies down the basement stairs to fend for themselves while constantly yelling mercilessly at them. They hurriedly searched for Chris and Dean encountering them in a dark dungeon in another area of the basement chained against the wall. They were unable to move with barely any food to keep them alive with their emaciated, bodily frames on the verge of collapse. Their conversation was incoherent when the vampires spoke to them with a response of, "uh huh! Uh huh!" Since Chris and Dean were unable to walk they had to be carried to the hearse by the vampires for the trip back home. When they arrived at 2125 Melbourne Street they carried Chris and Dean into the basement, depositing them in their respective coffins, until they are able to walk again. The vampires are monitoring their condition periodically since the gypsies failed in all respect. "What a life."

The Next Day

The vampires monitored Chris and Dean this morning indicating no eye contact and very shallow breathing. This afternoon they made an attempt to introduce food into their bodies but to no avail. They gurgled and the food spewed out of their mouths in the form of vomit. Earl said, "Chris and Dean need to be seen by a doctor and I have one in mind. He is a vampire doctor that makes house calls and I have known him for years. I will call his office immediately. Earl returned in a few minutes saying, "Dr. King will be coming by on his way home this evening to do a routine check on Chris and Dean. I'm sure all they need is a prescription for medicine to bring them back to normal." Dr. King evaluated Chris and Dean saying, "These two men are extremely weak and emaciated for lack of food, water, sleep and exercise, plus, the unusual conditions their bodies were exposed to. I will order their prescription this evening to be picked up at the pharmacy tomorrow. Thank you!" Earl thanked Dr. King, likewise, while seeing him to the door.

Chapter 78
A Speedy Recovery

Earl and the vampires arose extra early this morning to monitor Chris and Dean's medical condition according to Dr. King's evaluation. Their medical status was the same as yesterday, no change. Earl said, "I will hurriedly drive to the pharmacy recommended by Dr. King for the prescription medicine. Earl departed immediately and was back in an hour because of the distance with the prescription medication. Chris and Dean were very receptive with their medication besides eating a small portion of soup to their liking. This was, probably, the first morsel of food Chris and Dean had consumed in days. "A sad situation!" Several days have passed with Chris and Dean gradually improving after Earl administered their medication on a daily basis. By now, they are able to walk to their good advantage partaking their meals with the vampires and slowly responding to their conversation. Earl said, "Eventually, they will be back to their former selves in no time." They are also able to view a movie with the vampires on television in the evenings before bedtime which is usually 10:00 PM. At the present time, Chris and Dean's speech has improved dramatically considering the torment they were subject to at the hands of the gypsies. They are very coherent identifying their counterparts and their present surroundings. This speaks well of Chris and Dean deliberating the aforementioned

Calgary's Fall Festival, October 2017

This is the first year the city of Calgary, Canada will be hosting a street fair October 18, 2017 through October 22, 2017 in downtown Calgary on the main boulevard. It will consist of slashed price sales in all the businesses, vendor's booths, music, games, auctions, etc………… The parade is scheduled to start October 17, 2017 at 5:00 PM with Earl and the vampires participating. They are planning on furnishing a vendor's booth with barbecued flesh sandwiches, potato chips, cold drinks, etc………….for the public's culinary pleasure and relaxation. It is the afternoon before the parade with Earl and the vampires dissecting one of the two women that passed away several month ago. They were unaccustomed to the wild, sucking rampage inflicted upon them by the vampires besides being suspended from the ceiling in the aftermath of their encounter. The vampires are assisting Earl in the process, besides, pre-barbecuing the fleshy chunks to be catered and sold as sandwiches in their vendor booth titled, "Calgary's Best barbecued Sandwiches! "How do you like the title?" Earl and the vampires said, "We love it!"

The Parade

The vampires are in the process of bathing, shaving, attired to the nines with their hair meticulously groomed, flawless makeup and perfectly elongated, manicured fingernails. They have loaded their cooking supplies in a private vehicle to be transferred to the vendor's booth, after the completion of the parade. At present, they are hurriedly positioning themselves in the hearse for the entry into the parade. They are at the beginning of the parade, number 15, with their vendor's signs posted on either side of their car advertising their Calgary's Best Barbecued Sandwiches. The vampires said, "We are going to be walking on either side of the car passing out candy to the children that line the parade route." The Calgary High School Band is following the vampire's hearse performing to the music titled, "The Star Spangled Banner." Numerous floats are coasting down the parade route with masses of onlookers lining the sidewalks and streets to get a glimpse of their favorite float. The parade watchers are cheering, yelling and screaming as the floats pass by with the occupants smiling and waving to their delight.

Calgary's Best Barbecued Sandwiches

Eventually, the parade came to an end with the vampires saying, "We are, hurriedly, transferring our cooking supplies to our vendor's booth located in the downtown area." The vampires are assisting Earl, manning the vendor's booth, since festival goers are lined up for the tasty, barbecued sandwiches on display accompanied by potato chips, soda, etc............. A slight mist is beginning to drape the festival grounds but the lines continue to form at "Calgary's Best Barbecued

Sandwiches" vendor's booth in spite of the weather. Festival goers are relaxing on wooden, park benches on the parade route covered with a canopy enjoying their "Best Barbecued Sandwich, the fresh air, etc............ Besides, the sandwiches they are also enjoying the camaraderie of their neighbors, friends, and relatives they have come in contact with today. Finally, the lines have begun to dwindle as most of the dinner and supper crowd have dispersed with some people bagging one, more, last sack of sandwiches to take along home. "Sounds like a good idea, doesn't it?"At this point, the mist is getting heavier giving the festival surroundings a wet, soaked appearance compared to the beginning of a bright, sunny day. The vampires are gathering their cooking supplies, etc............. and depositing them in the hearse for their ride back to their home at 2125 Melbourne Street. Earl made the remark, "I want to, personally, thank every one of you that assisted me in the work involved in the preparation and sale of the "Best Barbecued Sandwiches" because I couldn't have done it without you! Thank you, once again!" The vampires said, "Thank you, likewise!"

Chapter 79
The Retrieval of Joe and Ryan!

Earl mentioned to the vampires, "Is anyone interested in revisiting the Rest in Peace Cemetery since we haven't frequented that for a while. Please raise your hand!" The vampire's hands shot up immediately saying, "Several of us have been thinking about the Rest in Peace Cemetery and Mausoleum wondering why we haven't been back there for a while?" Earl laughed and said, "Well, we can only visit so many cemeteries, downtown back alley haunts, etc............ at a time. So, I guess it's time to pay a visit to the corpses at the Rest in Peace Cemetery, hopefully, for our personal pleasure. How about tomorrow night at 6:00 PM? Please come at the appointed time, equipped with our tools, in the event the doors are heavily sealed." The vampires replied, "We'll be waiting!"

The Next Night

The vampires were raring to go since they were lined up by the hearse equipped with the necessary tools indicated by Earl. Everybody positioned themselves in the hearse since it can accommodate nine people for the trip to the Rest in Peace Cemetery. After they arrived they immediately paraded through the cemetery gates in search of the mausoleum to their advantage. As they approached the door they noticed it was slightly ajar with a dim light emanating from within and an incoherent babble of voices blabbering continuously. The vampires recognized the mummies immediately as they rushed toward them in violent anger grabbing them by their yellow, filthy, withered necks for a quick, blood sucking rendezvous. The vampires fought the mummies to the very end as they lay sprawled on the mausoleum floor with blood seeping from the tape encasing their bodies. Strangely enough, two mummies were huddled against the wall glaring at the vampires in extreme fear because of the violent rendezvous that ensued. Earl was suspicious of them as he asked, "Are you Joe, the vampire?" The mummy nodded and smiled and Earl said, "Is this your friend, Ryan? Both of the mummies smiled and nodded again as they said, "Arg!

Arg! Arg!" Earl asked them, "Do you remember us?" They finally uttered, "Yes!" Earl said, "Tell me your names again," to which they replied, "Joe! Ryan! Ryan! Joe! Ryan! Joe!" without stopping. Earl said, "You might as well go along back with us because you belong to our Vampire Club! Let's go!"The vampires extinguished the lights in the mausoleum and locked the door letting the mummies fend for themselves. Everybody took their respective seats in the hearse as they made the trip back to their home. After arriving back they were transferred to their original coffins which they remembered for a good night's rest. Tomorrow, the mummies will remove the mummy tape they were confined in and live the life of a vampire as before.

Happy Halloween, October 31, 2017

This year the vampires decided to prepare a Halloween Banquet on Halloween night for themselves only in their private, dining area in the basement. Actually, the main entrée has already been established and is in readiness in the freezer. The vampires will be devouring the leftover "Calgary's Best Barbecued Sandwiches" from the vendor's booth at the Calgary State Fair several weeks ago. It will be accompanied by potato chips, rotten Cole slaw, peanut butter vomit ice cream and goblets of red, savory, succulent blood.After dining on the aforementioned they will be going "trick or treating" themselves to see whom they encounter in the dark, misty, creepy hours of the night. They will be among the masses of children canvassing the streets of Calgary for candy handouts to fill their bags.

Trick or Treat

The aforementioned, Halloween night, has taken place including the banquet etc………… which was enjoyed by everyone. The vampires enjoyed the "trick or treaters that stopped by giving them abundant amounts of candy they had on hand. The vampires decorated the inside and outside of the house for everyone's pleasure including their own. Instead of hanging a fake body on display outside they hung an actual dead corpse in the front yard for the public's viewing pleasure. "Do you want to take a look?" No? Why not?"Eventually, the vampires returned from their "trick or treat" vampire encounters with several people as they proceeded to answer the door! As they answered individually the vampires grabbed them by their necks, not to be seen, sucking their left, jugular vein ravenously until their victim collapsed to the floor or the vampire's stomachs were bloated whichever came first. As the vampires trudged home, their stomachs full, sporting a ton of candy a heavy mist was beginning to form on the surroundings. By this time it was 9:30 PM as the vampires congregated in the basement relating their stories regarding their vampire encounters with the general public. How about all the sacks of candy on display that the vampires accumulated in the process? Earl said, "These snacks will come in handy when we are watching our movies on television during the winter evenings. How about that?" The vampires smiled and said, "That's right! We wished we would've gotten more!" After the afore mentioned conversation Earl and the vampires were exceedingly tired from their Halloween rendezvous and decided to retire a little earlier than usual for the evening.

Chapter 80
An Informal Meeting

Earl and the vampires were gathered in the meeting room in the basement this afternoon for a short, informal discussion on a variety of activities including the upcoming Thanksgiving Banquet. It will be held November 23, 2017 in the Community Hall on the Calgary Fairgrounds with Earl and the vampires participating in the National Holiday Celebration. Also, on the short agenda Earl asked the vampires, "Would any of you be interested in frequenting the Calgary Roller Skating Rink some night this week before we begin our holiday preparations?" The vampires were giddy with glee as they remarked, "Yes, we would all be interested in a skating rendezvous at the Calgary Skating Rink since we haven't been there for a long time." Earl answered, "How about tomorrow night since there isn't anything interesting on television in regards to movies etc……….. The vampires smiled saying, "We're ready to go anytime you say!" Earl said, "Then it's settled! Meet me at the hearse tomorrow night at 6:00 PM for a fun night at the Calgary Skating Rink." A few other activities were reviewed for consideration at this time.

A Skating Rendezvous

The vampires are bathed, shaved, dressed accordingly, flawless makeup, hair perfectly groomed and manicured, elongated fingernails. They have eaten supper earlier and are waiting at the hearse patiently for Earl's appearance. Here comes Earl five minutes late with a valid excuse. He said, "I fell asleep unexpectedly and just woke up! Sorry! It won't happen again!" The vampires said, "That's ok! We're plenty on time!"Earl and the vampires were escorted by attendants to the department where they are fitted with roller skates, to their specification, since they haven't frequented the Calgary Skating Rink for quite a while. By now everybody has been fitted with their skates and is trying to balance themselves on the skating rink at the same time. The vampires can barely skate around the rink once without falling three times to the floor Earl included. At the present time groups of skaters are joining hands and skating in a semicircle and full circle to see if they can keep up with their counterparts. The vampires cannot keep their circle afloat since they are constantly falling to the floor. Since the circle has dissolved they are skating with each other to see if they can control their balance any better. Heston made the remark, "I just can't seem to control my stability. I believe it's because we don't patronize the roller skating rink enough like other people do. I'm sure some skaters come every week to sharpen their skating skills. What do you think?" Joe said, "I believe your right! I never was that good of a skater! That's why everybody is skating circles around us!" Ryan said, "I agree with your conversation wholeheartedly because I am on the floor oftener than I am standing up!"By this time it was 8:00 PM and time for the snack of a sandwich, potato chips and an ice cold bottle of soda to quench their first. After they completed their snack they were back on their roller skates again trying to skate and control their balance at the same time which is impossible for the vampires to accomplish.For the remainder of the evening the vampires continued to practice their skating skill to the best of their knowledge. Besides trying to skate they also relaxed, sharing camaraderie with their friends they became acquainted with on prior skating encounters.By now it is 9:45 PM and a few of the vampires have removed their skates in a quest for any available stragglers, homeless people or transients lurking inside or preferably outside behind the Calgary Skating Rink. If so they would be interested in a possible, blood sucking rendezvous if they encounter anyone sneaking or slinking in the background of the Skating Rink. Most of the vampires are in the process of exiting the skating rink headed towards the hearse for their ride back home. Ryan, Joe and Heston have other ideas in mind. At the present moment they are following three, middle aged men that are walking behind the skating rink looking for their car. One man said, "I was sure I parked the car in this immediate area but we can't seem to locate it. We'll just have to keep on looking!" In the meantime, Ryan, Heston and Joe were already sneaking up behind them. They grabbed each of the men by their scrawny, dirt infested, slimy necks, thrusting their white, gleaming, canine fangs into their left, jugular vein. Volumes of red, delicious, savory blood spurt forth with the vampires sucking horrendously and greedily all they could muster in the allotted time. After they completed their blood sucking escapade they hurriedly dragged their bodies to the hearse for the ride back to their home. After they arrived they flung the three bodies to the bottom of the basement stairs until the next day at 4:00 PM. This was the standard procedure ever since Albert was the first President of the Vampire Club. Tomorrow, the vampires will monitor the three skaters as to their condition. If they are not up to par they will be kept in their coffins until they are able to share their meals, and communicate on a regular basis while living the life of a vampire.

The Next Day

This afternoon at 4:00 PM the vampires monitored the three men they transported home from the Calgary Skating Rink. They were hungry, coherent and able to communicate with the vampires. After Earl explained the vampire life they would be exposed to the three men were in agreement with the inevitable existence they would be committed to. Earl asked them, "What are your names and where are you from?" One man said, "My name is Alvin Ribordy, 52, and I am from Calgary, Canada." The other man said, "My name is Bernard Groff, 54, and I'm also from Calgary, Canada." The other man said, "My name is Wilbur Kenney. I am 56 years old and I'm from Ontario, Canada." Earl asked, "Are any of you currently employed? If so, where?" Alvin said, "No, none of us are employed anywhere. We basically live off the streets, eat out of garbage receptacles behind restaurants and private residences, plus sleep in my car every night." Earl said, "Very well, I believe that answers all of my questions for the time being. Later on this afternoon after Chris, Ryan and I return from our jobs as morticians at the Ronton Mortuary, I will personally transport you to the Calgary Skating Rink to retrieve your vehicle." Alvin said, "I would sincerely appreciate that. Thank you!"

Chapter 81
Thanksgiving Banquet

November 23, 2017

Since Thanksgiving Day is fast approaching Earl and the vampires are busy this evening dissecting the other female corpse that was suspended from the ceiling in the Death Chamber. It will be presented as a free Thanksgiving Day Banquet, November 23, 2017, in the Community Hall on the Calgary Fairgrounds. Earl and the vampires will be coordinating the National Holiday Celebration. The dissecting procedure consists of slicing the corpses' body parts into one inch serving size pieces of human flesh to be barbecued in a savory barbecue sauce for the upcoming Thanksgiving Day Banquet. The vampires will be barbecuing the human flesh on a low setting starting later on tonight while being monitored during the night until morning. They are also preparing moldy, mashed potatoes, creamed crock pot corn, a vegetable salad laced with the joints of a dead rattlesnake, burnt bread, rotted vanilla pudding, vomit, cherry vanilla ice cream and goblets of crimson, insatiable, delicious blood. The vampires have been hurriedly preparing the above mentioned meal accompaniments this morning while others are preparing the banquet tables in expectation of a massive crowd of hungry, starved people. Volumes of people are filtering into the Community Hall for the free Thanksgiving Banquet at their disposal. The vampires are catering plates of food to the tables accompanied by goblets of fresh, red, delectable blood to the people's liking. Everyone, alike, shared camaraderie with their fellowmen and friends equally as they participated in the free meal set before them for their consumption. Before everyone left they thanked Earl and the vampires saying, "Thank you for the delicious, well prepared meal that you served today. May God Bless you!" Earl and the vampires shook hands with the general public saying, "Thank you! We were glad to oblige!" By the time Earl and the vampires completed their regular, cleaning job, loaded the remainder of the food and utensils into the hearse, besides taking care of other incidentals, etc………..it was dark and close to 6:OO PM when they carried their supplies into the house. They were all exceedingly tired after the day's activities, therefore, they ate a light supper, watched a little television and retired to their coffins at 8:00 PM for a night of slumber. "Goodnight everybody!"Christmas Decorations Already?

Earl and the vampires were sitting around the fireplace in the basement this evening discussing a variety of issues at hand. Earl made the remark, "This week we will be adorning the house, inside and outside, with Christmas decorations in the event the elements turn disagreeable. Is everybody in favor of that?"Heston spoke up for the remainder of the vampires saying, "That sounds great! Rather too early than too late because you can never guarantee the weather. We will start putting up the decorations in the house tomorrow, then gradually move outside." Earl said, "I'm glad to see that everyone is motivated to start early again this year, as usual, because of the weather conditions." The next morning after Earl, Chris and Ryan left for their jobs as morticians at the Ronton Mortuary the vampires started sorting through the Christmas decorations in the basement storage room. They are in the process of adorning the house, upstairs and downstairs, with a variety of Christmas trees, large Christmas wreaths, window candles, etc………. Since all of the vampires are helping, except Earl, Chris and Ryan, they completed the decoration project at the end of the day.

Adorning the Outside

The vampires arose bright and early this morning, with a light snow falling coating the yards, streets and surroundings etc…………. with its white glaze. They are in the process, once again, of embellishing the house with Christmas lights on the exterior, besides adorning the front yard with their annual Santa Claus on a Sled display led by several reindeer. They have also decorated several Christmas trees in the front yard with colored bulbs, ornaments, etc……….. Even though Christmas is still a month away the vampires have completed a major job concerning the Christmas decorations. Considering the above mentioned there is still more work to be completed. Christmas cards need to be addressed, private food preparations in order, several nights of shopping, etc…………. By now the vampires have taken a break in their Christmas activities to sit back, relax and enjoy their evenings consisting of Christmas music, food, nightly movies etc………… Lately, their movies are consistent with the Christmas season which should make it more interesting to view. "That sounds reasonable, doesn't it?"

Christmas Eve, December 24, 2017

"My how the time does fly!" The Christmas season is upon the vampires again. This evening is Christmas Eve with everyone congregating in the All Purpose room in the basement for the annual gift exchange, Christmas snacks, music and camaraderie. At present the vampires are opening their gifts which consist of neckties, socks, chocolates, men's cologne, gloves etc……….. You name it somebody has it! Earl purchased a variety of Christmas goodies to munch on for the vampires delight! "Wasn't that nice?" In the meantime soft, Christmas music is flowing in the background to accommodate the vampires. At 8:00 PM they watched a two hour Christmas movie which held their interest until they retired.

Merry Christmas, December 25, 2017

Christmas Day, December 25, 2017, has finally arrived. Earl and the vampires are reheating the barbecued, human flesh pieces that were left over from the Thanksgiving Banquet at the Community Hall on Thanksgiving Day, November 23, 2017. They accompanied the meal with rotted, baked potatoes, a moldy, vegetable salad, creamed peas, frozen bread, angel food cake laced with beetles crawling through the center of the cake and goblets of red, flavorful, succulent blood. Everybody ate to their heart's delight enjoying every morsel and the camaraderie that accompanied it. After the meal was completed they watched another Christmas movie until it was time to depart for a good night's rest. "Merry Christmas, everyone!"

Chapter 82
New Year's Day

January 1, 2018

Today the vampires are lying around the fireplace in the basement in a relaxed mood and quiet, lazy atmosphere as they banter back and forth in a camaraderie fashion. The weather outside is in a frightful stage as the announcer said, "A severe snow storm is predicted for the Calgary, Canada area. The snow depth will increase with fifteen inches of snow and pending by tomorrow morning. The wind velocity will elevate to forty miles an hour with blowing and drifting snow up to five feet in some areas and a temperature hovering at twenty two degrees. Emergency crews will be on duty all night so that traffic will be passable in the early morning hours. Isaac made the following remark, "I guess we have our work all cut out for us this week. We might as well start taking our turns shoveling tomorrow morning. Since there are usually three of us shoveling at one time I will submit my name too." Heston and Blair also offered to help with the shoveling process since all of them were more readily available than Earl, Chris and Ryan Heston, Blair and Isaac crawled out of their coffins, earlier than usual this morning to start their shoveling procedure for the day after a hearty breakfast. They shoveled for two hours retreating back into the house to warm up then back outside again to shovel some more. Heston, Blair and Isaac are forced to brave the elements, including five foot drifts, plus constant snow draping the landscape and environment while they are shoveling. Tomorrow it will be Joe, Alvin and Wilbur's turn for a full day of shoveling. The next day is Saturday and it will be Earl, Chris and Ryan's turn to shovel, and so on, until the sidewalks, driveway, etc………..are cleared of all snow.

Calgary Ski Resort

At supper this evening Chris asked the vampires, "Would any of you be interested in frequenting the Calgary Ski Resort next week Wednesday when Earl, Ryan and myself would be able to participate? Remember we are not employed on Wednesdays." The vampires were ecstatic saying, "We would be very interested in visiting the Calgary Ski Resort again since it has been about a year since we've been back there. We wonder if any of our friends are still frequenting the Ski Resort. Chris said, "Very well! I will schedule a skiing session for this coming Wednesday afternoon from 1: 00 PM till 6:00 PM. Is everybody in agreement with the aforesaid?" The vampires smiled, nodded and said, "We're raring to go and we'll be at the hearse at the appointed time of 12:15 PM.

Wednesday Afternoon

The vampires are patiently waiting with their sleds for Earl to chauffeur them to the Calgary Ski Resort for an afternoon of skiing down the slippery slopes. They are in anticipation of meeting their skiing friends once again for a fun filled afternoon of sharing their camaraderie, plus hopefully, displaying their skiing expertise they have acquired these last several years! Here comes Earl carrying a sled saying, "It looks like everybody is raring to go, including myself. Please grab a seat in the hearse since we are ready to leave." By now everyone is positioned in the hearse besides Heston and Blair's vehicles to accommodate all of the vampires to the Calgary Ski Resort. At this point they have reached the ski resort and are tolerantly awaiting their turn to glide down the snow laden incline to the base of the slope racing against their counterparts and time. Once again their counterparts were their friends they became acquainted with last year and were looking forward to seeing again this afternoon. Finally the vampires, Heston and Joe, are getting positioned on the sled to race against their friends to see which sled will reach the base of the snowy slope first. As soon as the racing flag was lowered both sleds took off at breakneck speed as they glided toward the snowy, slanted surface expecting to win the race immediately. Which they did!!! The vampires won the first race of the afternoon against their friends but it won't be the last. "What do you think?" This time Earl and Chris decided to take their friends on in another race down the snowy, slippery slopes to see who will be the winner this time! Actually Earl and Chris won this race, also, by a long shot! "How fortunate can you get?" Chris made the remark, "We're starting out with a good record this afternoon! I hope we can keep on winning all day. Marvin and Mitchell made a comment, "Surely, we will beat them racing, at least seven times yet, before the afternoon is over. I hope so!" The vampires smiled and said, "It's a long afternoon! We have lots of chances yet!" In spite of Earl, Chris and the vampire's upbeat conversation in regards to their abilities their new acquaintances, likewise, are having the same discourse about their sledding expertise. One of the new vampires, Marlow, made the remark, "I think we are capable of beating them more times that they can beat us because we are experienced at sledding since we patronize the Calgary Ski Resort oftener than they do! That tells you something right there, doesn't it?" The other new vampires said, "Of course! We get the impression that they have not frequented the Calgary Ski Resort as often as we have!" Roger, one of the newer vampires, also said, "Let's approach them for another sledding race since we are all fired up and ready to go!"Lunch Time!After both vampire parties shared a lunch together they decided to embark on another sledding venture racing each other down the snowy, encrusted, slick, slope toward the base of the hill determining a winner once more. Both parties are in agreement and are climbing on their sleds respectively. Once again the racing flag was lowered with both parties taking off, side by side, with the new acquaintance vampires leading the race by a large margin. The new acquaintance vampires reached the base of the hill, basically, the finish line in advance of their counterparts to be declared the winner for the first time. Within fifteen minutes both vampire parties are racing each other again to the finish line to see what the outcome will be. The vampires are in the lead but the new acquaintance vampires are gaining speed and slowly passing them to win this race also. So far, the vampires have won two races and the new acquaintance vampires have also won two races. At the present moment both parties are taking a breather deciding which two will be seated on the sled for the next race. By now, both parties have selected the two racers that will accompany their sled to the finish line again. The vampire's two racers are Alvin and Bernard relatively new to the Vampire Club. The new acquaintance vampire's two racers that will accompany their sled are Richard and Gorman. Everybody is raring to go as the flag is lowered and the sleds are sliding down the slope at top speed, neck and neck, with the new acquaintance vampires leading again by quite a large margin. The new acquaintance vampires reached the finish line and we're declared the winners again. Both Vampire Clubs are taking a break while feasting on a snack before they resume their racing schedule again. The vampires are seated respectively in their sledding seats for the next four races they will compete in against each other. At this point the remainder of the races are being completed with the new acquaintance vampires winning a total of seven races and Earl's Vampire Club won a total of two races. Too bad!!! It seems like the vampires need to practice their sledding expertise repeatedly at the Calgary Ski Resort instead of just "on occasion."Earl and the vampires were upset and disgruntled on the trip back to Calgary with Chris saying, "We need to frequent Calgary Ski Resort oftener so that we can sharpen our sledding abilities to compete with our new found acquaintances. Right?" The vampires agreed wholeheartedly saying, "You bet!!!"

Chapter 83
Blood Sucking Escapade—Ronton Mortuary?

Since Earl, Chris and Ryan are morticians at the Ronton Mortuary they have access to a variety of activities that are ongoing at the mortuary. People have different funeral options to choose from, the standard embalming procedure, the normal method of (no-embalming) in which the blood is retained in the veins etc............ After supper this evening Earl, Chris and Ryan were discussing a variety of issues incorporating different subjects at the table. All of a sudden a little information entered Earl's mind which he forgot to mention to the vampires. He commented, "Incidentally, is anyone interested in a blood sucking rendezvous at an establishment not too far from here, no work involved and no transportation of bodies back to the house?" The vampires said, "Where would we have access to such a fortunate experience?" Earl remarked, "The Ronton Mortuary where Chris, Ryan and I are employed as morticians. At the present moment there are a large variety of corpses,' in various stages, not embalmed at the request of the family, reserved for final preparations prior to the funeral service. After you have completed your blood sucking rampage, at my request please clean any bloody particles on the corpse and immediate area. Is that understood?" The vampires smiled, nodded and said, "Which is the first evening available?" Earl remarked, "Friday night is the first evening available for this week at 7:00 PM. I will be at the back door entrance to escort you to the non-embalming room. Are there any questions?" Isaac asked, "Will the other morticians examine the bodies in regards to the non-embalming procedure involved?" Earl said, "No that will not be a problem. Thank you!"

Ronton Mortuary Escapade

Earl made arrangements for the vampires to meet him at the hearse at 7:00 PM this coming Friday night. He escorted them to the non-embalming room where a variety of corpses at the request of the families have not been embalmed. Their blood lies dormant in their veins for the vampire's pleasure. The corpses' are lying on bare, cement slabs, fully clothed, meticulously coiffed and manicured with a morbid atmosphere enveloping their surroundings. Each vampire singled a corpse, grabbing them by their yellow, withered, scrawny necks as they sucked their left, jugular vein ravenously and voraciously. This, in return, released volumes of red, succulent, savory, delicious blood for their personal desire. After the vampires completed their blood sucking rendezvous Earl transported them back to their residence at 2125 Melbourne Street. Earl asked them, "Did this encounter meet your expectations this evening?" The vampires remarked, "This was a rewarding experience with all of us interested in going again sometime in the near future if that's possible?" Earl said, "That's a strong possibility! I will inform you if that can be arranged. Thank you!"

Calgary Ski Resort Again?

Ryan asked the vampires at supper this evening, "Are any of you interested in a fun day at the Calgary Ski Resort this coming Friday?" The vampires laughed and said, "We are anxious and excited to go to the Calgary Ski Resort again to compete with our new acquaintance vampire friends in our sled races similar to last week. Since they defeated us in seven sled races we would like to reciprocate the favor! How about that? Ha! Ha! Ha!" Ryan said, "Very well! I will schedule a sledding session at the Calgary Ski Resort this coming Friday at 1:00 PM. Please meet me by the hearse at 12:15 PM." The vampires shouted with glee, "We'll be there with bells on! Ha! Ha!" When the vampires arose, later than usual this morning, they were greeted with a light snow that is beginning to infiltrate the yards, sidewalks and surroundings. Several of the vampires started shoveling this morning already to avoid an accumulation of snow for the days ahead. At the present moment the snow appears to increase including depth and wind velocity with Ryan asking the vampires, "Are you interested in having me cancel your sledding session due to the weather and reschedule another appointment for next week?" The vampires said, "No, this current sledding session will be fine. No one knows how the weather will be next week at this time!" Ryan said, "Very well. Our activity will proceed as directed! By this time the snowfall has receded and the velocity of the wind has decreased in strength making it easier for the vampires to defeat their counterparts in the sledding session scheduled for 1:00 PM this afternoon.

Yes, Calgary Ski Resort Again!

As soon as Ryan and the vampires entered the Calgary Ski Resort their new found vampire friends approached them saying, "We are seriously planning on defeating your Vampire Club again today in our sledding session the same as last week. No offense! Those are just the standards our Vampire Club lives by! Ryan and the vampires remarked, "That's okay! We know there was no offense intended! We are in the same position as yourselves. Since you defeated us last week it would be nice if we were to defeat you this afternoon, likewise! Because, then we would be even. Their new found vampire friends laughed and said, "We'll see" and walked towards their sled in preparation for the race. When the racing flag was dropped both sleds shot out of position as they raced against each other over the thick, white, flaky slope towards the base of the hill which is the finish line. Their new found vampire friends won this sledding race also while saying, "We weren't expecting to win this race because of the white, thick, flaky snow covering the track. Ryan made the comment to their new found vampire friends saying, "We're in for the long haul! We will compete against you for a total of nine races the same as last week to see who comes out the winner!" They continued racing intermittently against each other for the remainder of the afternoon. The results were: Their new found vampire friends—six wins and three losses! Ryan and the vampire's three wins and six losses! "What a shame! Ryan and the vampires lost again!"While Ryan was chauffeuring the vampires back to their residence he was obvious of a saddened, depressed atmosphere clouding the inside of the hearse with the vampires practically fighting back tears at the outcome of today's race. He remarked, "We need to have a brighter outlook on today's consequences regarding the race. We still have seven races to compete in regarding the final tally. Keep hoping and keep praying! Thank you for your perseverance!"

Chapter 84
Is There Any Interest?

Chris is aware of Valentine's Day drawing near as he approaches the vampires with the following question, "Would any of you be interested in hosting a Valentine's Day Banquet with a Valentine card exchange as a prerequisite for a free meal? If so I will need assistance, as usual, in the preparation of the dissection of the remainder of the corpses' suspended from the Death Chamber ceiling. Please raise your hand if you are interested." All the vampire's hands were extended immediately in favor of the aforesaid. Blair remarked," Let us know what day the dissection process will begin and we will be at your assistance." Chris commented, "Probably, February 13, 2018 the day before Valentine's Day. I will inform you when we get closer to the actual date. Thank you!" After the Valentine's Day Banquet has been completed all the Valentine cards will be distributed, at random, knowing whose card you will receive for your personal pleasure because there will be a signature required. "Sounds interesting, doesn't it?"An orchestra, Les Brown's Band of Renown, will accompany the banquet and card exchange with their beautiful, soothing, background music suitable for the occasion.

A Valentine's Day Banquet!

Chris, Earl, Ryan and the vampires are hurriedly making preparations today for the Valentine's Day Banquet to be hosted by themselves. At this time they are all assisting in the dissection procedure of a male corpse that was suspended from the Death Chamber ceiling. The vampires are diligently chopping numerous, one inch cubes of human flesh to be grilled and barbecued. They will be the main entree' to be consumed at the Valentine's Day Banquet accompanied by a variety of other delicacies. The remainder of the meal has been prepared and refrigerated until the day of the banquet. The vampires have arisen bright and early in preparation of the Valentine's Day Banquet hosted by themselves in the Community Hall at the Calgary Fairgrounds at

11:30AM. They have transported the main entree' and the balance of the meal to complete their cooking process to the kitchen of the Community Hall. In the meantime the vampires are busy adorning the dining tables suitably for the elaborate Valentine's Day Banquet that the general public will be devouring voraciously. People are beginning to filter into the Community Hall before 11:30AM, at breakneck speed, to partake of the scrumptious banquet that will be presented to them on this special occasion. The vampire waiters are distributing the main entrée, plus, the balance of the meal in various areas of the dining tables for everyone's access. The main entree' consists of chunks of human flesh, grilled and barbecued, plus, slimy, scalloped potatoes, rotted, moldy carrots, mushy bread, a vegetable salad laced with spiders, vomit vanilla ice cream and goblets of crimson, delectable, savory, succulent blood to complete their meal. After the meal was finished they immediately delivered the Valentine cards to everyone in attendance for their personal gratification. Everyone continued visiting remarking about the fabulous banquet they consumed and sharing in the camaraderie with their friends and relatives. In the meantime the Les Brown, Band of Renown is continuing to serenade the general public with their variety of soothing melodies they are known for. Dusk is fast approaching as those in attendance are beginning to leave the Community Hall thanking the vampires for the meal and returning to their means of transportation. The vampires are also cleaning and depositing left over food to the hearse etc…………..for the trip back to their residence at 2125 Melbourne Street. Chris commented, "I would like to thank everyone that participated at the meal site this evening. It was greatly appreciated. As usual, we couldn't have done it without you!"

Running Out of Corpses?

Several weeks have passed with the vampires going about their daily business of their household chores, etc……… In the evenings they watch the current movies that are displayed on the Calgary Television Station for their viewing enjoyment accompanied by a snack and a bottle of delicious, succulent, savory blood for their taste buds. This evening Earl suggested, "Would anyone be interested in frequenting the Poheta Cemetery since we haven't been there in quite a while? Please raise your hand!" All hands shot up in regards to the suggestion with Blair saying, "We remember visiting the Poheta Mausoleum for a blood sucking rendezvous on the corpses in the caskets. It was such a memorable time. Will the upcoming trip be similar to the other one?" Earl said, "Yes, this trip will be the same as the one before. We will be paying a call to the mausoleum, besides, unearthing a grave or two for our personal pleasure. We might even transport a corpse or two back home because we are running out of extra bodies for future banquets, events," etc………….. Blair mentioned, "What evening and time did you have in mind?" Earl remarked, "How about Thursday evening at 5:00 PM? The vampires remarked, "We will be waiting by the hearse at the appointed time! Thank you!"

Thursday Night

March 12, 2018

The vampires were waiting eagerly for Earl to appear at 5:00 PM for their "blood sucking encounter" at the Poheta Cemeteryand Mausoleum. Here comes Earl, raring to go, with the vampires piling into the hearse for a swift ride to the Poheta Cemetery! The vampires are traipsing through the Poheta Cemetery headed towards the mausoleum. They came equipped with tools in the event the mausoleum door was locked. As soon as they inserted the tool in the lock the door crept open exposing layers of caskets stacked four high lined up against the mausoleum walls. Earl and Ryan lifted several caskets to the floor pried the lids open and feasted on their left, jugular vein with volumes of red, savory, bloody liquid gushing forth. Earl and Ryan sucked violently and horrendously while slurping and smacking their lips in regards to the bloody flavor. The remainder of the vampires took their turn with a corpse, yanking them out of the casket, for a blood sucking rendezvous to their heart's content. After they were finished they deposited their frail, withered, emaciated frames back into the coffin. By now the vampires are strolling nonchalantly out the door as if nothing had transpired.

Unearthing a Grave!

March 12, 2018

At present the vampires are in the process of unearthing a grave that Earl, Chris and Ryan, morticians at the Ronton Mortuary are familiar with saying, "This body has not been embalmed because we were present at the final preparations." Since it is quite dark the vampires are shoveling furtively, as not to be seen, to the bottom of the grave. They are clamoring and banging on the casket lid as it slowly creeps open emitting a foul, rancid, vile odor, permeating the air. They are not interested in another blood sucking rendezvous because of their prior encounter at the Poheta Mausoleum this evening. But they are interested in transporting a corpse back home to be deposited in a casket or suspended from the ceiling in the Death Chamber to be used at a future date for an upcoming banquet, event, etc............, Someway the vampires were able to hoist the corpse up the grave and to the hearse for the trip back to Calgary. They shoveled the grave back up, smoothing the outer soil and hurriedly left the Poheta Cemetery for Calgary, Canada. When they arrived back they suspended the corpse's body from the ceiling in the Death Chamber. By this time, the vampires were exhausted and retired for the night immediately after supper. "Goodnight, everybody!"

Chapter 85
Roller Skating Anyone?

After supper this evening mild discussion ensued with Chris asking, "Is anybody interested in frequenting the Calgary Roller Skating Rink? Please speak up!" Heston decided to speak for the remainder of the vampires saying, "We would all be delighted to go for a change since we haven't been to the roller skating rink for quite some time. You set the day and time and we'll be at the hearse!" Chris said, "How about tomorrow night at 6:O0 PM at the Calgary Indoor Roller Rink?" The vampires nodded and smiled saying, "Sounds great!" The vampires were waiting by the hearse at 6:00 PM for their ride to the Calgary Indoor Roller Rink. When they arrived they immediately were fitted with their roller skates while conversing with their roller skating friends whom they encountered. The vampires were more adapt at maneuvering themselves on their roller skates this evening than they were last time. When they stood up they were able to skate, to and fro,, back and forth, in a circle with each other and single file without falling to the floor. They were even able to keep up with the tempo of the accompanying music hither and yon.The vampires and their friends took a break for a snack and an ice cold drink, to quench their thirst and then back to the roller rink again. Several of the vampires went outside after their break in the refreshing, cool breeze and stood behind the roller rink to see whom they could approach for a blood sucking rendezvous. All of a sudden two, young women came shuffling by in an indiscreet manner oblivious of the vampires in their presence. Blair stepped up to them quickly, grabbing the women's left, jugular vein, sucking voraciously and vehemently until it was depleted of its blood supply. Heston encountered the other woman, in the same manner, for his share of the ample blood supply that was still available in this case. In the meantime, both women were screeching and crying hysterically at the outcome of this encounter. They kept repeating, "Help! Help! Leave us alone! Who are you? Get away from us! Somebody, help us, please!" After a few minutes lapsed the bloody rendezvous ceased and the victims collapsed at Blair and Isaac's feet. They swiftly deposited their bodies in the back of the hearse for the ride back to their home. When they arrived back they flung their bodies down the basement stairs where they will lie until tomorrow afternoon at 4:00 PM. After that they will monitor them periodically to see if they qualify for the coffin or if they will have passed on to be suspended from the ceiling in the Death Chamber. "Time will tell!"After the ongoing activity had subsided Heston made the remark, "It seems like the back of the Calgary Roller Skating Rink is the ideal area to encounter victims for our blood sucking passion. What is your opinion, Blair?" Blair answered, "You're absolutely correct! It seems like, I remember, an encounter of this nature previously. Evidently a wide variety of the younger crowd stroll at random behind the roller rink in between sessionsor at intermission time to get a breath of fresh air. Heston commented, "Basically, every time we frequent the roller rink we have to keep this in mind in regards to the inevitable." Blair said, "That's right! We need to inform Earl, Chris and Ryan and the remainder of the vampires where this encounter transpired." We definitely need to keep patronizing the Calgary Roller Skating Rink to improve our skating expertise and supply our blood sucking demands.

Where are the Two Women?

At this point both of the women were confined to a coffin with their eyes closed, their lids barely fluttering, breathing sporadically and rambling incoherently. The vampires are making an attempt to force feed them but to no avail. The food either rolls out of their mouths or they regurgitate. As the evening draws nigh the vampires monitor the two women again checking their vital signs for any unusual or abnormal reports or findings in regards to their condition. Earl made the following remark to the vampires, "I am referring to the two women that we deposited in their respective coffins two days ago. Their vital signs are diminishing, therefore, cessation of life is imminent. Several hours later both women passed away and were automatically suspended from the ceiling in the Death Chamber to be dissected for future banquets, events, etc…………

Chapter 86
An Easter Banquet and Hunt

The vampires are in the process of conducting a Vampire Club meeting in regards to a variety of issues including an Easter Banquet at the Community Hall on the Calgary Fairgrounds and an Easter Egg Hunt adjacent to the immediate area. The date will be Easter Sunday, April 15, 2018 at 11:30 AM for the banquet followed by the Easter Egg Hunt at 3:00 PM. The above mentioned are free and open to the public. Further advertisements will precede the actual event and are forth coming. Earl has reserved the Community Hall today for the upcoming event plus the immediate area for the Easter Egg Hunt. At present the vampires are in the basement kitchen assisting Earl in the dissection of the female corpse that was suspended from the ceiling in the Death Chamber. They are busy cutting a large amount of one inch cubes of human flesh to be baked similar to a traditional, glazed ham, accompanied by mashed potatoes, laced with bloody eyeballs, white, watery gravy, chunky, glazed carrots, a vegetable salad with numerous ants scattered throughout, extremely, hot, rotted dinner rolls, slimy chocolate pudding, a vanilla cake with a vomit center and goblets of red, delicious, insatiable, scrumptious blood. The balance of this meal has been prepared and preserved in the freezer in advance of Easter Sunday. Earl and the vampires have jumped out of their coffins this morning at the rising of the sun for the ongoing preparations that it entails for the Easter Banquet to be held at the Community Hall on the Calgary Fairgrounds followed by an Easter Egg Hunt in the proximity of the Community Hall. The vampires have purchased dozens of plastic eggs filling them with a variety of candy to the delight of the youngsters. At this time they are in the process of transporting the main entree' and the remainder of the banquet meal to the Community Hall kitchen. The vampires are keeping busy arranging the banquet tables which incorporate the seating capacity besides tending to the general public which has already started filing into the hall. They are currently taking their places at various tables while the vampire waiters are distributing platters of food to their liking. At the present moment the vampires are getting a wide variety of comments in regards to the Easter Banquet presented before them. Mr. Jones remarked, "This is the best entree' and meal I have ever eaten at Easter time." Mrs. Jones also remarked, "You can say that again! This meal is scrumptious!" At the end of the table Mr. Holland commented," I have eaten many Easter meals over the years, but this is the best one yet, considering the complete meal." Mrs. Holland also commented, "I love the entree' and the variety of the meal which is something to satisfy everybody's craving."At the next table, several people were asking, "Who may I ask, prepared this Easter Banquet or was it catered?" The vampires said, "The President of our Club prepared the main entree' and the remainder of the club members made the preparations for the balance of the meal." A variety of people remarked, "This is a fantastic, remarkable meal, even though it was prepared at home and transferred to the Community Hall. Please relate to your main chef and assistants, "Congratulations" on such a great meal! "Thank You!"The vampires said, "thank you" knowing that most of the general public that participated in the "free meals" originally were vampires themselves. They were adjusted to the types of food and the preparation set before them. After the meal was completed everyone hurriedly watched the younger children hunt for Easter eggs filled with candy to complete their day. They scurried around to and fro, looking in tall grass and weeds, behind buildings, etc…………. carrying their already, half filled, baskets intended for more. When the Easter Egg Hunt was completed everyone was sharing and devouring their candy smacking their lips and displaying their camaraderie with anyone that was within distance. "At the end of the day, everyone departed the Calgary Fairgrounds with a full stomach, a happy heart and a basket full of candy!"

A Complete Rest

Earl and the vampires are taking a week's rest, starting today, from a whirlwind of activities they have been exposed to. Actually they are running behind on their household chores such as laundry, cleaning, vacuuming, etc…………. There large lawn needs to be mowed again, plus, the hearse needs to be washed and cleaned. Chris made a comment, "Everyone will be taking their turn on the household chores and the outside jobs that need to be taken care of. Is that clearly understood?" The vampires nodded and said, "Yes!" Their daily meals will come easy to the vampires because they will be feasting on the left over banquet meal that was not consumed by the general public. "Sounds good, doesn't it? No work involved!"Since the vampires have a lot of work that needs to be completed they are arising earlier than usual to get caught up on their chores. They eat breakfast together as a group at 8:00 AM in the morning. After that they disperse in different directions to tackle the chores they were assigned to complete. In the evenings there at liberty to view a television movie as a group before reclining for a peaceful night of sleep.

Chapter 87
The Alleyway Haunts

For years dating back to the time Albert was President of the Vampire Club they usually arose at 4:00 PM in the afternoon. Anymore they arise for the day in accordance with the chores that are scheduled for them. After the chores are completed their time is their own to do as they wish. This morning Heston suggested, "Is anyone interested in a nighttime haunt in the downtown alleyways some evening in the near future? We haven't canvassed the area completely yet because we were strolling, at random, through the alleyways between the business buildings." The vampires, as usual, were interested in another "Alleyway Haunt" to see whom they could encounter. There was always a variety of homeless people, derelicts, vagrants, social outcasts, etc............ in the proximity of the alleys, themselves. The vampires asked Heston, "What night did you have in mind for the "Alleyway Haunt?" Heston remarked, "How about tomorrow night at 8:00 PM? Please meet me at the hearse at 7:15 PM." The vampires said, "We'll be there!"

The Next Night

The vampires were raring to go and congregated at the hearse awaiting Earl's appearance. Here comes Earl, all smiles, as he motions for the vampires to climb into the hearse for their trip downtown. The evening was warm and balmy with a soft breeze rustling the trees, bushes, etc............ Since flowers were in bloom a fresh, sweet fragrance wafted through the air accompanied by a gentle, pleasant wind. As soon as Earl parked the hearse the vampires scattered in a variety of directions headed for the alleyways between the business buildings. They were anxious to see whom they could approach for a good old fashioned blood sucking rendezvous. There were numerous transients in the downtown area this evening because of the accommodating weather and the camaraderie they shared with other transients of the same caliber. Joe and Alvin traipsed nonchalantly through the alleyways between the business buildings with the only access to lighting at the end of the building. They encountered a man and woman meandering down the alley as they picked up speed to engage them in an escapade. Alvin commented, "Our chances look pretty good this evening since we are getting closer to them and they are unaware of us because of the slow gait they are walking. What do you think, Joe?" Joe agreed saying, "I believe you are absolutely correct, Alvin, because of their style and manner in which they are walking. They are taking a high risk!"As the vampires neared their victims they reached out and clutched their filthy, weathered, oily necks as they screeched and screamed in pain and fear, lamenting, "Who are you? Where do you come from? Help! Help! Leave us alone! What do you want? Money?" They threw a handful of bills toward Joe and Alvin which they grabbed greedily. They started sucking their victims left, jugular vein hungrily as volumes of blood gushed forth. They slurped their crimson, delectable, savory blood viciously and horrendously as they savored every drop that flowed from their left, jugular vein. After Joe and Alvin had completed their sucking sensation they noticed their victims collapsing at their feet, amidst the blood, dirt, etc............ in the alley. Since most of the transients have dispersed, amidst an unusually dark night, Joe and Alvin were able to transport their bodies to the hearse more readily. By this time the remainder of the vampires had congregated there for their trip to their home at 2125 Melbourne Street. When they arrived back they flung their bodies down the basement steps to lie there until 4:00 PM the next afternoon. After that they will monitor them intermittently as to their medical condition on a daily basis.

A Cessation of Life

The man and woman that were transferred back last night from the "Alleyway Haunt" are as follows: The man opened his eyes and is in good shape considering the violent escapade that he and his wife endured at the hands of the vampires. He has spoken several phrases but she has yet to breathe a word. At the present moment she is in the throes of yielding her life at the vampires will. Her condition leaves a lot to be desired since she has neither opened her eyes nor been able to breathe to stay alive. Her pulse is low and has almost stopped several times. Cessation of life is imminent. When the vampires monitored them this evening the man was able to eat supper but his wife had passed away sometime in the afternoon. Immediately the vampires transferred her to the Death Chamber where they hoisted her corpse to the ceiling to be suspended there indefinitely for future banquets, events, etc……… At suppertime the vampires made an attempt to incorporate the male victim into the conversation at the table. Earl said, "What is your name and where are you from?" He answered, "My name is Roman Boron and my wife's name is Gloria Boron. We are both from Calgary, Canada." Earl continued, "How old are you?" Roman said, "I am sixty two years old and my wife is sixty years old." Earl asked, "Are you and your wife currently employed here in Calgary?" Roman said, "Yes, I work at the Steele Manufacturing Plant here in Calgary and my wife is a nurse at the Calgary Regional Medical Center. Earl said, "Are there any children involved?" Roman said, "Yes, we have a son that is thirty years old and our daughter is twenty eight years old." Earl remarked, "Very well! This is just a routine interview. Nothing to get alarmed about!" Earl explained the nature and circumstances of the vampire's lifestyle and what Roman would be exposed to which he was in agreement with. Earl asked him, "Are there any questions involved on your part?" Roman politely said, "No."

Chapter 88
Memorial Day

Memorial Day, May 30, 2018, is here. The vampires are not having their usual free, holiday banquet this year like they ordinarily do. Instead Earl Chris, Ryan and the remainder of the vampires are going to the Calgary Steak House for a good old fashioned steak and all the trimmings. "How does that sound? Great!" At the present, the vampires are bathed, shaved and dressed to the nines in their black tuxedos, white shirts and black ties. Their hair are perfectly coiffed and their nails most recently manicured. Their makeup is flawless as usual. They are the epitome of good looks! Earl is chauffeuring the vampires in the hearse while the remainder of them are being transported to the restaurant by the vehicles of two other vampires. At this point in time all the vampires are browsing through the menu, but actually, their minds were already made up the minute they walked into the Calgary Steak House. They each ordered a large, well done steak with all the trimmings which consisted of a baked potato, vegetables, bread, several salads, chocolate cake with vanilla ice cream and goblets of red, flavorful, tasty blood. "Sounds delicious!" Since the vampires reserved a semi-private room for three different groups they were also serenaded by a live orchestra, the Les Brown, Band of Renown. Dancing was also available for those that cared to participate. A delicious, scrumptious meal and camaraderie was enjoyed by everyone present with Earl making the remark, "We'll have to do this oftener." The vampires smiled and nodded in agreement saying, "Now, don't forget that, Earl!" After the vampires arrived back at their home some of them decided to play a game of checkers, billiards, etc............. Some of the vampires took a nap and some viewed a Memorial Day program on television. "Anything to pass the time!" No one ate much supper because they were still full from dinner. This evening, Memorial Day, everybody watched a movie on television until 11:00 PM and then retired to their coffins for a good night's rest. "Tomorrow is just another day again! The beginning of another long, hot summer! Are you ready for that? I'm not! We had better get prepared!"

Fishing at Calgary Lake!

Earl, Chris, Ryan and the vampires decided to go on a fishing expedition this Sunday in Calgary, since the weather was a balmy seventy and very accommodating, for a sport of this nature. Maybe they will even encounter a victim or two engaging in a blood sucking rendezvous while transporting them back to their house. "You never know!" They arrived at Calgary Lake at 11:00 AM amidst a variety of families eating their lunch at the picnic tables before they try their fishing expertise at the lake. The vampires ate their lunch hungrily since they had not eaten breakfast yet. After they were finished eating they hurriedly positioned themselves on the piers, in different areas, to try their luck at seeing how many fish they can catch and take back to the house with them. By 1:00PM none of the vampires nary had a nibble and their luck was running out! Chris said, "It looks like we won't be catching many fish this afternoon. Is anybody having any luck?" Blair said, "I had several nibbles about an hour ago but they got away." Heston remarked, "I had a nibble just a few minutes ago, but that was it. Just a nibble!" Chris started strolling up and down the various piers checking on the vampires luck. Benjamin remarked, "I caught a small fish not large enough to take along back to the house. Chris said, "Let's all take a break from fishing and enjoy a snack and some much needed relaxation in the meantime. After that we can resume the sport of fishing again. Maybe we are taxing our bodies a little too much!" The vampires are following Chris' orders, laying low for about an hour, and then resuming fishing once again. This must have worked because all of the vampires have been reeling a variety of fish in on their poles. Blair reeled in a total of seven fairly large, fish that can be taken back to the house. Chris reeled in four, large fish and Benjamin reeled in fifteen fish on two poles within a half an hour! All the vampires were ecstatic in regards to the amount of fish they caught. At the present moment they each have their separate buckets with their fish flapping around in them. They continued fishing for several more hours stopping for a supper break and then resuming again until it got dark. In the meantime the next pier incorporated two, middle aged men, randomly fishing, while visiting, joking and laughing at the outcome of their expedition. One man commented to the other,

"I haven't caught one fish since we've been here this afternoon!" The other man retorted, "I've caught even less! Ha! Ha!"Chris made a comment, "Well, I guess we'll gather our personal effects which includes our poles, bait, buckets of fish, coolers, etc………….., and head back to Calgary. It looks like we will be eating fish for the next week!" The vampires said, "It sure looks that way!"Since there was no on the piers, in the immediate area, Benjamin and Heston strolled nonchalantly towards the two middle aged men they saw earlier. The sky was forbiddingly dark and treacherous looking as the darkness of the night totally enveloped their surroundings. Benjamin and Heston lurched towards them with their long, elongated fingernails clutching their spindly, slimy, yellowed, weather beaten necks. They immediately began to slurp voraciously and greedily until their stomachs began to fill up with the inevitable. Since no one was in the immediate area Heston and Benjamin were able to drag them back to the hearse for the ride back to the house in Calgary, Canada. After they arrived back they flung their bodies into the basement where they will lie until 4:O0 PM tomorrow afternoon standard procedure since Albert was presiding over the vampires. They will be monitored daily as to their condition. They will also be confined to their coffins until they are able to socialize and interact with the remainder of the vampires.

Chapter 89
Dancing, Anyone?

After the vampires had completed their supper this evening, Blair remarked, "I read an article in the Calgary Newspaper yesterday. It was in regards to a public dance which will be held, June 15th, 2018 in the Community Hall at the Calgary Fairgrounds from 8:00 PM to 12: 00 midnight. The admission is $5.OO per person which is reasonable enough considering the enjoyable time we had the last evening we attended a dance. If anyone is interested in the upcoming event please raise your hand." All the vampires raised their hands saying, "We're all interested in attending a dance again since that is an event we seldom frequent. Maybe we'll even get lucky and include a blood sucking rendezvous! How about that?" Blair commented, "That sounds great!"

Dancing! June 15, 2018

The vampires are hurriedly getting slicked up for their night out on the town, namely, a night of dancing to their heart's content to the serenading music of Les Brown's Band of Renown. They are shaving, bathing, attired in their white, dress shirts and black suits (minus the black capes for fear of being recognized by the Calgary Police Department.) Their hair are meticulously coiffed, their makeup flawless and their nails perfectly manicured. They are the epitome of a group of dapper young men out on the prowl this evening. At this point they are positioned in the hearse and the other two, private vehicles for their trip to the Community Center dance. When they pulled into the parking lot they became aware of a numerous amount of vehicles indicating many people in attendance. Throngs of dancers entered the hall as music was already blaring indicating the dance was in full swing. The vampires paid their dues while standing along the sidelines watching the dancers glide on by! Blair was the first vampire to make an attempt at approaching a young woman asking her, "Would you care to dance with me?" The young woman replied, "The pleasure is all mine!" Blair and his partner were engaged in a conversation as they glided along the floor to the music titled, "The Blue Skirt Waltz."

Heston and his partner were also dancing in the immediate area of the dance floor acting as if they were oblivious of everyone around them! Blair called Heston's name loudly, "Heston! Heston! I'm over here!" Heston did not acknowledge Blair! Maybe he was too interested in his dancing partner!Earl, Chris and Ryan are sitting this waltz out because they are tired and not used to dancing in the evenings instead of watching a movie on television every night. Besides, they have daytime jobs, employed as morticians at the Ronton Mortuary. So, Earl, Chris and Ryan's employment position is completely different. At the present moment, Earl, Chris and Ryan are conversing with each other with Chris commenting, "There is a large crowd of people frequenting the dance this evening considering all the other activities that are scheduled on the city's agenda that was posted in the Calgary Gazette Newspaper." Earl and Ryan were in agreement with Chris's statement saying, "There appears to be a wide variety of bachelor's twirling their partners around on the dance floor this evening with the greatest of ease as if this is an everyday occurrence which we know it isn't. Ha! Ha!"At 9:30PM the vampires accumulated at the snack bar for their favorite snack and a helping of soda. After that they strolled onto the dance floor with a new partner in tow to the beat of a two-step piece of music titled, "In the Mood," an old favorite even I can remember vividly. Also, scattered among Les Brown's, Band of Renown's music, were actually, my favorite piece of music, the "Beer Barrel Polka" which I love to this day and always will. Some of the vampires that were familiar with Polka music were out on the floor flinging their partners to and fro to the beat of the music. Others were nonchalantly strolling through the crowd sharing their camaraderie with friends and new acquaintances. Some of the vampires decided to step outside for a breath of fresh air, possibly, canvassing the back of the building for a stray person or two that they might engage in a blood thirsty rendezvous as the evening wears on. Benjamin and Alvin happened to meander behind the Community Hall never having been there before to get a glimpse of any stragglers shuffling along or hunkered down for a summer night's rest. All of a sudden they encountered two, young men desolately wandering behind the hall, slightly intoxicated, but managing to keep their balance, in spite, of their present condition. Benjamin and Alvin were about ten feet behind them, edging closer and closer, until they were within arm's length of yanking their spindly, emaciated, frail, withered necks toward them. They immediately started sucking their left, jugular vein with volumes of red, delectable, savory blood gushing forth. They kept up their violent, sucking rampage until their stomachs were totally ingested with blood and could tolerate no more. The stragglers collapsed at Alvin and Benjamin's feet in a dead heap as they struggled to drag them to the hearse depositing them in the back seat for the ride back to the house. Benjamin and Alvin exclaimed to each other, "This was our lucky night! We'll have to come back here again sometime!" After the dance ended Earl and the vampires proceeded back to their house at 2125 Melbourne Street in Calgary. When they arrived they dragged the two stragglers to the basement steps and flung them down the stairs to lie there until 4:00 PM the next afternoon. At this point the vampires, themselves, retired to their coffins for some overdue rest.

Chapter 90
A July 4th, 2018 Banquet

July 4, 2018 is just around the corner with Earl and the vampires, feverishly, in the planning stages for the free July 4th Banquet at the Community Hall on the Calgary Fairgrounds. This evening Earl and the vampires are dissecting the corpse of one of the men suspended from the ceiling in the Death Chamber. After the dissection process was completed they bagged the one inch chunks to be barbecued the next day for the main entree' at the banquet. In the meantime the balance of the meal is being prepared this evening such as burnt, scalloped potatoes with a tiny, dead lizard lying at the bottom of the serving dish, frozen, creamed, kernel corn, a vegetable salad endowed with dead ants and flies, chocolate chip cookies, chocolate chip ice cream, butterscotch pudding and goblets of savory, red, delicious, human blood. Upon completion of the meal preparation it will be transferred to the freezer and refrigerator for storage until tomorrow morning where it will be tended to by Earl and the vampires.

"Rise and Shine"

Earl and the vampires which are the waiters for today's banquet are up bright and early bathing, shaving, attired in their white shirts, black suits and neckties(no black capes, for fear of being recognized by the Calgary Police Department) Their hair are carefully coiffed, as usual, flawless makeup and perfectly manicured fingernails. Besides, immaculately, gleaming, white, canine fangs! They are busily scurrying , to and fro, assisting each other in all the tasks required to complete the free July 4th, 2018 Banquet. After the banquet is over, with dusk and darkness settling in, the vampires will furnish a firework's display for the general public to enjoy on the Calgary Fairgrounds which they rented for the day from the city of Calgary, Canada. After the fireworks display was completed the vampires hired the Les Brown Band of Renown, to furnish the music for the July 4th, 2018 free, public dance to be held from 9:00 PM to 12:OO midnight in the Community Hall on the Calgary Fairgrounds. In the meantime, the vampires are hurriedly removing the dining tables from the Community Hall so the Les Brown Band of Renown, can begin setting their orchestra in place, on the stage, for the beautiful music the public is accustomed to. Dancing

Earl, plus, the remainder of the vampires attended the dance as did other numerous singles and couples. The vampires were swinging and swaying, to and fro, with their partners to the beat of the Les Brown Band of Renown Orchestra. They played a variety of 1950's music such as the Polka's, Waltzes, Two Steps, Elvis Presley music, Fats Domino, Jerry Lee Lewis, anything dedicated to that era of time. Intermission was announcedby Les Brown saying, "Intermission will begin at 10:30 PM. Our orchestra will resume playing at 11:00 PM. Thank you! At 10:30PM Earl and the vampires, plus numerous other people, headed for the snack bar for a sandwich, chips, etc.............. and an ice cold drink. Immediately after that the Les Brown Band of Renown resumed playing their first piece of music which was "Blue Suede Shoes" by Elvis Presley, followed by "Blueberry Hill" by Fats Domino and "Great Balls of Fire" by Jerry Lee Lewis. At the close of the dance the last number that was played by the Les Brown Band of Renown was "My Happiness."Before everyone departed Earl said, "We want to thank everyone for coming to the banquet, fireworks display and dance this evening. We also want to thank the Les Brown Band of Renown for the wonderful music they provided which was enjoyed by everybody. Thank you!" All the people in attendance clapped their hands and kept yelling, "Thank you! Thank You! Thank You!"As the throng of people exited the Community Hall, numerous well wishers personally thanked the Les Brown Band of Renown and Earl and the vampires for the time, effort and finances involved. As usual, they promoted the dinner, fireworks display and dance for the fun and relaxation of the general public.

Time to Swim

August, 2018

Summer is back in full force and the vampires are raring to go swimming again as soon as Earl sets an appointment date at the Calgary Swimming Pool. As soon as supper was over this evening

Earl announced, "I set an appointment date at the Calgary Swimming Pool for tomorrow night at 6:00 PM which will be our departure time. Please be at the hearse at the appointed hour. Is everybody in agreement with the aforementioned? Everyone smiled and said, "We are anxious to go swimming once again because it's been awhile since we have frequented the Calgary Swimming Pool. We'll be at the hearse at 6:00 PM." The vampires have bathed, shaved and donned their trunks for their swimming excursion at the Calgary Swimming Pool. They are waiting with their towels by the hearse even though it is only 5:30 PM. "The vampires are very time conscious! Right?"

A Variety of Swimmers

Upon arriving at the Calgary Swimming Pool a large variety of swimmers of all ages were frequenting the pool on this hot, steamy evening which I'm sure is weather related. The vampires immediately headed for the highest diving board waiting in line for their turn at plunging into the cool, crisp, clear water that beckoned them with the occasional splashes of water erupting around the pool. When they finally descended into the pool they were overcome with laughter at the outcome of the initial plunge that they pursued. Blair remarked, "That seemed like quite a high dive, didn't it?" Earl commented, "It seemed to appear that way, Blair, because we haven't been here for a while!" The vampires raced each other, back and forth, across the length and width of the pool to see who the winner was. They also dived off the diving board a number of times with their friends and new acquaintances they encountered the length of time they were at the pool. Everybody took a snack break at 8:00 PM, including the vampires, munching their chips and devouring a bottle of cool, refreshing soda to quench their thirst. After the snack break the vampires returned to the swimming pool for another two hours of fun before the pool closed for the evening. They bashed and splashed, to and fro, attempting a variety of swimming maneuvers they have become familiar with over the years. Eventually, Earl reminded them, "At 10:00 PM we will be departing the Calgary Swimming Pool. Please congregate at the hearse at the appointed time. Thank you!"

Chapter 91
The Calgary Bowling Alley

While Earl and the vampires were watching a dull, boring television movie last night they decided to switch to several, different channels for a documentary, an interesting movie, etc……………All of a sudden they accidentally exchanged channels winding up with a channel depicting a game of bowling in progress at the Calgary Bowling Alley. Earl and the vampires watched the bowling game much to their delight although none of the vampires have ever played a game of bowling in their lives. Earl asked the vampires, "Would any of you be interested in taking bowling lessons at the Calgary Bowling Alley sometime?" The vampires faces lit up beaming from ear to ear saying, "None of us have ever bowled in our lives and we would be, sincerely, interested in taking bowling lessons so that we can master the art of bowling for our own recreational pleasure." Earl retorted, "I will establish an appointment for all of you tomorrow after the bowling alley opens up for business. Today Earl called the Calgary Bowling Alley arranging an appointment for the vampires and himself to begin bowling classes in the near future providing they purchase their own bowling ball or rent a bowling ball from the Calgary Bowling Alley. After Earl and the vampires completed their dinner Earl made the remark, "I called the Calgary Bowling Alley this morning setting up an appointment for our first bowling lesson which will be Wednesday night at 6:OO PM. Please be at the hearse at 5:15 PM. If you so desire to purchase a bowling ball downtown that will be fine. If you are interested in renting a bowling ball that is acceptable also. Whatever you wish to do!" The vampires were in agreement with the aforesaid saying "We are all interested in buying our own personal bowling ball for future use before Wednesday night." Earl asked, "Would Monday evening be a good time to purchase your bowling balls to which they replied, "Yes, that sounds like a favorable time. Let us know when we are to meet you by the hearse." Earl retorted, "12:30 PM will be fine." The vampires nodded in agreement saying, "Very well! We will be there!"

Chapter 92
New Bowling Balls!

Chris, Ryan and the remainder of the vampires gathered at the hearse at 12:30 PM patiently awaiting the arrival of Earl to transport them to Donald's Department store. They will likely purchase numerous bowling balls for their upcoming bowling lesson this coming Wednesday at 6:00 PM at the Calgary Bowling Alley. Earl is running a few minutes late, apologizing, but he made it nevertheless! After the vampires purchased their bowling balls Earl suggested, "Who is interested in a fresh hamburger, fries and an ice cold drink as opposed to a warmed over microwave meal when we get back to the house?" The vampires were all excited about frequenting a local Burger King saying, "We would rather eat at Burger King than at the house! We hardly ever eat at a fast food restaurant!"

Wednesday Night Bowling

The vampires are waiting in expectation of Earl's arrival to chauffeur them to the Calgary Bowling Alley downtown for their first lesson in the art of bowling. Here comes Earl remarking, "Is everybody ready for their first lesson in bowling?"The vampires screeched, "Yes, we are ready to master the art of bowling! We're raring to go! Hurry up! Let's get going!" When they arrived at the Calgary Bowling Alley they were escorted inside by an attendant and introduced to Mr. Conner's, the bowling instructor. Likewise, the vampires introduced themselves, also receiving explicit instructions as to whereabouts at any given time. They will also receive additional training, in spite, of the other vampires in attendance. Personal training also includes picking up the bowling ball, your grip on the ball, tossing the bowling ball down the lane etc............. A variety of bowling issues have surfaced in the course of the afternoon which will be addressed by Mr. Conner's, the instructor. According to Mr. Conner's, actual bowling lessons will be conducted every Wednesday night from 6:00 PM to 8:00 PM for six weeks in a row. The extent of their lessons will be six weeks of basic, bowling lessons. The vampires have tried their hand at tossing the heavy, bowling ball, at random, which was hard to control without the aid of the instructor, Mr. Conner's. The vampires practiced their bowling skills until 3:00 PM when it was time to depart. As the vampires walked out the door they all exclaimed, "This is a game the vampires all think they are going to enjoy immensely, even though, six weeks of lessons are involved." According to them they are enjoying the exercise as well.

Chapter 93
A Nightly Haunt

Chris, Earl, Ryan and the remainder of the vampires were relaxing in the back patio chairs when Ryan asked a question, "Is anybody interested in going on a nightly haunt in Riley Park similar to years ago when Albert and Jean were still among us? Remember? We usually got lucky behind the band shell!" The vampires smiled and said, "Yes, we remember that very well. Those were the good old days! Ha! Ha! The best haunts were usually behind the band shell in the latter part of the evening when most of the park walkers, stragglers, transients, derelicts, etc…………..had nothing better to do with their extra time than walk. Like we always say," We're ready any evening you are! Just say the time and day. We'll be at the hearse waiting." Ryan said, "How about tomorrow night, at 10:00 PM after the Calgary High School Band Concert is over?" The vampires replied, "That sounds great! We'll be waiting by the hearse at 10:00 PM.

Riley Park

The vampires were waiting for Earl, Chris and Ryan by the hearse in the dark at 10:00 PM for a nightly haunt they will participate in at Riley Park. Here they come, ready to go! The vampires positioned themselves in the hearse and one extra vehicle for the ride to Riley Park in the eerie, dead, creepiness of the night. Owls can be heard hooting in the trees in the stillness of the night. When they arrived at Riley Park the band concert had just ended. The band concert members and the general public were dispersing in every direction en route to their homes. By this time Earl, Chris, Ryan and the vampires were meandering behind the Riley Park Band Shell while others were scouting the wooded area adjacent to the entrance. Still others were scouring the shelter houses for anything abnormal or unusual at this time of the night. Benjamin and Heston were walking stealthily behind two men engaged in conversation oblivious of anyone behind them. They gained enough speed to thrust their hands around their necks, while grabbing their left, jugular vein. They sunk their white, gleaming, canine fangs into their veins while sucking the moist, savory, delectable blood to their heart's content. Their victims screeched and screamed demanding to know who they were but they did not release their names. Benjamin and Heston continued their blood sucking rampage until the two men became disoriented, weak and fatigued, collapsing at Heston and Benjamin's feet in a morbid, deadly heap! By now, Riley Park was totally deserted as Heston and Benjamin dragged them through the park to the vehicle that was parked the closest. They flung them into the back of the hearse and drove off in the dead of the night to their house in Calgary, Canada.

Chapter 94
"Joseph and Mike"

When Heston and Benjamin arrived back at the hearse they flung the two men down the basement stairs to lie there until 4:00 PM the next day. The vampires will monitor the two men attending to their basic needs until they are able to function on their own. The two men were in bad shape, not expected to live, until for some unknown reason they drastically improved and are able to conduct themselves on their own. They ate supper with the vampires at 5:30PM with Earl interviewing them saying, "What are your names and where are you from?" They said, "My name is Joseph Volton, 46, and I'm from Calgary, Canada." The other man said, "My name is Mile Levin, 48, and I'm also from Calgary, Canada." Earl continued, "Do you reside here in Calgary?" They replied, "We do not have any living quarters in Calgary because we are homeless. We eat food scraps out of trash receptacles behind restaurants and sleep in my car at night. We have a mutual, male friend that gives us the use of his shower at his apartment to freshen up besides do our laundry. Actually, "we kind of have it made." The information that Earl gleaned from the two, homeless victims gave him quite an insight into their private lives. "What do you think?"Earl decided the currently mentioned was sufficient for Joseph and Mike to reside as part of the vampire household including their meals, sleeping accomodations, laundry, household chores and participation in all the haunts, city wide events, banquets, etc............, for their relaxation and pleasure.

"Get Out the Bowling Balls"

It's Wednesday night again and time for the vampires bowling lessons at 6:00 PM at the Calgary Bowling Alley! When they arrived they immediately entered the bowling alley of their own accord, positioning themselves for their first bowling game of the evening. Before the bowling game was in progress Mr. Conners, the bowling instructor, explained explicitly and in detail the art of bowling in all its different phases. The vampires won the first, short, bowling game against the "Night Riders" while they received last minute instructions from Mr. Conners, in regards to new ideas and concepts formed in the art of bowling. They also met some of their old friends and new acquaintances from the week before sharing their camaraderie as time allowed. The vampires took their turns at their bowling expertise until it was departure time at 8:00 PM. As they left they remarked to one another saying, "This is one game we are all going to thoroughly enjoy even after our bowling lessons have been completed. After we have completed the inevitable I'm sure we'll be back to continue our bowling skills, thereafter."

Chapter 95
"Time to Swim Again?"

The summer season is slowly waning, the heat is less intense and the clouds are least forbidding and less stormy as the warmest days are drawing to a close. The Calgary Swimming Pool will be closing in a week so the vampires are going to frequent the pool one more time since Earl scheduled an appointment for this coming Friday night from 6:OO PM to 10:OO PM. The vampires are looking forward to the swimming session with Mike and Joseph remarking, "We are really looking forward to our swimming escapade this coming Friday night at the Calgary Swimming Pool because it's been years since we've been to a swimming pool!" The remaining vampires said, "You will absolutely love this swimming pool, the environment, plus the swimmers we can assure you!" Friday night is beckoning and the vampires are bathing, shaving, their hair meticulously coiffed, flawless makeup, freshly cleansed, gleaming, white, canine fangs, donned in their swimming trunks carrying a beach towel. They have eaten a light supper, due to the fact, they will be gallivanting around in the Calgary Swimming Pool for four hours. Everybody is ready to leave at 5:15PM, as usual, with Earl chauffeuring them and two others transporting vampires also. The swimming pool is crowdedtonight because of the three remaining days left to remain open. In the generalized, public pool the swimmers are laughing, frolicking and splashing to and fro to the beat of the music in the background if you can use your wild imagination! Ha! Ha! After the vampires hurriedly paid their swimming fee they immediately immersed their bodies into the cool, refreshing, clear water of the Calgary Swimming Pool. They romped around playfully in the pool to their heart's content. Several of the vampires climbed onto the highest diving board available and plunged, head on, into the cool water of the pool. They landed with a big splash as it sent ripples to the edge of the pool with the vampires laughing with glee at the effect. Heston said, "The amount of the ripple effect was the same as if an elephant had dived into the swimming pool. Ha! Ha! The vampires laughed and remarked, "You can say that again!" The vampires continued bashing and splashing in the cool, clear water throughout the evening, cavorting to and fro, as their body temperature cooled in response to the refreshing water. At this time the announcer suggested over the intercom, "That everyone depart the pool for a snack and drink before returning for the remainder of the session," which the vampires did. While the vampires were at the Calgary Swimming Pool they met up with their good friends, meeting them at prior swimming sessions they had attended. They all visited with each other, sharing their camaraderie, while romping through the water in a lively, frolicking way. Eventually, the announcer mentioned over the intercom, "The Calgary Swimming Pool will be closing in fifteen minutes. At 10:00 PM please retrieve your personal effects and depart from the swimming area. Thank you!" The vampires obeyed the announcer, collecting their personal effects and departing from the Calgary Swimming Pool. They positioned themselves in the hearse and two vehicles for the ride back to their house at 2125 Melbourne Street. When they arrived back they viewed television for a while and then reclined in their coffins for the remainder of the night.

Chapter 96
Mausoleum Rendezvous

September 6, 2018

Earl asked the vampires at the supper table this evening, "Would any of you be interested in a blood sucking rendezvous at a mausoleum in the Poheta Cemetery some night this week?" The vampires said, "Yes, we would be interested because we haven't been there for quite a while. What day and time did you have in mind?" Earl said, "How about tomorrow night at 6:15 PM at the hearse?" The vampires said, "That will be great! We'll meet you there!" The vampires are ready and raring to go to the mausoleum in the Poheta Cemetery this evening for a blood sucking rendezvous. When they arrived they passed through the iron gates headed for the three mausoleums in the proximity of the tombstones that were scattered throughout the cemetery. Earl posted Heston outside the mausoleum to keep a watchful eye on the immediate surroundings in the cemetery. It would be in regards to any intruders, stragglers or displaced people, frequenting the cemetery at any given time possibly crouched or hiding behind a tree, tombstone or building. The vampires slowly started to pry the mausoleum door open, but to no avail, because it wouldn't budge. The vampires used all the force they could muster but it didn't make any difference. Eventually, they tried different varieties of tools designed for those special purposes which didn't help the situation anyway. Finally they remembered from years past that if nothing else opens a door or lock etc…………..a slightly, moist cloth or tool with increased pressure on the lock will inadvertently create the lock or door to open of its own accord. Luckily Blair had a bottle of water on his person and proceeded to moisten the cloth and tool which caused the door to open slowly accompanied by a creaking noise, facilitating matters more readily. Ryan glanced at the vampires saying, "I guess this is what it takes! A little moisture on a cloth, tool, etc…………… making things more flexible or pliable to manipulate." The vampires replied, "It sure appears that way! Who would've thought of that? Although we vaguely recall hearing something to that effect years ago which we had forgotten since."

Chapter 97
Blood Sucking Rendezvous-2018

Since the door is opening readily to facilitate the vampire's entrance they immediately locked the doors again and dimmed the lights. There might be intruders or wayward people that could be frequenting the Poheta Cemetery or lurking behind a tree, tombstone, etc………….. "You never know!"By now, Earl, Chris and Ryan know which bodies have not been embalmed since they are employed at the Ronton Mortuary as licensed morticians for two years. According to them they assisted in the preparation of the bodies for the wake, etc………….. plus assisting in the funeral service at the Poheta Cemetery. Earl chose three bodies that were not embalmed, therefore, letting the vampires suck the red, savory, succulent blood, gluttonously and greedily until their stomachs became distended with blood. After the vampires completed their blood sucking rendezvous on the three bodies, upon Earl's recommendation, they gathered in the hearse for their trip back to their house at 2125 Melbourne Street. After arriving back they reclined in their coffins immediately due to the blood sucking rampage they exposed themselves to and the over exertion and over exhaustion on their bodies.

Chapter 98
Silent Meditation Only

September 9, 2018

This afternoon, Wednesday, while the vampires were taking care of their household chores Chris approached them asking, "Would any of you be available or interested in frequenting the Mohegan Cemetery for an hour of silent meditation at the tombstones of our friends, comrades, relatives, etc………….. It will be silent meditation only, no haunts, blood sucking rendezvous, or anything else involved. Please raise your hand if this appeals to you at this time. All the vampires raised their hands in regards to Chris' suggestion besides asking "What time are we leaving and what day?" Chris said, "We are leaving tomorrow night, Thursday, at 6:30PM and will be congregating at the hearse. Please be there at the appointed time!" The vampires nodded and said, "We will be there at the appointed time you designated. Thank you!"

Chapter 99
Lurking Behind the Tombstones!

September 12, 2018

Earl, Chris, Ryan and the vampires arrived at the Mohegan Cemetery at 7:00 PM with nary a soul in sight. They strolled through the cemetery grounds in search of familiar names of friends, comrades and relatives. They discovered Albert Benson's tombstone where Albert's ashes were buried. Earl, Chris, Ryan and the remaining vampires meditated at the tombstone for some time and then moved on. The next tombstone they knelt and meditated at was where Jean Benson, Albert's sister's ashes were buried. They also discovered Sue Benson's tombstone which was Albert and Jean's mother that was electrocuted for her misdeeds with her ashes buried at her gravesite. They knelt and meditated at the currently mentioned names of their friend's gravesites which were Mortimer, Armen, George, Andrew, Oliver and Phillp. "Do you recognize any of the above names? I do!" After kneeling and meditating at their friends, comrades and relatives graves they continued strolling through the Mohegan Cemetery to see if they could recognize any more names etched on the tombstones. Since it is a very large cemetery it is impossible for the vampires to remember all the names that coincide with all the tombstones. Eventually Ryan mentioned, "Since we have meditated at quite a few tombstones of our beloved friends and relatives it is time to leave the Mohegan Cemetery. Everybody was in agreement with Ryan's statement saying, "We are ready to depart the cemetery whenever you are. Thank you!" As they were ambling towards the cemetery gates, unbeknown to Earl, Chris and Ryan, several of the vampires happened to glance quickly towards the side noticing two people dressed in black clothes lurking behind two tombstones. By the time they notified Earl, Chris and Ryan they were nowhere in sight! The vampires continued on their trek to the hearse with Heston and Benjamin glancing back periodically saying, "There they are! There they are! The two people that were lurking behind a tombstone watching us in the Mohegan Cemetery. Now they are watching us walk towards the hearse for our ride back to Calgary, Canada." As the vampires were driving off they could still see the two, black clothed people watching them in full view from the Mohegan Cemetery. The vampires questioned, "Who are they? Why are they doing this? What are they up to?" The vampires remembered the same occurrence happening to Albert when he was at the cemetery one evening. There was one man in black clothing lurking behind a tombstone presumably watching Albert and the vampires. When Albert and the vampires left in the hearse the man clothed in black was watching Albert from the cemetery as the vampires looked back. Not long after that Albert visited the cemetery one night by himself. When he was in the mausoleum the man in black, similar to a vampire, grabbed a silver stake thrusting it through Albert's heart once with a shovel which automatically killed Albert never to be reincarnated again. Albert's ashes were found in the casket later placed there by the killer.

Chapter 100
Next to the Last Chapter

September 22, 2018

Earl approached the vampires telling them, "I am planning on visiting the Mohegan Cemetery again within a couple of days but Chris and Ryan have other activities to tend to and will not be able to accompany me. Actually I forgot to take dozens of flowers along that night to adorn the graves we meditate at. Are any of you interested in going along to help place the flowers on the graves?" Most of the vampires raised their hands and said, "Yes, we will go along since the movies on television this week will not hold our interest. You name the night and the time. Earl said, "How about this Friday night at 5:00 PM while it's still light?" The vampires said, "Sounds great! We'll be at the hearse at 5:00 PM. By the time they arrived at the Mohegan Cemetery it was 5:45 PM. Earl and the vampires meandered through the rows of tombstones, placing the flowers at the various gravesites of their friends, acquaintances and relatives. They hurriedly finished the placement of the flowers while departing the Mohegan Cemetery. Once again as they were leaving they noticed a man clothed in black hiding behind a tree and another man dressed the same hunkered down behind a tombstone glaring towards Earl and the vampires. As Earl and the vampires sped off into the night the vampires glanced back noticing the two men standing and watching them in full view until Earl and the vampires were out of sight.

Chapter 101
The Last Chapter

September 25, 2018

Earl, Chris and Ryan decided to go to the Mohegan Cemetery, also, for private meditation since Chris and Ryan were unable to attend last week. When they arrived at the Mohegan Cemetery it was totally deserted at 7:00 PM at night. They knelt and meditated at several gravesites saying to each other, "Well, I guess it's time to go since it is getting quite dark earlier now. I also notice a soft, misty film draping the tombstones and immediate surroundings." As they departed the Mohegan Cemetery they became aware of soft footsteps padding behind them. By the time they turned around, three men in black attire accompanied by a shovel and spade approached them. One man grabbed Earl another grabbed Chris and the other man grabbed Ryan. The first man thrust a spade through Earl's heart with a shovel killing him immediately never to be reincarnated. The second man thrust a spade through Chris' heart with a shovel, killing him immediately never to be reincarnated. The third man thrust a spade through Ryan's heart with a shovel killing him immediately never to be reincarnated. The ashes will appear later!!!

Earl, Chris and Ryan are DEAD!!!

"Will the vampires find their bodies? What will they say? What can they do now?"

THE END

"THE DEATH CHAMBER" Blood Sucking Series 5